"You were married for less than two years. What happened?"

She remained silent.

"Macy…"

"He divorced me, okay?" With angry movements she walked over to the bassinet in the corner.

"*He* divorced you?" Beau was thrown for a second. "Was he having an affair?"

"No." She fingered the lace on the crib.

Beau hated to keep on, but their future was at stake. "Then why?"

"As I said, it's none of your business."

"You know I'm not stopping until you tell…"

She swung around, eyes flashing. "Because I'm not perfect."

That made no sense to him. She was perfect in every way. "What are you talking about?"

"This conversation is over." She headed for the door. "Go home, Beau."

He caught her arm. "I love you and I'm not leaving until you tell me why you can't love me."

Her eyes clouded over. "Because I'm the reason my baby is dead."

Dear Reader,

I have enjoyed creating the McCain family. I wrote about Jake in *A Baby by Christmas,* Eli in *Forgotten Son* and Caleb in *Son of Texas.* Thank you for your many letters inquiring about the other brothers. This is Beau's story.

I'm often asked where I get my ideas. The germ of an idea for this book began one day when I was talking to our niece about how traumatic the first few months of life had been for her daughter, Taylor. She was born with laryngomalacia. When I was plotting Beau and Macy's story, I thought about Taylor's problem and knew I had to put it in the book.

Simple, right? It was far from simple. When I write I make up things, and if I can make you believe it really happened, then I've done my job. But turning fact into fiction proved to be more difficult than I'd planned. It was hard not to let the little girl take over.

The story was about Beau and Macy and their relationship. They'd been best friends forever. My thought as I plotted this book was: Can friends become lovers? And what happens next? If you want to find out, you'll have to read further.

Thank you so much for reading my books, and I hope you enjoy this visit with the McCains.

Warmly,

Linda Warren

P.S. It always brightens my day to hear from readers. You can e-mail me at Lw1508@aol.com or write me at P.O. Box 5182, Bryan, TX 77805 or visit my Web site at www.lindawarren.net or superauthors.com. Your letters will be answered.

THE BAD SON
Linda Warren

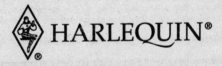

TORONTO • NEW YORK • LONDON
AMSTERDAM • PARIS • SYDNEY • HAMBURG
STOCKHOLM • ATHENS • TOKYO • MILAN • MADRID
PRAGUE • WARSAW • BUDAPEST • AUCKLAND

ISBN-13: 978-0-373-71375-2
ISBN-10:   0-373-71375-4

THE BAD SON

Copyright © 2006 by Linda Warren.

This edition published by arrangement with Harlequin Books S.A.

® and TM are trademarks of the publisher. Trademarks indicated with ® are registered in the United States Patent and Trademark Office, the Canadian Trade Marks Office and in other countries.

www.eHarlequin.com

Printed in U.S.A.

ABOUT THE AUTHOR

A Waldenbooks series bestselling writer, Linda Warren is the award-winning author of fifteen books for Harlequin Superromance and Harlequin American Romance. She grew up in the farming and ranching community of Smetana, Texas, the only girl in a family of boys. She loves to write about Texas, and from time to time scenes and characters from her childhood show up in her books. Linda lives in College Station, Texas, not far from her birthplace, with her husband, Billy, and a menagerie of wild animals, from Canada geese to bobcats. Visit her Web site at www.lindawarren.net.

Books by Linda Warren

HARLEQUIN SUPERROMANCE

Don't miss any of our special offers. Write to us at the following address for information on our newest releases.

Harlequin Reader Service
U.S.: 3010 Walden Ave., P.O. Box 1325, Buffalo, NY 14269
Canadian: P.O. Box 609, Fort Erie, Ont. L2A 5X3

To Taylor Tharp—the inspiration for this story.
She is now a happy and healthy nine-year-old.
And to her parents, Melissa and Ken Tharp,
for being such loving parents.

ACKNOWLEDGMENTS

Nelda F. Williams—thanks for being a
good friend and offering your legal expertise,
and especially for answering my many
questions with such kindness and patience.

Amy Landry—neonatal nurse—thanks once again
for sharing your knowledge of babies so graciously.

Any errors are strictly mine.

CHAPTER ONE

IN THE WESTERN SKY, an orange sun sank slowly toward the hazy net of trees low on the distant horizon. It reminded Beau McCain of a large basketball sailing toward a basket. Bam. Three points. The light was gone and a shadowy dimness crept over central Texas.

He gazed through the beam of his headlights, a slight grin on his face. He'd been playing too much basketball with his brothers. He changed lanes and shifted uncomfortably in his seat. The grin faded. He was returning to Waco after visiting a law firm in Dallas where he'd been offered a senior partnership, an offer he had no intention of refusing.

It was a drastic move. Living all of his forty-two years in Waco, except for a law internship in Dallas, he had his own firm practicing family law and was doing quite well. His personal life was the problem. All because of Macy Randall. He was tired of waiting for her to see him as more than a friend.

At his age, he wanted a home and a family and he had to finally acknowledge that wasn't going to happen with Macy. He had to move on, start a new life and forget her. Moving to Dallas was a big step in that direction.

Taking an exit off I-35, he turned by a McDonald's then onto the street leading to his subdivision. He and Macy lived next door to each other and Beau had known her all her life. She'd lived down the street when they were kids. He was eight years older, but he was a sucker for those big blue eyes and her sad little stories. Single-handedly, she was trying to save every animal on the planet.

Macy was a neonatal nurse who worked nights and Beau had babysat her strays more than once. She was never going to love a man as much as her animals. Beau wasn't sure she saw him as anything more than a very good friend. She cried on his shoulder, told him her problems, but not once in all the years he'd known her had they progressed beyond friendship. He kept waiting, though. Like a lovesick fool, he kept waiting.

Not anymore.

Beau McCain was moving on.

He turned onto a cul-de-sac that housed several condos. When he'd bought the place, he'd no idea Macy lived next door. She'd married and moved away to Dallas, but now she was back—without a husband. He'd asked her about it, but in the last seven years she'd only said the marriage hadn't worked out. They talked about everything else, but her marriage was a subject she avoided.

He remembered her wedding vividly. He, his younger brother, Caleb, and their parents had attended. Though he'd acted like a normal friend, all the while his heart had been breaking.

Everyone in the neighborhood knew the scrawny, curly-haired girl who was always searching for a home for the endless array of animals she rescued. When Beau returned after his internship, the scrawny girl had turned into a leggy beauty with alabaster skin he'd never noticed before. But he knew where the freckles were on her nose, even though makeup hid them flawlessly.

Following the divorce of her parents, he'd become her confidant, her friend. That was his first big mistake. The next thing he knew she was engaged—someone she'd known in college and had met again. Beau had never told Macy about his real feelings and he never planned to. Their lives went in different directions, then a short two years later they were living next door to each other and the cycle started again.

His brothers teased him all the time about Macy and her ability to wrap him around her finger. He was too good for his own well-being—that's what his brothers said. But that's not how he felt. His father, Joe McCain, had called him "the bad son" because when Beau's parents had divorced, he chose to go with his mother. His brother, Jake, stayed with their father and spent years estranged from the family.

Joe McCain was a jealous, abusive man who drank heavily. When he did, he became angry and mean, and hit Althea, their mother. When Althea became pregnant with their third son, Caleb, Joe accused her of sleeping with Andrew Wellman, a man from their church. He said the baby wasn't his and beat Althea until she was black and blue. His mother knew she had to get out or risk losing her unborn child.

But Althea hadn't counted on Joe spreading his lies to their oldest son, Jake. When the sheriff came to take them away, Jake refused to go. It broke Althea's heart, but she left one of her sons behind. She tried and tried, but Jake remained steadfast in his loyalty to his father.

Beau saw his father from time to time as a kid, mainly running into him by accident. Joe had refused any contact with his younger son. On those rare occasions, Joe never missed a chance to tell Beau what a bad son he was and how disloyal he was to his own father. Those words stayed with him all his life, but he never changed his decision. It only instilled in him a need to prove his father wrong—to prove he was a good son.

As a kid, he grew up wanting Jake back in his life—and Althea's. When Joe passed away, Beau went to the funeral, determined to make contact with his older brother. Jake resisted at first, but Beau never let up. He kept talking and visiting, wearing Jake down, and he didn't stop until he brought Jake and their mother back together. They were a real family now. Even Elijah Coltrane, a son Joe had with another woman, was a part of their big family.

Eli and Caleb were Texas Rangers and Jake ran the McCain farm. Beau knew from an early age that he was going to be a lawyer. Since his parents' divorce, he'd become passionate about keeping families together. He was good at negotiating and working out problems. This was his life's work.

Caleb had just married and was ecstatic. Jake had a wife and a family, and Eli was also married. He and his wife Caroline were expecting their first child. Beau wanted a bit of that happiness—with his own family.

His friend, Jeremiah Tucker, known as "Tuck" to the family, was also still single and the same age as Beau. Tuck was Eli's foster brother and the McCain brothers had accepted him as one of their own. Since Tuck and Beau were the two single sons in the group, they'd become good friends.

Beau started to call Tuck to see if he wanted to commiserate over a beer, but he decided it would be best to go straight home. It had been a long three days and he had to tell his family about the job offer.

And he had to tell Macy.

AS HE DROVE INTO HIS GARAGE, he saw Macy sitting on her front step with her animals around her—Lucky and Lefty, two mixed-breed terriers, and Freckles, a spotted orange tabby.

He unlocked his door and went inside, thinking he'd talk to Macy later. After three days and nights of being wined and dined, he wanted time alone to rest and to regroup. And he was tired. He yanked off his tie and threw his suit jacket onto the sofa. He ran his hands over his face, feeling drained. Was he getting old, or what? He couldn't take three days of partying? What was wrong with him? He had to exercise more—or something.

He usually ran every morning, but had missed his routine in Dallas. That's what he needed, to work up a little sweat. As he headed for the bedroom to change into shorts and sneakers, the doorbell rang.

He grimaced. It had to be Macy. No way around it— he had to see her tonight. Just as well. He needed to get this over with, to start severing the ties that had kept him bound for so long. He took a deep breath.

Swinging the door open, that breath of fortitude dissipated like smoke into thin air. Tears trailed down her cheeks and she quickly wiped them away with the back of her hand. His fingers tightened on the doorknob and he willed himself not to react, not to let his emotions take control. The tears were probably for another pet she'd rescued. The abuse of animals always broke her heart.

"Hi." She smiled through her tears, making her blue eyes appear that much brighter. "I saw you drive in." Lucky and Lefty trotted inside and Freckles trailed behind them.

"What's wrong?" he asked, doing what he always did—supporting her no matter what. His brothers were right. He was putty, soft and malleable, in Macy's hands. Any reservation he'd had about moving just vanished. He had to salvage what was left of his self-respect, his pride. And he couldn't do that when he was around her.

"You're not going to believe this." Macy followed her animals into the living room and curled up on the sofa, her bare feet beneath her. Petite and energetic, she had shoulder-length strawberry-blond hair that had a natural curl and a life of its own. Today it seemed to be everywhere and he knew the cause. When she was upset, she was prone to running her hands through it repeatedly.

Macy wasn't beautiful by anyone's standard, but to him she was. She had a natural, honest appeal that was hard to resist. She was everything he'd ever wanted in a woman—kind and caring, with a great sense of humor, and never afraid to admit when she was wrong. She was perfect in every way, except she thought of him as her best friend. And nothing more.

"Delia's back." Through a stab of pain, he heard her soft voice.

"What?"

"Delia, she's back. She showed up this afternoon out of the blue."

Delia was Macy's sister, ten years her junior. As a child, Delia had been diagnosed with attention-deficit hyperactive disorder. She'd been uncontrollable until they'd put her on medication. Even though the medicine calmed her, her rebellious, bossy nature still shone through.

After the Randalls' divorce ten years ago, Delia became more of a problem. She couldn't stay focused in school and started skipping classes. At fourteen, she ran away and their mother, Irene, had a hard time disciplining her, especially without the influence of their father, Ted. At sixteen, Delia moved out for good and they'd had no idea where she was. Months later she'd resurface only to leave again. But Delia had always been at the center of Macy's soft heart.

"She's eight months pregnant and I don't know what to do. When I tried to talk to her, she became angry and stormed upstairs to the bedroom." Her fingers slid through her hair in a nervous gesture.

"Delia's pregnant?"

Beau sat in an oversized leather chair and Freckles

hopped onto his lap. Freckles had half a tail and one ear missing. Stray dogs tried to make a meal of her and Macy had rescued her from the animal shelter. He stroked the cat and she purred at his touch. At least someone missed him.

"Yes."

"Have you contacted your parents?"

That was a sore subject with Macy. After twenty-five years of marriage, Ted had walked out, moved to Houston, and later remarried. After Delia ran away, Irene sold the house and moved to Denver. She soon remarried, too. Macy's relationship with both her parents was strained. She didn't understand how her father could do what he'd done or how her mother could give up on their marriage and Delia.

"Not yet. Not too sure it will do any good. They're too busy with their new lives to be bothered with her, but I'll call anyway. They need to know. I don't understand either one of them and how they can just turn their backs on…" Her words trailed away as she fought to control her emotions. Beau resisted the urge to go to her.

Lucky, hearing the distress in Macy's voice, crawled into her lap. Lucky had a ring around his neck where his hair wouldn't grow anymore. Some kids tried to hang him. Once rescued, he was taken to the animal shelter, the rope still around his neck. Macy's number was on file and whenever they received an abused animal they called her, knowing she would nurture it back to health and find a home for it. The vet had said he was lucky to be alive, so that's what Macy named him.

She'd found Lefty on the side of the road after a car had hit him. His right paw was so mangled that it had to be amputated. He hobbled on three legs and Macy had had him for years. Both dogs whimpered in her lap and Macy's face changed completely. The stress disappeared and her face softened. Her animals brought her a peace that no one else could.

"In a way, your parents are right," he told her. "Delia's been on her own for a long time and she's never taken kindly to interference in her life, from them or you."

"I know, but there's a baby involved now and she won't even tell me who the father is. She won't tell me anything."

"She probably never will, and come a new day Delia could just as easily be gone again."

"Yeah." Macy stroked the dogs.

"Try not to argue with her because it's not going to make a bit of difference. It never has."

"You're right." She tried to smile and failed. "I always feel better when I talk to you." She ran her hands through her hair again. "Oh, crap, I should have combed my hair before coming over here. I must look a mess. Or like a Brillo pad."

You look beautiful.

He grinned. "It is sticking out in different directions."

"Beau McCain." She lifted an eyebrow. "You could at least say something flattering."

I do, but you never hear me.

"I think it's rather fetching like that."

Her hand stilled. "You do?" For a moment she paused and he wondered if his opinion of her looks meant something to her, then she came back with one of her usual remarks. "You're such a diplomatic lawyer and an even better liar."

He winced. "Ouch."

"Don't pretend your feelings are hurt." She stood with both dogs in her arms. "I better go back to the war zone and see what Delia's visit is all about."

Beau walked her to the door. "Let her talk and try not to pressure her. Just be patient."

"I'll try. I just worry about her." At the door, she stopped. "How was your trip?"

"Fine." He refrained from saying anything else.

"I miss you when you're not here."

For a brief second, his heart knocked against his ribs in excitement, then he had to remind himself that they were just words. Nothing else. Now was the time to tell her he was planning on moving, but she was too upset about her sister. He'd do it later.

MACY WALKED BACK to her condo, feeling the dried grass beneath her feet. She'd forgotten to put on her shoes. Oh well. She took a moment to breathe in the crisp February air. Soon spring would arrive, heralding new life and new beginnings. Maybe there was hope for her and Delia to start again.

Delia came down the stairs, her corn-colored hair orange in spots from being bleached so much. Why Delia had to do that to her hair, Macy didn't understand. She never understood a lot of things about her sister, but she loved her and was going to be patient and listen like Beau had said.

She was so glad he was back. Her world just wasn't right when he wasn't around. There weren't many people in her life she could trust, but Beau was…

Her thoughts stopped as Delia went to the refrigerator and grabbed a Coke, some chips and cookies. "I'm starving," Delia said, and plopped her large frame into a chair.

"I can fix you something to eat," Macy offered.

"No, thanks. I live off junk food."

But it's so bad for the baby. No, don't say a word. Be patient.

She took a long breath. "So, how are you?"

"Big as a cow. My back hurts and I can't sleep. I hate being pregnant."

Macy sat at the table and stopped herself from running her hands through her hair. "It'll be over soon."

"Yeah." Delia wolfed down two chocolate chip cookies. "The sooner the better because this is hell."

Macy counted to three. "Have you talked to Mom or Dad lately?"

Delia stopped in the process of stuffing food into her mouth. "How likely is that?"

Macy let that pass. "We worry when we don't hear from you."

"Yeah, right." Delia chuckled in disbelief. "You're happy when you don't hear from me. At least I'm not bugging you for money."

"That's not true."

"Well, the last time I visited dear ol' Mom, I met her new hubby. He has to be ten years younger than her. She couldn't wait for me to leave—I think she was afraid

I'd make a pass at him. And when I saw Dad and his young wife, they wanted me out as soon as possible. Didn't say it, but every question, every nervous glance, made that crystal clear. So please don't try to make me believe that my so-called family is worried about me."

"I am," Macy said quietly. "I worry about you all the time."

"But that's you, Macy. You worry about everyone, including every animal on this earth." Delia took a swallow of the Coke. "Thought this place would be like a zoo, but you have only three critters. That has to be a first."

Macy let that pass, too. "You're my sister. I love you." She paused. "Are you still on your meds?"

"Nope. Don't see the need."

Macy bit her lip. "Are you having an easy pregnancy?"

"I feel so keyed up, I can't sit still and sometimes I feel as if I'm going crazy."

"You're not," Macy assured her. "I'd like for you to see a doctor while you're here. I'll help all I can."

Delia swung back her yellow hair and stretched her back, her large stomach protruding. "Don't razz me. I just need a place to stay for a couple of days. I'm waiting for a deal to go through and when it does, I'll be outta here."

Macy frowned. "Deal?"

"No questions, because you wouldn't like the answers."

What was Delia up to? *Be patient.* "Do you know the sex of the baby?"

"A girl."

"A little girl. How nice." Warm, precious memories surfaced and she quickly forced them away.

"You would say that." Delia pushed to her feet, her hands rubbing her back. "God, my back is killing me. Do you have any pain pills? I could use something, the stronger the better."

"You shouldn't take anything without a doctor's advice. It could hurt the baby." Her patience ran out and she couldn't stop the censure in her voice.

"Don't tell me what to do. That's what I hate about you—you're always trying to run my life."

Macy sucked in a deep breath. "It's for your own good. You have to think about the baby. I'll give you a massage, that will help to calm you."

"Go to hell," Delia said in anger, then waddled to the stairs and soon Macy heard a door slam.

Macy sat there for a moment. Like Beau had said, Delia had been living on her own for a long time and there wasn't much she could do. But an innocent baby was involved. That's what got Macy the most—the baby. Who was going to love her, care for her and give her a home? She didn't think Delia was capable of doing any of those things. No, she corrected herself. She *knew* Delia wasn't capable of doing any of those things.

Before she could change her mind, she picked up the phone and called her mother. Irene wasn't too concerned.

"Macy, I'm not sure what you expect me to do. Delia has made it very clear that she doesn't want me to interfere in her life."

"What about the baby?"

There was a long pause, then her mother replied, "That's Delia's responsibility."

"I see."

"Macy, you know how Delia is. She won't listen to me or take her meds. I've been through hell with her and I'm not putting myself through that again."

"Okay. I just wanted to let you know that you're going to be a grandmother." Saying that, she hung up and realized she was trembling. And she was angry.

That anger driving her, she phoned her father, something she wouldn't normally do. Ever since he'd walked out on their mother, Macy had a hard time talking to him. But this was important.

His wife answered and tension coiled inside her at the thought of her father's new life. A life that neither Macy nor Delia had a part in. It was hard to get past the resentment, but she kept trying. Soon her father was on the line. His response was the same as her mother's.

"Delia never listens to me. There's nothing I can do."

She gritted her teeth. "I just thought you might like to know."

"Macy…"

She hung up, not wanting to hear anything else. She had to take several deep breaths to calm herself. Picking up Freckles, she walked to the window. It was dark, but from the streetlight she saw Beau jog by.

Beau usually asked her to run with him. Why hadn't he tonight? Because of Delia—that had to be it. Beau had seemed different earlier. He didn't have a lot to say and he usually told her all about his business trips. Maybe he was just tired.

Dear, sweet Beau—her knight in shining armor. When everyone else in her life had let her down, Beau was always there. He'd been her best friend forever. She wondered what he'd say if she told him that she'd had a gigantic crush on him when she was a teenager. She and his younger brother, Caleb, were the same age and she'd make all kinds of excuses to see Caleb in the hopes of seeing Beau.

When Beau went to college, he lived in the dorm and when she'd spot his car at home she made sure she got to see him. Then she started college, then nursing school and met Allen. They dated but he graduated and moved on to a job in Baltimore. He worked for a large drug company and a year later they met again and renewed their relationship. Soon they were in love and planning a future. She forgot about Beau and her silly crush.

But at the wedding, when Beau had wished them well, for a brief moment she remembered thinking *it could have been you*. Because he was older, she was sure he only saw her as the kid down the street.

And she'd thought that Allen was the answer to all her dreams. He wasn't—far from it. She shuddered and forced herself not to remember. Not tonight.

Fate had landed her and Beau in condos next to each other. It had been a big surprise when they realized they were neighbors again. That had been seven years ago. And not once in all those years had either of them crossed the line of friendship. At times, she wanted to and she couldn't explain why she hadn't. She wasn't a kid anymore, but she sometimes wondered if Beau still saw her that way. She was an adult woman and a part of her needed more. Beau never seemed inclined to change their relationship. That was fine with her. Their friendship was more important.

Was that it? Was it safer as friends? That way she could never be hurt again. She nuzzled Freckles. With animals it was so simple. You shower them with love and attention and they return it tenfold. There were no feelings of rejection—the way it should be with humans.

She'd given her father her love and he'd walked out on them without one word of explanation. He wasn't happy. Big deal. She never would understand that. How could a man turn his back on his wife? His daughters?

Allen had done the same thing, she reminded herself. He'd left, but at least she'd known why. She was less than perfect and he didn't want a flawed wife. Tears stung her eyes and she resolutely refused to cry.

Freckles purred and she cuddled her. Would she ever trust a man again? Probably not. But she trusted Beau. That felt strange to her, especially since she'd sworn off men for the rest of her life. Beau was different, though. She knew him inside and out and he was wonderful and nice and sometimes too damn handsome for his own good. He made her laugh and he made her feel good about herself. Then why had she never told him that?

Fear. Like monsters under the bed. You know they're not there, but when it's dark and the silence mingles with your breath, your mind believes. If she told Beau her true feelings, the light would come on and expose her for the woman she was. A woman a husband couldn't love. A young girl a father couldn't love. She couldn't take anymore rejections—especially not from Beau.

So where did that leave them? Friends.

As that thought warmed her heart, Beau jogged to his condo. She watched until he disappeared up the walk. Sweat poured down his face and his breathing was labored. She didn't need to be close to him to know that. That's the way he was every time they ran and she teased him about his age. He teased her about her frizzy hair. They laughed a lot. Macy needed that and a part of her knew that she needed Beau.

Would she ever be able to tell him? Would she ever be able to expose the monster under her bed?

CHAPTER TWO

BEAU TOOK A QUICK shower, pulled on pajama bottoms, grabbed bottled water out of the refrigerator, and flopped onto the sofa. He wasn't hungry so he didn't bother with food. Picking up the remote control, he found a basketball game and settled in for the night. He kept his mind a blank, concentrating on the plays instead of what he had to do tomorrow—tell Macy goodbye.

The sound of the phone ringing woke him. Opening one eye, he looked at his watch—2:00 a.m. Who was calling this late? He quickly clicked off the TV and yanked up the phone.

"Beau, Delia's in labor. Could you please drive us to the hospital? I'm too nervous."

"Sure," he answered without a second thought. "I'll bring the car to your front door. Be there in a minute."

He slipped into jeans and a T-shirt. Within minutes he was parked in front of Macy's condo. She came out holding on to Delia and Beau hurried to help. He hadn't seen Delia in a while and she looked as bad as he'd ever seen her.

"Hey, Beau," Delia said in between groans.

"Delia." He took her arm. "Doesn't look like you're feeling too good."

"Got knocked up. Can you believe that?" A desperate laugh escaped on a moan.

"Yep."

Delia laughed. "At least you're honest." She clutched her stomach and cried out in pain. Between the two of them they managed to get Delia into the backseat. Macy sat with her and Beau crawled into the driver's seat. They sped toward the nearest emergency room.

Delia continued to scream with pain.

"Take deep breaths," Macy instructed.

"Don't tell me what to do," Delia snapped. "You know I hate it when you do that. And I'm not in labor. It's too early." She let out an earth-shattering scream that said otherwise. "Dammit. I can't have this baby now. Macy, do something. You're a nurse. Make it stop."

"We'll be at the hospital in a minute," Macy replied in a calm voice, but Beau caught a thread of panic in her tone.

"I can't have this baby now. Macy, do you hear me?"

"Yes. People three blocks away can hear you. Calm down."

"Dammit, this hurts."

Beau pulled into the emergency area and a nurse was waiting with a wheelchair. Evidently Macy had called ahead. Smart woman.

"Beau, thanks," Macy called as the nurse wheeled Delia away.

He drove around, looking for a parking spot. What was he doing? He should go home and let Macy handle her own life. When he left for Dallas, she would have to. This is where he drew the fictional line in the sand. This is where he walked away.

But Beau had learned something about himself. He couldn't leave a person in need. His mother raised him to be kind and caring and he wasn't the type to abandon a friend.

He hated himself for that—for caring too much. Nice guys finished last. Isn't that what they said?

In the maternity ward, he looked around but didn't see them. A door opened and Macy, dressed in scrubs, came out talking to a doctor. She noticed him and immediately came over.

"Beau, I thought you'd gone home."

"No. I wanted to make sure Delia was okay."

"As much as she denies it, she's in labor. She's dilated ten centimeters and it shouldn't be much longer."

"Isn't the baby early?"

"Yes. But who knows? Delia could be further along than she realizes." Macy tucked a stand of hair behind her ear. Beau noticed her hair was tamed and clipped behind her head. "I've asked about the father and all she'll say is that he's not in the picture anymore."

"That explains why she showed up at your house."

"Mmm."

"She knows you'll take care of her and the baby."

"Yeah. She keeps muttering something about a plan and I don't have a clue what she's talking about. When I ask about her plans for the baby, she gets angry." She glanced toward the hall. "They're giving her an epidural so I better get back in there. I want to be present when the baby arrives."

"I'll wait out here."

She gave a warm smile that felt as soothing as a towel fresh from the dryer. "Go home. I'm sorry I bothered you, but I didn't know who else to call."

"No problem." He eased onto a sofa in the waiting area. "Let me know when the baby comes."

"Beau…"

"What?"

"Go home. You can't rest here."

"I've slept on worse." He leaned his head on the cushion. "Go back to your sister."

"You're a special man, Beau McCain."

"Mmm." He closed his eyes. "I'll remind you of that one of these days."

Her lips brushed his forehead and his eyes flew open. The scent of her filled his nostrils—lilacs and fresh soap—and for a moment he was lost in the sensation. But damn, his mother kissed him like that. He didn't want those kind of kisses from Macy. He wanted the real thing.

Macy disappeared around the corner and he made himself as comfortable as he could on the hardest sofa he'd ever slept on. He stared up at the ceiling, sleep the furthest thing from his mind. Here he was with Macy because that's where he wanted to be. He blew out a hard breath, knowing he was in so deep that putting distance between himself and Macy was not going to make a difference.

Why was he trying to fool himself?

BEAU NAPPED ON AND OFF. At six he stretched and went in search of coffee. A nurse finally gave him a cup. As he sipped it, he saw Macy down the hall talking to a doctor. He walked over and realized she wasn't talking, but arguing in a way he'd never seen her do before.

"I insist you run a full battery of tests," she was saying.

"I've been doing this a long time and in my opinion I feel it's unnecessary," the doctor replied.

"I want the tests done," Macy repeated in a stubborn voice Beau knew well. Evidently the doctor did, too.

"Fine, Macy. Just calm down and let me do my job." The doctor strolled away to the nursery.

"What's wrong?" Beau asked.

"The birth went smoothly and the baby seemed fine. But when we checked her in the nursery we detected a low-pitched intermittent inspiratory sound. Dr. Pender feels it's stridor which we see in some newborns."

"And he doesn't feel it's anything serious?"

"No." Her chin jutted out.

"And you do?"

"Yes. Something's wrong. I know it is." Her voice wavered slightly.

"What do you think it is?"

"Her heart. Dr. Pender feels I'm overreacting. I told him how our sister died from an atrial septal defect when she was two days old but he thinks I'm just being paranoid." She paced back and forth in agitation. Beau had never seen her quite like this. She didn't trust the doctor and he wondered why.

He caught her by the forearms and stopped her. "Calm down and take a deep breath. They'll run the tests and find out for sure."

"I suppose." She drew in deeply several times. "The baby is so tiny, a little over five pounds."

"But otherwise healthy?"

"Yes. Her blood sugar is fine and there's no fluid on her lungs."

But he heard a note of distrust again. "Then trust him." Her expression didn't change. "I need another cup of coffee. Come with me to the cafeteria."

"No. I want to be here for the baby."

Beau took her elbow. "Let the doctor do his job, and you need a break. We'll only be gone a minute."

She removed her scrubs without a word of protest and followed him to the elevator. In the cafeteria, she took a seat and he ordered the coffee. This early the place was empty except for two nurses in a corner. He noticed a couple of boxes of fresh donuts that had just been delivered.

Macy loved donuts. It was her weakness. He paid for two and carried them with the coffee to the table.

She looked at the donuts, then at him. "Are you trying to make me fat?"

"Impossible." He took a seat. "You burn off more energy than anyone I know. These are to cheer you up."

"You're eating one." She made a face at him.

"Deal."

She dipped one into her coffee and ate it delicately, like a child. He enjoyed watching her. She licked the icing from her lips and eyed the half-eaten donut on his plate. "Aren't you finishing that?"

He pushed it across to her. "You can have it." It was common for them to eat off each other's plates and he considered if maybe they were too comfortable with each other. Maybe there was no excitement or mystery left. He didn't believe that, though. A whole new dimension of emotions was just waiting for them, if only she'd let it happen.

She finished it in record time and wiped her mouth. "Now I feel better. I'll be on a sugar high for the rest of the day, but I'm better."

Sipping his coffee, Beau turned his thoughts to something else. "Why don't you trust the doctor?"

She looked at him over the rim of her cup. His eyes were dark and warm, like the coffee, and just as stimulating. Now was the time to tell him her secret, her insecurities and her fears. Something held her back. She trusted him more than anyone, but she still wasn't ready to expose the monster under her bed.

"I guess I'm too closely involved."

"She's your sister."

She nodded. "I know what you're going to say—not to get emotionally attached because Delia and the baby could be gone tomorrow."

"Yes."

She twisted her cup. "It's not easy for me. My parents turned their backs on Delia. I can't do that. I have to be here for her and the baby."

"I know." He drained his cup.

She reached out and ran the back of her hand across his cheek, feeling his stubble against her sensitive fingers.

He rubbed his jaw. "I need a shave."

"I like it."

"Really?"

"Sure. You're like a rugged he-man you see in the

magazines." But Beau looked better than any man she'd ever seen in a magazine because he had a kind heart and a loving soul.

"You like those type of men?"

She grinned. "I'll never tell." She pushed back her chair. "I better get back to Delia. She's probably awake by now."

He followed her to the elevator. "Think I'll go home, shower and change."

"Would you mind checking on my gang and make sure they have enough food? And if you have time, let them out for a few minutes." Beau had a key to her house and often checked on her animals.

"Okay. I'll be back later." He strolled away with his smooth, easy strides and she watched him with a heavy heart. She had to do something about their relationship and soon.

THE TIME SEEMED TO CRAWL as the baby was undergoing tests. Macy paced and watched the clock. Finally she went to Delia's room. She was awake, drinking juice.

"How are you?" Macy asked.

"Sore from head to toe and ready to get out of this place. The doctor said the baby's undergoing some tests. What's wrong?"

"She's making a squeaky sound when she breathes. They're trying to determine the cause."

"Dammit. I can't even have a kid right. What the hell am I going to do with a sick baby? Macy, what am I going to do? I can't handle this."

Macy tucked Delia's hair behind her ears and love for her sister filled her heart. So many memories surfaced from Delia's childhood. *Macy, help me. Don't tell Mom and Dad. Just one small favor. I love you, Macy.* And Macy never said no. She would always be there for Delia.

"Just love her," Macy said simply.

Delia squirmed in the bed. "I don't know how to do that. Macy, please help me."

"You know I will. I'll show you how to take care of her. I'll show you everything."

"I don't think I can. I just can't do it."

She knew Delia was confused and overwhelmed at the enormous responsibility, not to mention that her hormones were out of whack.

"They'll bring the baby in a little while for you to nurse. Once you hold her, you'll feel completely different."

"Nurse?" Delia pushed up in the bed, a look of terror on her face. "No, no. I can't do that. This baby was an accident and I don't plan on nursing it."

Macy stroked Delia's arm. "A lot of mothers choose to use formula."

Delia squirmed again. "She won't be like me, will she, Macy? Impulsive, foolish and a little crazy?"

"You only think of yourself that way. I see someone who could be an unbelievable young woman if you'd just let it happen."

Delia sighed. "Go away, Macy. I have to decide what to do."

"You don't have a lot of options."

"That's where you're wrong."

Macy didn't know what to make of that so she put it down to hormones. Delia would feel differently once she held her baby.

"I'll go check on the baby. Get some rest. You've had a rough night."

"Macy?"

She turned back.

"I'd like to name her Zoë."

Macy felt a moment of relief. Delia was showing an interest. That was very good. "Would you like the father's name on the birth certificate?" She might be pressing her luck, but she tried anyway.

Delia shook her head. "You just don't give up, do you? Just put Zoë Jane Randall on the birth certificate."

Macy was taken aback. Jane was her middle name, named after Irene's mother. "I like it."

"Thought you would. It's for Grandma."

"Grandma Jane would be proud."

"Yeah. She was the only one who ever took an interest in me."

That was very true. Delia had defied discipline as a kid, but Grandma Jane had a way with her. She passed away when Delia was twelve and after that Delia's problems had escalated out of control.

"Is there anyone you'd like me to call?"

"Like who?"

"I haven't seen you in a year, so you had to be living with someone, someone who might be worried about you."

Delia scooted down in the bed and pulled a pillow close. "You're the only one who worries about me.

That's because you don't know any better and you never seem to learn."

Delia drifted off to sleep and Macy walked out with a sigh.

BEAU CHECKED ON Macy's animals and fed them—a ritual he was quite used to. When Macy worked and he was at home, the trio stayed at his place. He often let them out and took them for walks. Freckles didn't believe in exercise, but the dogs jogged with him sometimes.

They followed him to the door, so he let them come to his house, knowing they wanted some company. They curled up on his bed while he showered and shaved. Putting on clean jeans, he watched them.

Macy had taught them all sorts of tricks. One was making up the bed. He'd just thrown the sheet and comforter back last night, intending to crawl into bed after the game. But he'd never made it.

Lucky caught the corner of the sheet with his teeth and pulled it across the bed, slipping off the side of the bed and hanging by his teeth until the sheet pulled tight. Lefty did the same with the comforter. Then both dogs jumped onto the bed and sniffed and pulled until they thought the job was done. Freckles hopped into the center, curled into a ball and promptly fell asleep.

Lucky and Lefty barked at her and Beau smiled at their antics. "Thanks, guys," he said. "Time to go home." They followed him to Macy's. He hated to leave them, but Macy would be home soon. Or at least he hoped she would.

He drove to his mom and dad's. He had to tell them about the move, which he wasn't all that sure about anymore. The aroma of something good cooking greeted him as he entered his mom's big kitchen, her haven. She loved to cook. Katie, his five-year-old niece and Jake's daughter, sat on a bar stool pulled up to the island staring at some cookies that obviously had just been taken out of the oven. Bandy, a small black-and-white dog and one of Macy's rescues, looked up at Katie, waiting for a morsel of food.

"Uncle Beau." Katie jumped off the stool and ran into his arms.

He swung her around and kissed her cheek.

Katie pointed to the cookies. "Granny and me made peanut butter cookies. Want one?"

"You bet."

Katie slipped to the floor and he smiled at his mother. Her brown hair was turning grayer every day, but she still looked the same to him, petite with a few extra pounds and a heart of gold. She stood on tiptoes to kiss his cheek.

"Hi, dear. How was your trip?"

"Pretty good."

Katie came toward him walking very carefully with a cookie held in both hands. Bandy hopped up and down behind her. Althea grabbed a napkin and Katie deposited the treat gently on the table. Beau sat down and took a bite, Katie's big brown eyes watching him.

"Is it good?" she wanted to know.

"The best ever."

"It's got lots of love in it. Granny and me always put it in."

He kissed her forehead. "And I taste it."

Andrew walked in, his glasses perched on his nose. "Beau, son, I didn't know you were home."

Beau stood and hugged him. Accepting his stepfather, Andrew Wellman, into his life after living with Joe McCain hadn't been hard at all.

Beau was afraid of his father and his temper, but he'd never been afraid of Andrew. Everything he'd learned about kindness and caring, everything that wasn't inherited, he learned from Andrew. He taught him about life and how to be a man with a sensitive heart and a strong faith. Church had been the cornerstone of his new life and he needed that just as his mother had. Without her eldest son, she was lost, and so was Beau.

Now they all had a second chance and he'd never seen his mother happier. She thrived on being a grandmother.

Andrew turned to Katie. "I've got the movie all set to go. Ready?"

"Yay." Katie clapped her hands. "Is it about the donkey?"

"Yes."

Katie looked at Beau. "Want to watch it?"

"No, thanks. I'll talk to Granny."

"Okay. Grandpa, Bandy and me will watch the movie."

After they left, Althea brought more cookies to the table. "How about a cup of coffee?"

"Sure. Where's Jake and Elise?" Katie was now in school so there had to be a reason she was here today.

"It's a teacher workday so the kids didn't have

school, but Jake, Elise and Ben had a meeting with Ben's teacher."

"Is he okay?" Ben had developmental problems and they all worried about him.

"He's fine. He wants to play Little League baseball. Elise and Jake are cautious and I don't blame them. They just want to make sure he's up for it." She set a cup of coffee in front of him.

He took a sip. "Have you heard from Caleb?"

"They're visiting Josie's family in Beckett. They should be back tomorrow." Althea smiled. "Caleb walks about six feet off the ground these days."

"He's very happy," Beau commented.

"Yes, and it's wonderful to see. I wish all my sons were as happy."

Beau shifted uneasily. "Who's not happy?" But he knew what was coming next. He'd opened a can of worms and he prepared himself for the stink. It took about a split second.

"You're not happy. You're my single son, my unmarried son."

He gritted his teeth. "Not all men have to be married to be happy."

"You do."

"Mom." He took a deep breath and shifted gears. "Macy's sister, Delia, is back and she had a baby girl last night."

"What!" Althea drew back, thrown completely off guard, as he'd intended.

"She gave birth last night," he repeated.

"How is Macy taking this?"

"She hasn't seen Delia in a year and she's trying to be supportive."

"Yes. That's Macy." Althea shook her head. "So sad what happened to that family. They just broke apart after the divorce, then Macy married that man. Don't even remember his name, but he was all wrong for her. I haven't talked to Irene in years. Macy said she's remarried?"

"Yes. Divorce is sad. I deal with it every day. Maybe that's why I'm not so strong on marriage. So far it hasn't lived up to its billing."

"Don't be cynical. That's not you."

It wasn't. He always suggested counseling to people who came to him wanting a divorce. If he could get them to talking, communicating, it helped with the process. Some only wanted to talk to him and he gladly obliged, saving a few marriages. When he did that, he knew he wasn't a bad person, a bad son.

He decided to change the subject. "I have a job offer from the law firm I visited in Dallas. Senior partnership, big office, unbelievable perks—the works."

She patted his hand. "How nice. Everyone knows what an excellent attorney you are and I'm sure there are a lot of firms who'd love to have you. But I'm also sure you refused."

"Not yet. I'm giving it some thought."

Althea's eyes opened wide in disbelief. Without a word she got up and walked into the kitchen, putting dishes into the sink. The rattle of pans was deafening in the silence of the room. Beau was dumbfounded. Clearly his mother was upset. He never dreamed she'd react like this.

Andrew strolled in. "We need cookies and milk to watch the movie."

His mother grabbed a plate and threw cookies onto it. "Beau's moving to Dallas," she said curtly.

"What?" Andrew looked from his wife to Beau.

"I had a great job offer," Beau explained.

"Dallas is so far away," Andrew mumbled, then caught himself. "But if it's what you want, son, we'll support you."

"How can you say that?" Althea flared. "I need Beau. I depend on him, we all do." His mom swung to face him. "I've depended on you since I had the courage to leave Joe McCain. You were just a kid, but very responsible for your age. After Caleb was born, I depended on you to help Caleb understand why his father denied who he really was. Most of all I depended on you to bring Jake back into the family. It took years, but you never let up on your brother."

"Mom…"

"Jake was stubborn, though, believing all the lies Joe had told him about me. It wasn't until Jake found out he had a son by another woman and needed your help legally that everything fell into place. You fought tirelessly to make that happen. That's the type of person you are."

"Thea," Andrew intervened. "Why are you dredging up the past?"

"Because Beau is the foundation of this family. When Ben's mother kidnapped him, Jake and Elise were beside themselves, not knowing if they'd ever see their son again. Then Jake turned to me needing my solace and comfort like he had when he was a boy. Ben was safely returned and old wounds began to heal. I had my son back and we became a family again. All because of Beau."

Andrew put his arm around Althea. "Thea, we all recognize what a wonderful person Beau is, but he has a right to live his own life. I'm sure he has a good reason for considering this job offer and we should support him."

His mother looked directly at him. "This is about Macy?"

"Mom…"

"She's the reason you've never married. It's always been Macy for you. Leaving isn't going to change any of that."

Beau got to his feet. "I came for support, but I can see I'm not going to get it."

"Your family needs you," Althea said.

Beau saw that for what it was—a guilt trip. He wouldn't let his mother do this to him. "Maybe it's time they needed someone else. I have my own life to live. I'm sorry if you don't agree with my decision."

"Your mother's just upset."

Beau looked into Althea's clouded eyes and the urge was strong to tell her that he'd always be here for everyone, mending bridges, mending hurt feelings and attending to everyone's needs but his own. Today wasn't one of those days, though. He turned and walked out.

"Not my Beau," he heard his mother cry. "Andrew, go after him. Tell him he can't leave."

"Thea, get yourself under control. We've never interfered in our grown sons' lives and we're not starting now."

Beau didn't wait to hear anymore. He'd spent his life nurturing his family, being the good son his mother wanted him to be. The good son he had to be. He never wanted to be like Joe McCain, unfeeling and uncaring.

As he drove away, for the first time, he felt a trace of Joe inside him. He'd hurt his mother and he'd never meant to do that. But he wasn't going back to apologize. He'd call her later. For now he needed some space, some time.

It's because of Macy.

His mother knew him well.

CHAPTER THREE

HE WENT BY HIS OFFICE and checked in with his secretary, Liz Meadows. The older woman was an invaluable asset. She'd been with him since he'd opened his practice fifteen years ago and her direct, no-nonsense manner kept his office running smoothly.

She handed him several messages. "Those need your attention. The rest I took care of."

"Thanks, Liz." He flipped through the names. There was nothing that couldn't wait.

"Since it's late, I assume you're not planning on working."

"No." He didn't feel he needed to explain further.

Liz stood with her hands on her hips, waiting.

"What?" He looked up.

"You know what I'm anxious to hear, so let's have it." She pushed her glasses up the bridge of her nose with one quick movement.

Liz knew the Dallas law firm might make him an offer—she was the only person who did and he trusted her discretion. But sometimes her avid curiosity, or just plain nosiness, got under his skin.

"The meetings went fine."

Liz rolled her eyes. "Oh, please, don't give me that bull. Did they make you an offer or not?"

"Yes."

There was a long, awkward pause.

"Are you taking the job?" Her eyes narrowed to tiny slits.

"Liz…"

"There's a lot of people in this office who depend on you for work and I'm one of them. You're just gonna up and leave us high and dry? What are we going to do for jobs? At my age the job market is not all that appealing. This isn't like you, Beau McCain. You're responsible, dependable and…"

If he heard that one more time, he was going to scream or hit somebody. And that really wasn't his nature. Liz's voice drummed on inside his head like a steady, relentless rain, annoying the hell out of him.

"I haven't made a final decision. But I will take care of everyone who works for me. No one will be without a job."

"Yeah." She snorted. "Like I want to work for someone else. I'm too old for this, Beau."

"Change is good. Haven't you heard that?"

"Ha." She waved a hand. "You're going through a midlife crisis, that's what's wrong with you. Take your family and your next-door neighbor off speed dial and go on one of those single's cruises. Have a fling. Hell, have several flings. It'll get that restlessness out of your system and make you feel young again. Then come home to your family and friends in Waco. Not Dallas. Dallas isn't for you. Take it from someone who has known you for a very long time."

He picked up a pencil and resisted the urge to break it in half. "I wish people would stop making assumptions and decisions about my life. Bottom line—it is my life, so butt out, Liz."

Indignant, she stiffened. "Whatever," she mumbled under her breath.

He stood and Liz knew just how far she could push him and when to stop. That's why she still had a job.

"Jon is handling the Powers' case and Natalie has the Coleman case." Liz shifted to business. "Anything you'd like to tell them?"

"No. They do their jobs very well." He stuffed the messages in his pocket. "I'll be back on Monday."

"Beau?"

He turned.

"You've earned this big fancy job, but I'll miss you. We'll all miss you. That's all I'm trying to say."

"I know. Thanks."

"But…"

"No buts, Liz. Stop while you're ahead. I'll let you know as soon as I decide." With that, he walked out.

IN HIS CAR HE TOOK a couple of deep breaths. He wasn't expecting this kind of opposition and it was starting to get to him. His whole life was here and he had a good job, good family and friends. Why was he running away? Why did he feel that leaving would change his feelings for Macy?

Before he could answer the questions, his cell buzzed. He saw the number. Jake. His mom had found reinforcements.

"Hey, Beau, what's going on? I just left Mom's and she's pretty upset. She said you're thinking about moving to Dallas."

His hand tightened on the cell. "It's a very good job offer. I haven't decided yet."

"This is awful sudden, isn't it?"

"I was hoping for some support, big brother."

There was a moment of silence. "Hell, Beau. I'm sorry. I was thinking about myself and my kids and the family. We all depend on you. You keep us all together and never fail to remind us about the brothers' meeting every month. We never worry about the date because we know you'll call us. But if this is something you really want to do, then I'm there for you."

"I appreciate that."

"Beau?"

"Hmm?"

"You sound strange. Are you okay?"

No. He wasn't okay. He felt like a traitor—deserting his family and friends.

"I'm fine. This is just a difficult decision."

"Don't worry about Mom. I'll talk to her."

"Thanks, Jake. How's Ben?" Beau wanted to change the subject.

"He's fine. We talked to his teacher and the coach and we've agreed to let him play in Little League. It's past the sign-up day, but we got everything okayed. We were worried because he doesn't have great coordination, but the coach thought it would be good for him. Ben is so excited that he's going to get a uniform and play with some of his friends. I told Ben you and I would practice with him, but since you might not be here Elise will have to help. Can you imagine that?"

Beau closed his eyes briefly. This was his family and he'd never let them down. He made sure he was always there for them. A paralyzing pain shot through his heart. What was he doing? Why was he feeling so guilty about the choice in front of him?

"She might be better than you think."

"Yeah. Now wouldn't that be something. I'll call you tomorrow."

"Okay."

Beau stared at the phone for a few minutes then headed for the hospital. Now that his mother was aware of his plans, it was only a matter of time before Macy found out. He had to tell her before that happened.

For his mother to enlist Jake's help, she had to be really upset. That reaction still floored him. All his life she'd encouraged and supported everything he'd done. But he'd been within easy access, not far from her. This was different. Dallas was two hours away.

She'd said that she depended on him. And she had. It had been just him and her in that one-room apartment after she'd left Joe. She'd tell him that everything was going to be okay, but he'd cry at night because he missed Jake. She cried, too. Then somehow their positions shifted and he was the one telling her everything was going to be okay.

Althea depended on him to keep them together, as did Jake. Even though they were busy with their own lives, he made sure they all stayed in contact. Suddenly he knew what his mother was so afraid of. With him in

Dallas, she was afraid the family would fall apart again, as the Randall family had.

He could call her, but he couldn't tell her with certainty that he wasn't leaving. That was still a very real possibility. He'd go over in the morning and have a long talk with her, reassure her that the family was strong and stable and nothing was ever going to break them apart again. Of that he was certain.

WHEN HE REACHED the maternity ward, he saw Macy coming out of the nursery. Her hair was pulled back and held with a clip. Loose strands curled around her face. With no makeup, the sprinkling of freckles across her nose and cheekbones was visible. And she looked beautiful. His heart knocked like a faulty engine. She pulled off her scrubs and stared at a baby in an incubator.

"Is that her?" he asked quietly, walking to her side.

Macy glanced at him. "Yes, that's Zoë, Delia's daughter. To maintain a normal body temperature, Dr. Pender decided to keep her in the incubator for a few days."

Beau stared at the tiny infant with wisps of strawberry-blond hair. She wore only a diaper, and round stickers attached cardiac and respiratory monitor cords to her small chest. His gut tightened at the sight.

"Is she okay?"

"Yes."

"What's that contraption she's wearing?" A clear plastic bubble surrounded her head.

"She's getting some extra oxygen through an

oxyhood. Dr. Pender says she's four weeks early and all she needs is time to grow and to become stronger."

He watched the concern on her face. "Do you agree with that diagnosis?"

"I'm not sure. It makes sense, but I'll feel better when we have the results of the tests." She placed her hand on the glass, her eyes on Zoë. "Isn't she adorable? And she has big blue eyes."

Beau knew that tone. He'd heard it a million times as she cooed over some dog or cat who was battered and bruised. She was that type of person, and she was already so in love with her niece that any words of caution would be pointless.

"She's so tiny," he remarked.

"She's five pounds and two ounces. Delia doesn't want to nurse her. I just fed her and she feels like nothing in my arms. So precious."

At that moment, Zoë's body jerked and became stiff. Macy immediately tensed. The nurse on duty was standing over her and put her hand through the hole on the side of the incubator to Zoë's chest. She gave the thumbs-up sign to Macy, signaling everything was okay.

"What was that?" he asked.

"Babies sometimes do that in their sleep. She's fine." Macy didn't seem worried so he wasn't, either.

"When can Delia take her home?"

"The doctor hasn't said and we have to wait for the test results. But Delia can go home in the morning."

"Is she fine with leaving the baby?"

"Yes, but she's nervous and anxious. I'm trying to get her back on her meds."

"Good luck with that. It never worked before."

"She's twenty-four now and has a baby to raise. She might be more responsible."

He watched the glow on her face. "You just never give up."

"No, not with someone I love. And with Zoë here, it will give us time to buy a baby bed and things Zoë will need."

"Macy…"

She raised a hand to stop him. "I'm helping my sister any way I can and, yes, my heart will be broken when she takes the baby and leaves. But my heart has been broken before and I'll survive."

He wondered if she was talking about her ex-husband. How much had she loved him? And what had happened in that marriage? He'd probably never know.

"When are you going home?" He had to tell her about the job offer and he didn't want to do it here.

She cocked her head to one side. "I was hoping a tall, dark and handsome neighbor would give me a ride."

That teasing light in her eyes warmed his insides. He didn't understand how two people who cared so much for each other could be miles apart in their desires. He wanted a life with her, but she just wanted him around— like his mother. Oh yeah, that was a dose of reality.

He bowed from the waist. "He has arrived, ma'am. Are you ready?"

She smiled broadly and linked her arm through his, so naturally, so right. Yet there was a tension building in him that wasn't natural or right.

"The baby's fine and Delia's sleeping. That will give

me time to make space for a baby bed in the upstairs bedroom and do some shopping. Zoë's going to need a lot of things. Delia doesn't have anything prepared." She talked as they headed toward the elevator.

"Don't you think you should rest first? You've been up all day and night."

They stepped onto the elevator and she touched his cheek. He wished she wouldn't do that. It made it that much harder for him to remain detached.

"Thanks for worrying, but you know how I am. I'm on an adrenaline rush and there's a lot of things I want to get done before Delia comes home."

Yes, he knew how she was—a bundle of energy. Sometimes she worked twelve hours, then came home, cleaned the house, shopped, took care of her animals, snatched a few hours sleep and went back to work. She was always going at a breakneck speed, as if she had to stay busy. Maybe to keep from thinking. And he wondered what she was trying to avoid.

"This will give Delia and me a chance for some time together. Maybe we can talk as sisters again," Macy said as they walked from the hospital to the parking area. "Delia has this wall of anger and resentment that's hard to break through. I'm hoping Zoë will change all that. I'm looking forward to having them with me for a while."

They climbed into his Expedition. "For a while?"

"Yes. I know this is short-term so you can stop looking at me like that."

"Yes, ma'am." He smiled inwardly at how she was trying to look at the situation realistically. But they both knew she was a cream puff when it came to animals and babies.

"Maybe, just maybe, Zoë will change Delia."

"Maybe," he murmured, but he had his doubts.

She playfully hit his shoulder. "How's my gang?"

"Fine. I let them out for a bit then they stayed at my place. Lucky and Lefty made my bed."

"Aren't they smart?" Her eyes glowed with love.

"Absolutely. But I'm sure I have teeth marks on my sheets and comforter."

"They're love marks."

"Mmm."

"You see, you need a pet. It would be so much company for you."

"No, no, no. We've been through this a million times. I work all the time and sometimes late at night."

"But…"

"No."

"Pets are wonderful. They greet you at the door with affection and they don't care if you're late. They're just glad to see you. They lick your hands, your face and steal your heart with their unconditional love."

"No." He remained strong.

"Beau, you love my pets and you'd be crazy about one of your own."

Now was the time to tell her his plans. He was moving and wouldn't have time for a pet. Driving into his driveway, he turned off the engine. "Could we talk for a minute?"

"No." She opened the door and got out. "You're not convincing me you don't have time for a pet. It's a

waste of your breath and my time. Talk to you later."
Closing the door, she ran to her condo.

Damn! He hit the steering wheel with his hand. On
a scale of one to ten, his day was hovering at a one. He'd
try again tonight—that's all he could do.

Later he saw her drive away. She hadn't even rested.
Her mind and energy was now on the baby and Delia.
He wasn't even on her radar screen of interests.

BEAU ANSWERED his messages then thought of calling
Tuck to see if he wanted to go out for a beer tonight.
Tuck lived outside of Austin and they usually met
halfway, but he had to talk to Macy. He couldn't
concentrate on anything else.

He grabbed a can of beer out of the refrigerator and
found a bag of peanuts in the cabinet. As he opened the
can, he saw the box of bacon-flavored dog biscuits. He
kept treats for Macy's animals. Their lives were as
entwined as married people, except they weren't
together. And he couldn't keep going on as if they were.

Clicking on the TV, he found a basketball game, sat
down to enjoy his beer, and forced himself not to think
about Macy. He was so engrossed in the game that the
sound of the doorbell startled him. Hitting the mute
button, he went to answer it.

Macy stood there with her arms full of shopping
bags. She charged in and deposited her load onto the
sofa, her animals following her. "I had to show you
what I found," she said, her cheeks flushed with excitement. "Once I started shopping, I couldn't stop. And
Delia's going to need all of this." She pulled a tiny pink

outfit out of a bag. "I bought this to take Zoë home in. Look, it has lacy ruffles on the back. Isn't that cute?" She didn't give him time to answer. "It has booties, a cap and a blanket to match. I got sleepers, bibs, bottles, a diaper bag and several cases of diapers, just about everything a baby will need." She kept pulling items out of the bags.

Bored, Lucky and Lefty trotted into the kitchen and reared up on the cabinet, whining. Beau gave them a treat.

"I bought a bassinet, but I have to put it together. I was hoping you'd help."

He walked back into the living room. He had to do it now. "Sure, but I'd like to talk to you first."

"I know I'm getting too involved, but I can't help it." She folded the pink outfit very carefully and he wondered if she ever thought of having children of her own. He was getting sidetracked.

"This isn't about Delia and the baby."

"It isn't?" She folded a sleeper.

"No." He took a moment. "I wanted to tell you before you found out from anyone else. My Dallas trip was about a job offer—a very good offer. I'm thinking of taking it."

Her head jerked up. "What?"

"It's a senior partnership, a salary to match and a corner office with a view of the city. The perks are unbelievable."

Her eyes narrowed. "You're moving to Dallas?"

"I have to let them know by the end of the week."

"But your life and your family are here."

"It's not an easy decision to make."

She tucked a strand of hair behind her ear and he noticed her hand shook slightly—the only sign that his leaving bothered her. His pulse skipped a beat.

She stuffed the clothes back into the bags, the neatly folded ones jumbled together. "You're my best friend. I depend on you for so many things. I whine on your shoulder and tell you my secrets."

This was it. He had to say out loud what he'd been avoiding for years. She had to know how he felt. He swallowed, never realizing how hard this would be. "Have you ever thought that we could be more than friends?" He waited, and his breath lodged in his throat like sawdust.

Macy didn't answer. She just kept stuffing the baby items into the bags. That made him angry. He deserved an answer.

"Macy, did you hear me?"

"Beau, please, I…ah…" She didn't look at him and that fueled his anger and his frustration.

"I don't want to be just your friend. I want more. I want to have a life with you in every way that counts— a home and a family."

She picked up the bags and her blue eyes met his. "I realize you've worked hard for this advancement."

He frowned. "Is that all you can say? I just told you that…"

"I'll miss you," she muttered.

It took a few seconds for him to catch his breath. "I'll miss you, too." He sighed, waiting for a miracle he knew wasn't going to happen. This was it. The final goodbye.

"I better get this stuff to my place and find room for it." She moved toward the door and glanced back.

They stared at each other. Beau wanted to say so much but for a man who was used to talking, words suddenly seemed useless.

"Will you be leaving soon?" she asked.

"I have to let them know by the end of the week, but it will probably be a month before I leave Waco."

"You'll let me know."

He didn't answer. He didn't feel he needed to.

They kept staring at each other. Years of friendship hung in the balance. Those years melted away into a moment of intense pain. Without another word, she turned and headed to her condo.

Beau flopped onto the sofa and buried his face in his hands. His leaving was about Macy, just like his mother had said. But he already knew that. He'd tried to take their friendship to another level, but she made it abundantly clear that wasn't happening. He was never going to have a life with her, share her bed, her hopes, her dreams and her future.

It was over.

And the truth of that hurt more than he ever thought possible.

MACY PACED in her living room, Lucky and Lefty matching every step. *Beau was leaving*. That was all she could think. She never saw it coming and she should have. She should have known she couldn't have Beau forever. Not this way. He needed more and so did she.

I want to have a life with you in every way that counts—a home and a family.

When he'd said those words, she'd wanted to accept everything he was offering. But she couldn't. *Why not?*

The monster under the bed reared its ugly head and fear gripped her, held her a prisoner of her own emotions. *Tell him about your marriage. Tell him the truth.* The thoughts tantalized and teased, but the monster still held her captive. She couldn't do it. She couldn't handle another rejection. It was time to let Beau go so he could find a woman who could give him everything he deserved—like the family he wanted.

To keep from torturing herself, she opened the box with the bassinet and realized her hands were shaking. Sucking in a calming breath, she decided to put it together herself. She could do it. She didn't need Beau. After reading the instructions, she grabbed her tool- box—something Beau had insisted she have for when he fixed things at her place.

A sob escaped and she fought tears. No. She wouldn't cry.

She forced herself to study the instructions. All she had to do was connect the stand to the body of the bassinet. Simple. A Phillips screwdriver was required. She stared at the set of screwdrivers. Which one?

"Mmm." She glanced at Lucky. "Which is the Phillips screwdriver?"

Lucky barked and sniffed the tools. "Don't know either, do you?"

Lucky barked louder and Lefty got in on the act.

"Quiet," she ordered. "I have to think."

It couldn't be all that hard. Studying the screws, she picked a screwdriver to match the grooves. She shouted for joy and the dogs barked again.

"Shh." It took a lot of strength and patience, but she worked on until she had the bassinet attached to the base.

Sinking back on her heels, she looked at her handiwork. It was beautiful—all white and delicate. Through her defenses slipped another memory of a precious bassinet trimmed with satin and lace.

No. No. No.

She leaped to her feet, shoved the memory away and collapsed onto the sofa. Gathering her dogs into her arms, she felt as if her world had just collapsed. The monster under the bed now controlled her and she was the only one who could turn on the light and reveal the secret she'd kept hidden in her heart.

Beau wanted her to ask him to stay. She saw it in his eyes—that's how well she knew him, and she'd wanted to. But she didn't have anything to offer him, except friendship.

Sometimes late at night when she wished his arms were around her, she'd wondered how long she'd have him. How long would they be friends before he'd want more? He was a man, after all. She'd seen him go out on dates and though it broke her heart she never did anything to stop it. Just like she'd do nothing to stop him leaving.

A tear trickled out of the corner of her eye, then another followed. She tasted the saltiness on her lips and the dogs whined at her distress. Freckles slinked along the back of the sofa and rested on her shoulder. She stroked them so they'd know she was okay.

But she wasn't.

Beau had said that she had more energy than anyone he knew. She had to keep going, doing until she exhausted herself. That way her mind was too tired to dream dreams she shouldn't—like having a husband and a family. She'd had the fairy tale. Now she lived with the nightmare.

She would never marry again, but she would always love Beau. How she wished she could tell him that and share her secret. Allen was the only one who knew. Not even her parents had known what had happened in her marriage. It was her own personal pain.

Beau was leaving.

More tears followed and she didn't bother to brush them away. She needed to cry, to cleanse away the heartache and to find the strength to say goodbye to Beau.

That night as she lay in bed her arms ached to hold him, to see the warmth in his eyes, feel his body against hers and to fulfill a need in her that she'd been denying for a long time. She wanted Beau in all the ways a woman wanted a man she loved.

Tell him.

The silence mingled with the darkness and the fear in her was very real, holding her back. Turning the light on wouldn't help. She'd still be the same person, a person no one could love.

Living without Beau was better than living with his rejection, which inevitably would come. Tomorrow she'd be better. Tomorrow she'd be busy with Delia and the baby. Tomorrow she would find the strength to face a future without Beau.

CHAPTER FOUR

TOSSING AND TURNING, Beau had a restless night. Toward dawn he gave up the struggle, showered and dressed. Today was the beginning of a new Beau—a new life. He wasn't pining for Macy anymore. The pain of her rejection was still very raw, but he'd survive.

He had several things he wanted to do today. First, he intended to buy a baseball glove for Ben, drive out to the farm, and teach him how to use it. He would enjoy that as much as Ben. Second, he planned to talk to his mother again and try to make her understand that the McCain family was strong and stable.

As he backed out of his drive, he didn't see a light in Macy's condo. She'd probably already left for the hospital. He knew she'd have a constant vigil there and wear herself out completely. He grimaced at his thoughts. Rule number one—he had to stop thinking and worrying about Macy. Rule number two—same as above.

He checked in at his office, then headed for a sporting goods store.

MACY SLEPT VERY LITTLE. As the sun crept through the clouds, she was jogging through the neighborhood breathing in the early morning breeze. At fifty degrees the air was fresh and invigorating. The oaks, elms and ash trees stood stiffly from the brunt of winter, but renewed energy filled the atmosphere with the inviting taste of spring. The stiffness would give way to a burst of new life, color and growth.

As uplifting as the outdoors was, it couldn't stop her thoughts. She cursed herself for being a coward and not telling Beau the truth. In not doing so she'd hurt him and that kept her in turmoil. But she'd done the right thing. Letting Beau go was best for him. Now she had to make herself believe that.

When she returned to the condo, she got ready to go to the hospital. She was eager to see Delia and the baby. The phone rang just as she grabbed her purse. It was the lady at the animal shelter—they had a dog that needed help. She quickly made the trip to the shelter.

"Hi, Judy," she said, walking into the building that always smelled of disinfectant. Barking dogs could be heard from the back.

"Macy." Judy stood at a counter writing something in a notebook, her features marked with sadness. "I was just fixing to call you."

"Why?"

"The dog died about five minutes ago."

"Oh." Her expression crumbled and a tear slipped from her eye. "What happened?"

"Two neighbors were arguing over the dog. He kept getting into the neighbor's yard; digging in the flower-beds and making a mess. The neighbor repeatedly told the owner to keep the dog in his own yard. But the owner didn't comply. The neighbor caught the dog digging again and he kicked him into the fence, injuring him. The dog was lifeless, so he called us. When we phoned the owner, he said we could keep him. Nice, huh?"

Macy only nodded.

"A report has been filed with the police department, but other than that there's nothing we can do. The vet said his internal injuries were too severe. I'm sorry."

Macy nodded again, her vocal cords locked.

"Thank you, Macy, for caring so much. I knew if the dog had a chance, it would be with you."

She turned toward the door.

"Macy."

She looked back.

"Are you okay?"

"Yes." She found her voice. "I'm fine, but sometimes this kind of cruelty gets to me. I'll talk to you later."

In her car, the tears flowed freely and she made no effort to stop them. After a moment she gained control. She was stronger than this. She had to be. And it was tomorrow—a new beginning with Delia and her baby.

Her mind set, her resolve strong, she drove to the hospital anxious to see how her sister and niece were doing. The hospital administrator and Macy's supervisor were in the office next to the nursery. Macy wondered what was going on. As she reached for scrubs to go into the nursery her supervisor, Harriet, called to her.

"Macy, may I speak with you, please?"

Macy followed her into the office and shook hands with Mike Goodman, the administrator. "We have a problem," he said.

She immediately thought the tests had come back and something was seriously wrong with Zoë. A feeling of déjà vu came over her. She braced herself for what she knew was coming.

Mike handed her a note. "The night nurse found this on your sister's bed this morning."

She stared down at the paper in her hand. Scribbled in large letters was: *Macy, I can't do this. I can't deal with a sick baby. Take care of Zoë. Delia*

Trying to calm her erratic pulse, she took a deep breath. Delia had left—without her baby. Macy hadn't expected this, but then Delia had been acting strange since she'd showed up on the doorstep. Had she planned this all along? Or had fear gotten the best of her? Macy experienced a moment of anger and sadness.

"We've contacted Child Protective Services," Harriet said. "It's standard procedure when a baby is abandoned. You know that."

A deep sense of unease filled her. If they called CPS, that meant they were turning the baby over to them—to strangers. No way would she let that happen. She would take care of Zoë until Delia returned.

"I'm the baby's aunt and my sister says in the note for me to care for Zoë. Doesn't that count for something?"

"The hospital has to follow procedure or we could be liable if something happened to the baby." Mike made his position clear. "If you want the baby, I suggest you hire a lawyer and make it legal. I'm sure CPS will be willing to work with you and I'd be happy to vouch for your character." His cell rang. "Excuse me." As he took the call, Harriet pulled her to the side.

"I'm sorry, but there's nothing we can do. If you really want to keep the baby, call a lawyer. But it's the weekend and you won't be able to hire one until Monday."

"Thanks, Harriet. I'm aware of the rules, but this is my niece and I don't want her to go to strangers. I can take care of her."

"Well, the baby's test results haven't come back yet so you probably have until Monday before they move Zoë."

Macy walked out into the hall feeling numb. How could Delia do this? What was she thinking? This was typical of her sister, though. She always ran when things got rough, but she just had a baby and needed rest and care. Where was she? *Delia, what have you done? Please call me. I'll help you.* She turned her thoughts to a more pressing matter—finding a way to keep Zoë.

She knew a lawyer—a good one. Calling Beau was out of the question, though. She'd hurt him enough. She couldn't just pick up the phone and call as if nothing had happened between them. She'd find another lawyer.

Walking to the large picture window of the nursery, she watched Zoë, her little chest moving up and down. If she did have a heart problem, she would need someone to love and care for her, to give her their undivided attention. In foster homes, there were usually several children and special attention wouldn't be a priority. Zoë moved her tiny hand and Macy's heart contracted. She couldn't allow her to go to strangers. In that instant, she knew she'd do anything to keep her.

Even call Beau.

BEAU CAME OUT of the sporting goods store with the best baseball glove he could buy. He'd even bought a new ball, the kind used in Little League. Now he'd drive out to the farm and surprise Jake and his family. That would help him to feel better and to get another perspective on his decision.

As he climbed into his car, his cell rang. *Macy.* Why was she calling him? He started to ignore it, but he wasn't sixteen. He was an adult and could handle talking to her.

"Hello."

"Beau, I'm sorry to bother you, but I need your help."

He inhaled deeply. "What is it, Macy?"

"Delia has left the hospital during the night without the baby. CPS has been called and they're on the way. I need a lawyer to gain temporary custody of Zoë. Please help me."

"I'm on the way." Even though he should have hesitated, he didn't.

Delia was gone. That was sooner than Beau had expected. She'd definitely had a plan when she came to Macy. Macy would love that baby with everything in her. But what was going to happen when Delia wanted the baby back?

He clicked off thinking that some things never change. He'd make sure Macy had custody of Zoë. Macy'd ripped his heart out and stomped on it and still he was there for her. And probably always would be. That's what real love was all about. Why couldn't Macy see that?

He knew her well enough to know that she was hiding something—something about her marriage. How did he get her to talk to him? Poking out a number, he realized he was already breaking rule number one. But not thinking or worrying about Macy wasn't going to be an option. Maybe the next rule should be to admit that and go from there.

Liz answered her phone.

"Morning, Liz. I need you in the office in about an hour."

"Beau McCain, it's Saturday and I was planning on going to a movie."

"Sorry, Liz. It's important. I could do it myself, but you know how you hate me messing with your filing system."

She sighed. "I'll be there."

Beau made his way into the hospital and found Macy pacing in front of the nursery. Her hair was loose and disheveled, as if she'd been running her hands through it. Delia had just dealt her another blow. Macy's arms were folded around her waist as if to ward off the pain.

His gut twisted at the sight and he walked closer to her.

"Beau," she said in a breathless tone. "Thank you for coming."

Before he could respond, a voice said from behind him, "Beau McCain, are you working on a Saturday?"

He turned toward the voice. "Morning, Joanne. Seems you're working, too."

"I'd introduce you, but evidently you know each other," Macy said.

"Oh, yes. Beau and I have worked a lot of cases," Joanne replied. "So you're Ms. Randall's attorney?" She didn't give him time to answer. "You know the rules as well as I do. Once a baby is abandoned, she becomes a ward of the state and put into foster care until a stable home can be found."

"You also know that there are always extenuating circumstances. Macy Randall is the baby's aunt and wants to care for her. I'll have the papers in your hands by the end of the day, appointing Ms. Randall the child's legal guardian."

"Not only handsome, but a miracle worker, too?"

Beau grinned at the harmless flirting. He'd known Joanne a long time. They understood each other and they both worked for the good of the child. "Face it, Joanne. This baby is better off with Ms. Randall."

"The sister did leave a note to that effect." She shifted the pile of papers in her arms to show him the note. "But I need more than a note. I need an order signed by a judge."

"You'll have it."

"The baby has health problems and I'll have to have something sooner than this afternoon."

"That's almost impossible."

She shrugged. "My job is to look after the welfare of the baby. Sorry, Beau."

Beau looked into Macy's worried eyes and he knew he had to pull out all the stops. "May I have a copy of the note?"

"Give me a minute." Joanne shifted the papers again and walked into an office.

"You think you can get something done today?" Macy asked, her voice anxious.

"I'll try, but Zoë's not going anywhere for a few

days. That'll give me plenty of time. It'll just be a lot more paperwork and I'd rather get it done now."

"Me, too." Macy glanced toward Zoë.

Joanne came back and handed him a copy. "You have two hours. That's all I can give you."

Beau strolled away with the note in his hand. He needed a miracle. In his truck, he called Liz.

"See if you can locate Judge Brampton. I'm on the way to the office." Judge Roland Brampton was known for his fairness and being a diligent advocate for children's rights. If Beau had a chance of getting the guardianship paperwork done today, it would be with Roland.

"He's going to love being bothered on a Saturday."

"Just do it, Liz."

As he arrived at his outer office, Liz was on the phone. In a minute she followed him into his office.

"The judge's wife said he's playing golf this morning." She laid a piece of paper on his desk. "That's his cell if you have nerve enough to call him."

"Did his wife give you his cell number?"

"Of course not." She lifted an eyebrow. "Remember the Dobbins case?"

"Sure."

"The judge's daughter was having a baby and he gave me his cell to call when I had the papers ready for him to sign. I jotted it down for future reference."

"You're a marvel." He picked up a pad and handed it to her. "We're going to file a motion for temporary guardianship with these names on the document."

Liz stared at the names. "Macy…"

"I don't have time to explain. Just get the paperwork done."

She gave him an indignant glance and walked out.

Without a second thought he poked out the judge's number. He'd been on the receiving end of a judge's ire before and this was probably not going to be an exception. It rang several times before he heard the judge's voice.

"McCain, this had better be important." Obviously he'd looked at the caller number before answering.

"It is, judge." He told him about Macy, Zoë and Delia's disappearance.

"The mother left a note?"

"Yes, and I have a copy of it. The baby makes a wheezing sound when she breathes and the doctor has run tests to determine the cause. The results aren't in yet, but this child may need special attention. In foster care, you know that's not going to happen. Macy Randall is her aunt and a neonatal nurse who will love and give the baby all the care she needs. I'm sorry to bother you on a Saturday, judge, but a child's welfare is at stake."

"I'll be in my office in an hour. You better have the paperwork in order. I'll go over it and if it reads to my satisfaction, I'll sign it."

"Thanks, judge. I'll see you in an hour."

In less than an hour, Beau walked into the judge's office. The motion was granted in less than ten minutes. He then hurried to the hospital.

Macy was in the nursery, sitting by the incubator watching Zoë. He didn't bother her. He walked on to the supervisor's office, where he'd agreed to meet Joanne. He handed her a copy of the signed papers.

She glanced through it. "You are a miracle worker."

"I'll need a copy for our records," Harriet said, handing the papers to a nurse. "I'm so glad Macy will have custody of this baby. She'll be well taken care of and that is everyone's main concern."

Joanne picked up her briefcase. "I'm glad I don't have to find a home for her. Foster homes for babies who require special attention are scarce."

Beau headed back to the nursery with a copy of the papers in his hand. Macy was coming out and her eyes grew big when she saw him.

"What happened?"

"It's done. You have legal guardianship." He gave her the papers.

"Oh, my." Her hands trembled against her mouth. "Thank you." She threw her arms around his neck and hugged him.

He breathed in her scent and felt the softness of her skin, her body. For a moment he allowed himself to enjoy the sensation. Then he removed her arms and looked into her eyes. "Don't thank me. I would have done it for anyone." With that, he walked toward the elevator.

"Beau."

He stopped and hated himself for that reaction. Why didn't he just keep walking?

As he stared at her, she brushed back her hair with a nervous hand. "You're angry with me."

"Yes." He had to be honest. "I've known you forever and I thought we could talk about anything. But when things get personal like last night, you shut me out and back off. I know it has something to do with your marriage, yet you refuse to talk about it. That means we don't have much of anything—not love or trust and certainly not friendship."

She bit her lip and didn't speak.

"Goodbye, Macy." He took the stairs, needing the exercise.

MACY GAZED AFTER HIM, trying to still the quakes in her. She gulped for air. Dredging up every ounce of strength she had, she went back to Zoë. She'd made a choice and she now had to see it through—no matter how much it hurt.

Slipping into her scrubs, she saw Dana, a friend. Dana was petite with dark hair and eyes. She used to work nights with Macy, but after the birth of her daughter she'd switched to days.

"Hey, I just heard. That's a bummer about your sister, but that little baby is going to have a great mom."

"Thanks. I'm a little in shock at the moment. I didn't expect Delia to bail this early."

"How are you going to handle working nights and a baby?"

"I haven't even thought about it, but I haven't taken a vacation in years. I'll probably take some time now and hopefully Delia will surface."

"Good luck. If you need some help, just holler."

"Thanks. Has Dr. Pender been by this morning?"

"I haven't seen him, but he did call earlier wanting a report. He'll probably come by later."

"Yeah." But Macy wanted to talk to him now. "How does Zoë seem to you?"

"Her breathing is raspy, but all her vitals are strong. We see these cases occasionally and she'll outgrow it. You know that, so stop worrying. And everyone is keeping a close eye on her."

"Thanks, Dana." Taking a seat by Zoë, Macy never felt so alone in her life. She'd pretty much alienated everyone close to her. Tears burned her eyes and she forced them away. No more tears. She would survive. She always had.

BEAU HEADED FOR Jake's farm outside of Waco. He crossed the cattle guard and drove to the old farmhouse with the dark green shutters. Jake had renovated the place, but it looked much the same as when Beau was a kid. He'd lived the first years of his life here, learned to ride a bike down the dirt road, jumped out of the hay loft as a super hero, breaking his arm, and spent many days running through the cotton fields playing with his dog, Willie. So many memories—some good, but most were bad.

Although it seemed a lifetime ago, Joe McCain's abusive nature was still imprinted upon his memory— the yelling, cursing and hitting. He never wanted to be that kind of man, feared by his family. He didn't have to worry about that. The way things were going he'd never have a family. Unrequited love was hell.

CHAPTER FIVE

STOPPING AT THE GARAGE, Beau saw Ben, Katie and Wags, their dog, playing in the backyard. Ben and Katie were throwing a baseball to each other. With Ben's coordination, he missed it almost every time, but he'd improved so much over the years and he was always eager to try new things, much to Jake and Elise's dismay and worry.

With the glove and ball in his hand, he got out. Ben and Katie came running, Wags loping behind them.

"Uncle Beau! Uncle Beau!" They threw themselves at him and he held them for a moment, knowing it was going to be hard not being able to see these two every week. He pushed such thoughts away and drew back.

"Look what I brought." He showed Ben the glove.

"What is it?" Katie asked.

"Your dad said that Ben was going to play in Little League so I bought him a baseball mitt to fit his hand. I bought a new ball, too."

"Wow!" Ben's brown eyes grew enormous. "A real baseball glove like…like real players use. Thanks,

Uncle Beau." Ben sometimes had problems with words and he often paused to finish a sentence.

"It sure is," Beau told him. "Try it on and see how it fits."

Jake and Elise came out the back door. "Hey, Beau," Jake called.

"Daddy, Mommy, look…look what Uncle Beau got me." Ben held up the mitt. "It fits…good." His face all smiles, he worked his fingers in the glove.

The brothers' eyes met. "Thanks, Beau," Jake said.

"That was so sweet of you," Elise added, giving Beau a hug.

"Now let's see if you can catch with it," Beau said. He, Jake and Ben walked off into the yard. Elise, Katie and Wags watched from the sidelines.

They spent the afternoon playing ball. Though Ben could barely catch the ball with his hand, he did much better with the glove. And that surprised all of them, especially Ben. The boy's enthusiasm made up for anything he couldn't do.

By the time Beau left he was in a better mood, but now he was having more than second thoughts about moving to Dallas. Family was important to him. It always had been.

He needed a beer and a friend to talk to, so he called Tuck. They agreed to meet in Salado, a small historic town between Waco and Austin. When Beau walked into the diner, Tuck was already seated at a table.

Beau pulled out a chair. "You beat me."

"As a Ranger, I've traveled all these back roads and I know all the shortcuts." With dark hair and eyes,

Jeremiah Tucker could easily pass for a McCain. He also had a tender heart and he and Beau got along well. "How about a steak? I haven't eaten much all day."

"Me neither. Sounds good."

They placed the order, and a waitress brought two beers. "How are Eli and Caroline?" Beau asked.

"Fine. But Eli is about to drive Caroline and me crazy. He's bought every book he can find on childbirth and pregnancy and has actually read them, reciting parts to Caroline, who is about ready to strangle him. I've never seen anyone so nervous about having a baby. We might have to sedate him before this is all over."

Beau smiled. Eli and Tuck were foster brothers and lived not far from each other on the same property where they were raised. Big Eli was frightened to death of a little baby. It had taken Caroline two years to get him to think about being a parent. It was probably the way he was raised as a young boy—without a father. Joe McCain left scars on all his sons. But Eli and Tuck had incredibly good foster parents who loved them and had given them all that had been missing in their lives.

"He'll make a great father."

"Yeah." Tuck took a swallow of beer. "So how was your week?"

Beau told him everything that had happened in the past few days, even the part about Macy.

"Hell, man, we need something stronger than beer." Tuck leaned closer. "You told Macy how you felt and she basically said goodbye."

Beau nodded. "That's about it. She acted as if she didn't hear what I'd said."

"That's cold. It doesn't even sound like the Macy I've met."

"It isn't. I know something happened in her marriage that she won't talk about. I'm not sure how to get her to open up."

Tuck leaned back. "I've seen a lot of abuse cases and women that have been hurt tend to avoid another relationship, unable to handle the pain again."

"Macy knows I would never hurt her."

Tuck nodded. "Women who have been sexually abused avoid intimacy. Maybe that's what Macy's afraid of. As long as the two of you are friends, she's fine."

Beau swiped a hand through his hair. "Man, I don't even want to think anything like that happened to her. That would tear me up."

Tuck twisted the beer bottle. "Maybe that's why she hasn't told you. She knows you can't handle it or feels you might think differently about her."

He took a big gulp of his beer. "Macy knows me better than that. She knows...hell, I can't say anything for sure. For two people who are so close, we seem to be miles apart."

Tuck didn't say anything for a moment. "You think moving to Dallas is going to change the way you feel about her?"

"Nope. But I have to get away. I can't live the rest of my life like this—seeing her every day and not..."

"Then move across town. That way you won't be so close to each other."

Beau fiddled with label on the bottle. "This offer in Dallas is a deal like I dreamed about in college."

"I dreamed about being a rock star in high school, but I adjusted my thinking."

Beau laughed. "You? Quiet, unflappable Jeremiah Tucker, wanted to be a rock star?"

"I play a pretty mean guitar."

Beau held up his beer. "Here's to dreams."

Tuck raised his. "And change."

The waitress laid two sizzling steaks in front of them. "Can I get you boys anything else?" she asked.

"No thanks, ma'am," Beau replied.

The waitress pinched Beau's cheek. "You're so sweet. Holler if you need anything." The woman had to be in her sixties with heavy makeup and bleach-blond hair.

Beau cut into his steak. "Don't say a word," he warned.

Tuck complied with a silly grin.

After a moment Tuck changed the subject. "Have you told Caleb you're planning on moving?"

Beau swallowed and took a swig of beer. "No. Telling my family is like walking through a minefield. They keep exploding in my face without warning."

"Your mother didn't take the news well?"

"No, and neither did Jake."

"Then stay in Waco and make everyone happy."

"Mmm." That's what he always did—tried to make everyone happy, but himself. Maybe it was time to change that, too.

He glanced at the adjoining poolroom, where country music hummed on a jukebox. A couple of cowboys were playing at one table, but the other was empty. He didn't want to think anymore. He needed action. "Finish your steak and I'll beat your ass at pool."

"In your dreams."

Beau downed the rest of his beer and headed for the pool table.

MACY STAYED at the hospital until Dr. Pender arrived, but he didn't have any information. He hadn't received the test results and he didn't expect them to show anything. Zoë was doing fine. He said if that continued Macy could take her home at the end of the week.

End of the week.

That's when Beau had to make a decision about Dallas. She tried not to think about that as she fed Zoë. She didn't take the nipple well and a lot of milk ran out her mouth. But it was the raspy breathing that bothered Macy. Being a nurse, she had seen this before, so why couldn't she shake this internal fear?

Zoë was so tiny and Macy held and cuddled her. This was Zoë's time out of the incubator. Babies needed that human touch. A baby needed a mother. Zoë needed Delia.

How could Delia leave her own child? How could she expect Macy to take on this responsibility? This was a human life, not a goldfish Delia wouldn't feed or a chore she wouldn't do. When Macy thought about it, she just became sad.

Delia had never learned responsibility or how to deal with life and its ups and downs. And she was ill-equipped to cope with a new life. Delia knew her limitations. That's why she ran. *Please come back. I will help you.* Macy pushed the plea out of her mind, concentrating on the fragile life she held. It was late when she finally went home.

There wasn't a light at Beau's so he must be out. It was almost ten and he was usually home by now. She wanted to thank him again for what he'd done today. Maybe that wasn't a good idea. But she still wondered where he was.

Though it was late, she called her mom so she'd know about Delia.

"That's typical Delia. What else did you expect?" Irene asked.

"I expected her to care for her own child."

"Macy, she's not like you. When are you going to see that?"

Probably never, Macy thought, because she loved her sister. Her mother seemed to have washed her hands of her youngest daughter.

"I have legal guardianship of Zoë," she said in a rush.

There was a long pause. "Oh, Macy. Is that wise?"

"They would have put her in foster care."

"Macy, what are you going to do when Delia returns for the baby? She won't think about your feelings. "

"I know, but Zoë has a wheezing sound in her chest when she breathes and the doctor has run some tests. We don't have the results yet." She took a breath. "I was concerned it might be her heart."

"Oh, no."

"The doctor says it's stridor that she will outgrow, but I have to be sure."

"Macy, the doctor would know immediately if it was her heart. You're a nurse, you know that. Don't over-react because of what happened with Sabrina."

"I'm trying not to. I deal with babies every day, but this is different. I feel this uneasiness."

"Would you like me to come to Waco for a while?"

Macy was surprised by the offer. "No. I can handle it."

"I might come for my own peace of mind."

Her mother said the right thing for a change and Macy felt uplifted by her concern. "Thanks, Mom. For now I don't think it's necessary, but you might want to see your granddaughter. She's very tiny and has this patch of strawberry fuzz like Delia had when she was born."

"She sounds very sweet. Please keep me posted."

She hung up and thought she should call her father. It didn't take her long to decide against it. If he were concerned, he would have called back to check on Delia, but he hadn't. He knew Delia was pregnant, yet he chose to ignore them once again.

Hearing a noise, she hurried to the window. It wasn't Beau—only a neighbor across the street. Where was he?

She sank onto the sofa and gathered her animals into her lap. "We've going to have company in a few days," she told them.

Lucky whined. Lefty looked up at her. Freckles didn't move a muscle.

"It's a baby and you have to be on your best behavior."

Lefty barked.

"I know you will be." She stroked his head and stared at the bassinet—all delicate and white, ready for a new arrival. Memories beat at her.

No. No. No.

How long could she keep pushing painful thoughts

away? She took a deep breath and walked over to the bassinet. Sitting on the floor cross-legged, she fingered the silk of the skirt.

Don't overreact because of what happened with Sabrina. It wasn't Sabrina she was overreacting about, but she couldn't tell her mother that.

She and Allen had searched and searched for the perfect bassinet. They knew the baby was going to be a girl and Allen wanted it to be one-of-a-kind. A specialty shop had one on an antique brass stand that swung back and forth. The crib itself was brass, too, but the bedding and skirt were made of delicate cotton, silk and lace. She thought it was a bit much, but Allen loved it so they'd bought it.

She drew a ragged breath. They buried their baby girl in it.

Her chest tightened in pain and she gulped for air. Her immediate instinct was to push the thoughts away like she always did. Tonight, though, she needed to remember. To remember a little girl she'd loved beyond measure and a husband…

She gulped in more air. A few months into their marriage, they began to have disagreements. He didn't support her need to help animals and refused to allow her to have any more pets in the house. That angered her and they often had words. In the end he relented because she agreed not to pick up any more strays. When she did, she took them to the animal shelter.

Then she found out she was pregnant and they were thrilled. They were happy again waiting for the birth of their child. The pregnancy went smoothly. She didn't have any problems until…

She pushed to her feet and walked to the window. Pulling back the curtain, she saw everything was dark except for the streetlights revealing an empty street. Beau still wasn't home. She would have heard him if he had come in. The curtain fell softly into place. Beau wanted her to talk. What would he say if she told him she'd killed her precious beautiful baby? He would look at her differently. Allen had. It was better to live with the monsters than to see that look in Beau's eyes.

IT WAS AFTER ONE when Beau drove into his garage. He and Tuck had each won two games at pool. They decided to play the tiebreaker next week. Next week. He had to make a life-changing decision by then. To stay or to go. He threw his keys onto the kitchen counter. To stay or to run.

That's what he was doing—running away. As that thought settled in his mind, the decision was clear. His job, family and friends were here and this is where he needed to stay. He wasn't pulling up roots and starting over. But first, he and Macy were going to get a few things straight.

He'd been kind, gentle and caring—all the qualities he'd been taught. To get Macy's attention, he might have to become the bad son his father had called him, even though he'd spent all his life proving that statement wrong.

As a kid he'd believed his father's words and at times shouldered the blame for the breakup of his family. If he had stayed like his father had ordered him to, then his mother wouldn't have left without her sons.

But that was a child's guilt, a child wanting his

family to be what it wasn't. As he grew older, he realized that staying wouldn't have made things better. His mother knew what was best for her, her sons and her unborn child. Still, the bad son was branded upon his soul. That's why he had the need to keep the family together now—to keep everyone happy.

He wondered, though, if the need arose because a part of him was afraid that he was a bad son. And that he had to keep proving over and over that he wasn't.

He dragged his hands over his face. Maybe it was time to find out the truth—to see if he could be selfish and hard like his father. And maybe for once think only of himself and his feelings

It was a foreign emotion to him, but he'd tried everything else with Macy and nothing had worked. He wouldn't force her to do anything, but he was going to pressure her to talk. He knew how to do that, he did it in court. She had to tell him what was holding her back. What had happened in her marriage? And he had to be prepared for the answers.

That settled, he fell into an exhausted sleep.

THE NEXT MORNING Macy was at the hospital early. She wanted to feed Zoë so she'd know someone who loved her was there. Even as an infant that was important.

Dr. Pender came in with the test results. There was nothing wrong with Zoë's heart. She was just a preemie and had a laryngeal problem found in newborns known as stridor. As Zoë grew stronger, the raspiness would stop.

"So you can rest assured it's not her heart," Dr.

Pender said. "Just watch her closely. You know what to look for and if the symptoms change, just call me."

"Thanks. I had to be sure," she replied. Macy still had her doubts, but for now she had to trust the doctor.

Later, she spoke with Harriet about time off and Harriet agreed to an indefinite period with pay. Macy didn't want to stay away from work too long, but she had the time and she took it. She and Zoë would need a period of adjustment. Macy prayed that Delia would soon return before she became so attached to Zoë that she wouldn't be able to let her go. She always kept that at the back of her mind—this was only temporary.

THAT MORNING Beau went to visit his mom and Andrew since he didn't get there yesterday. He had breakfast with them and Althea was much more relaxed, not pressuring Beau and trying to be very supportive. He didn't tell his parents that he'd changed his mind. His plans weren't final and he didn't want his mom to think she had any influence over his decision.

Caleb and Josie arrived mid-morning. Caleb was all smiles and Josie didn't even resemble the woman he'd met over a year ago. Today she was radiant. Back then she was hollow-eyed and pale. She'd been found wandering the streets of Austin, without a name, without a memory and with a bullet in her head. A cult had taken her in and Eli had rescued her from them. But Caleb was the Ranger who stole her heart.

Caleb worked tirelessly to bring her back from all the pain and to help her recover her memory. It had taken over a year for Caleb to unravel the mystery of Josie's identity. The hardest thing Caleb ever had to do was to leave Josie with her family and return to Austin alone. Beau had never seen his brother so low. But Josie had found her way back to Caleb and they'd now been married four months.

Leaving Josie had not changed Caleb's feelings for her. Real love was like that—everlasting. In a moment of clarity, Beau realized moving to Dallas wasn't going to change his feelings for Macy, either. Away from Macy and his family he'd be disheartened and lonely. He knew then that he would be turning down the offer on Friday.

After lunch, Beau and Caleb sat on the patio each drinking a beer. Josie and Althea were in the kitchen and Andrew was watching golf on TV.

"So you're planning to leave Waco?" Caleb said out of the blue.

Beau looked up. "Mom called you?"

"Sure did. All in a panic."

"Yeah." Beau watched Bandy playing with a ball. "Never knew I was so important to the family."

"You're the biggest mother hen I've ever met."

Beau cocked an eyebrow. "Smile when you say that."

Caleb grinned, then leaned forward. "So why the change of scenery all of a sudden? What's going on with you?" Caleb held up a hand. "No. Let me guess. Macy."

Beau nodded. "I told her about the job offer."

"And…" Caleb prompted when Beau stopped speaking.

"Nothing. Absolutely nothing. She wished me well."

"Wait a minute." Caleb shook his head. "Something's not right."

"I told her I wanted us to be more than friends and that I wanted a life with her, a home and a family."

"And still nothing?"

"No. She just wanted me to let her know when I was leaving."

Caleb leaned forward, his elbows on his knees. "That took guts, big brother. I'm proud of you."

"For all the good it did me."

Caleb's eyes narrowed. "Beau, I hate to ask this, but you did tell Macy that you loved her?"

"What?" His mind quickly went over the scene with Macy. Oh, God! He hadn't.

"You didn't, did you?"

Beau squeezed his eyes shut for a moment. "No. But she knew what I meant."

"You have to say the words, Beau." Caleb spoke slowly and succinctly. "I'm not a walking encyclopedia on women, but I know they need to hear those three little words. Hell, men do, too."

"It wouldn't have mattered. When I brought up the subject, Macy couldn't get out of my condo fast enough." Beau knew those three little words wouldn't have changed a thing. "Besides, Delia's back. She had a baby and quickly abandoned it."

CHAPTER SIX

"WHAT!"

"Delia appeared after a year of not a word. She was eight months pregnant and had the baby. The next morning Delia was gone. I filed a motion to have Macy appointed the legal guardian and it was granted. So you see, Macy's mind is now on other things."

"You made sure Macy is the guardian of Delia's baby?"

"Yep."

Caleb shook his head. "You just keep opening yourself up for more pain."

"I think it's a legacy."

"Mmm." For a moment they both thought about a father who caused nothing but pain. Caleb studied the tips of his boots. "Well, from your baby brother who knows you better than anyone, you'll hate it in Dallas."

"Just about figured that out for myself."

"So what are you going to do?"

Beau ran both hands through his hair. "Push Macy until she tells me what's bothering her. I have to hear her say that she doesn't love me or want a life with me." He moved uneasily. "Do you know anything about Allen Graves?"

"No. Only met him a couple of times. Seemed like a nice enough fella."

"Something happened in that marriage."

"Want me to do some checking?"

"Yes, and see if you can find out anything on Delia, an address would be nice. The hospital contacted the police so there's a warrant out for her arrest, but I doubt if anyone will actively try to find her."

"Probably not. There's too many major crimes to be solved."

"I just know she's coming back for that baby and it's going to break Macy's heart."

He could feel Caleb's eyes on him. "What about your heart?"

Beau looked at him. "Made of steel."

"Yeah, with marshmallow filling."

They both laughed and Josie walked outside and slid onto Caleb's lap. She slipped an arm around his neck. "What's so funny?"

"Beau trying to be tough when I know he's a cream puff."

"Women like a sensitive man." Josie trailed a hand through Caleb's hair. "That's one of the many reasons I love you."

They shared a long, deep kiss and Beau cleared his throat to no avail. They kept kissing. "Don't you two have a bedroom?" he asked.

They drew apart, both grinning. "We forget that sometimes," Caleb replied.

Beau stood. "Must be nice. I'll catch you later."

Before Beau entered the house, Caleb called, "I'll call you tomorrow."

"Thanks."

He said goodbye to his parents and headed home to wait for Macy. Tonight she was talking to him—one way or another.

WHEN BEAU REACHED HOME, there was no sign of life at Macy's. He knew where she was—the hospital. He was about to go there to see how Zoë was doing, but changed his mind. He wanted to talk to Macy somewhere private. Flipping on the TV, he made himself comfortable to wait for her.

It was almost nine when he heard her car. He gave her a few minutes then made the short distance to her front door and rang the bell.

Macy opened it almost instantly, Lucky and Lefty at her feet, Freckles in her arms. Her hair was neatly pulled back, not a strand out of place, but the worry in her eyes told a different story.

"Oh, Beau, come in." She stepped aside. "I'm glad you came by. I wanted to thank you again for…"

He squatted to pat Lucky and Lefty. "I told you at the hospital that you don't have to thank me. I would have done it for anyone."

"Still, it saved me a lot of worry."

Beau stood. "I came over to talk to you."

"Oh? Are there papers for me to sign?"

"No. I want to talk about you and me."

She frowned. "I don't…"

"I do." He walked over and sat on her beige sofa that

was covered with flowered throw pillows. He took a deep breath and looked directly at her. "Something is bothering me and I need to get this straight for my own peace of mind." He paused. "I tell you I want a life with you and you show no emotion at all. That was cold— not the Macy I know. I could have been telling you the time of day. Why, Macy? Why did you choose to ignore my feelings? I need to hear an answer from you."

"Beau…"

"We've known each other for a long time and I deserve more than that."

She sat on the edge of a straight-backed chair. "I'm sorry. I'm not ready for a life with anyone."

"Why not?"

Her eyes narrowed. "You just have to accept my decision."

He rested his elbows on his knees, his hands clasped together. "Sorry. I can't. I need more." He took a deep breath. "I love you, Macy. I have for a very long time. Tell me you don't love me and I'll leave and never come back."

She looked down at the carpet and he couldn't see her eyes. He kept pushing, not willing to give up so easily.

"Tell me about Allen."

Her head jerked up. "That's none of your business."

Her protest didn't stop him. "What happened in your marriage? You and I both know your reticence has something to do with your marriage. You never talk about it. Did Allen abuse you?"

Her eyes flared. "Of course not."

"Then tell me about Allen. Do you still love him?"

"Beau…"

"He seemed like a nice man and he seemed to care for you, yet you were married less than two years. What happened?"

She remained silent.

"Macy…"

"He divorced me, okay?" In an angry movement she stood and walked to the bassinet in a corner.

"*He* divorced you?" Beau was thrown for a second, but quickly recovered. "Was he having an affair?"

"No." She fingered the lace on the crib.

Beau hated to go on, but their future was at stake. "Then why did he divorce you?"

"As I told you, it's none of your business."

"And you know I'm not stopping until you tell…"

She swung around, her eyes flashing. "Because I'm not perfect. He wanted a perfect wife and I wasn't."

That made no sense to him. She was perfect to him in every way. "What are you talking about?"

"This conversation is over." She headed for the door. "Go home, Beau."

He caught her arm before she reached the door. "I love you and I want a life with you. I'm not leaving until you tell me why you can't love me."

Her eyes clouded over. "Because I'm the reason my baby is dead."

If she had slapped him, he couldn't have been more shocked. He shook his head, wondering if he'd heard her correctly. "What baby?"

"Go home, Beau. Please." Her voice was thready and weak.

"You can't say something like that and expect me to leave." He took another deep breath. "When did you have a child?"

Macy walked back to the bassinet, knowing the monster under her bed was out in broad daylight and she couldn't pretend it didn't exist or wasn't real. But could she tell Beau what had happened? She touched the lace again, also knowing that she had to. She couldn't keep living with all this pain inside her. And she owed Beau an explanation.

"I had a baby girl four months before I returned to Waco." Her voice was shaky but she got the words out.

"You never mentioned having a child."

"It was too painful to talk about."

A long silence followed.

"What happened to the baby, Macy?"

"She was born with a congenital heart defect known as atrial septal defect, meaning she had a hole in her heart and had to undergo open-heart surgery. She died four days later. I held her as she took her last breath."

"Macy." His voice was soft, comforting, but she didn't feel it. All she felt was the pain in her chest.

"You wanted to know, so I'm telling you."

"Why do you think you're responsible for her death?"

She looked at him and wished she hadn't. It was there—the disbelief, sadness and the shock. "The defect was genetic and I carry the gene. My sister Sabrina died the same way. I passed the defect to my baby and that's the reason she died."

"Macy, you can't blame yourself. You…"

She rounded on him. "I can and I do. You wanted to know and now you do, so please leave."

He took a step toward her. "Macy…"

She backed away. "No. This is the reason I've never told you or anyone. I don't want to hear what you have to say. My pain is private and my own. I will never marry again or have another child so you have no future with me. Please accept that." She ran to her bedroom and slammed the door.

Beau stood for a moment, feeling numb and helpless. *Macy had a baby.* He never expected anything like this. He'd been her best friend yet she hadn't shared her deepest pain. She'd endured this all alone. His first instinct was to go after her, but he recognized she needed time to herself.

Old wounds had been reopened and now he cursed himself for forcing the issue. He slowly made his way back to his place. He wouldn't rest tonight, though. Too many painful revelations, but at least he understood Macy a little better. He knew why she wouldn't allow herself to love him and why she showered so much attention on abused animals. She was hurting and nothing was ever going to heal that pain. Except pouring her love on someone she couldn't hurt.

And she was afraid of hurting him. He knew his instincts were right in deciding to stay in Waco. Macy needed him and there was no way he'd leave now. He'd bide his time, be there for her—as always, because now that Zoë was in her life she was going to need someone. Predictably, she would push him away, but as his brothers would attest he was never good at taking no for an answer.

He and Macy were meant to be together. Now he had to convince her of that. Deep down he wondered, though, if she were still in love with her ex. She hadn't said she wasn't. The loss of a child had torn them apart, but how did Macy feel about Allen now?

TELLING BEAU had a cathartic effect on Macy. She didn't cry herself to sleep or have horrible nightmares. Beau knew. Someone else knew her pain. For years she'd kept the secret from as many people as possible, even her parents. Their friends in Dallas had known, but other than that, no one she was close to had shared her pain. That was the only way she could deal with it. Beau was different. He wouldn't judge her or think differently about her.

She wasn't sure why she thought people would think differently about her. When her baby had been born, everyone at the hospital, even their friends, had been very understanding and supportive. Maybe she thought differently about herself. That was a sobering thought.

She'd always wanted children and having that taken from her changed her perception of herself. She didn't have that choice anymore and she felt flawed.

Beau had asked if she still loved Allen. She didn't. After losing the baby all they did was argue. He wanted her to go to counseling, but she refused. The pain was so deep she couldn't share it with anyone. Allen didn't understand her reasoning. Talking is what they needed, he'd said, but she saw the way he looked at her—with blame and guilt. Or maybe that's the way she saw herself because Allen had really tried, but she was unresponsive.

When Allen filed for divorce, she didn't blame him. Their marriage was in shambles and she was inconsolable. Allen had said it was her fault the marriage had fallen apart. It was. She was to blame for everything.

That's why she cared for abused animals. It gave her a sense of self-worth and she loved being a caregiver. Now she would have Zoë to care for and love. She would be busy. Maybe a miracle would happen. Maybe her heart would begin to heal.

But what did she do about Beau? *He loved her*. Selfishly she allowed herself to feel the joy of those words, then stored them in her heart as a keepsake of all that she was losing.

She'd leaned on Beau for too long. That was a big mistake. She had no future to offer him, yet she couldn't let go. Now he'd brought their relationship into the open and she had to back off and let him have a life—without her.

BEAU SPENT MOST of the night thinking about Macy. He hadn't understood her paranoia about Zoë, but now he did. How painful it must be for her to deal with another baby girl. However, she showed no signs of shirking the job Delia had bestowed upon her. He fervently prayed that nothing happened to Zoë.

He was in his office by eight. After being away, he had a stack of phone messages to return. Macy was never far from his mind. He kept missing her most of the week and it wasn't intentional. His firm had two important trials going that required his attention. When he returned home at night, the lights were always out at Macy's and he knew she was spending every moment at the hospital.

He was giving her time, but he didn't intend to do that much longer.

BY THE END OF THE WEEK the doctor removed Zoë from the incubator. They would monitor her and if she did well, Macy could take her home. She had a few nervous jitters, but she knew a lot about babies and knew she could handle it. The wheezing didn't seem as bad and she began to believe the doctor was right. She had just overreacted because of what had happened to her.

At the back of her mind she kept thinking that it was the end of the week. Had Beau taken the offer in Dallas? Had he made the call? As much as she wanted him to go, she just as strongly wanted him to stay. All week she had purposely avoided him and she was glad he hadn't insisted on talking to her again. Torn by conflicting emotions, she concentrated solely on Zoë.

BEAU MADE THE PHONE CALL on Friday and turned down the job offer with his regrets. Afterward he felt a sense of peace about his life. He was fighting for what he wanted. He was fighting for a life with Macy.

ON SUNDAY, Macy took Zoë home. A new addition to the household caused a bit of excitement with her animals. Freckles had no interest in her at all. The dogs sniffed and whined and Macy gave them a stern lecture about baby Zoë being off-limits. They were good dogs and she knew they wouldn't bother the baby.

As she placed Zoë in the bassinet, the doorbell rang. Beau stood there and her pulse leaped with excitement. He wore jeans and a T-shirt, his at-home clothes, and she thought he never looked more handsome.

"Hi. I saw you bring Zoë home. May I see her?"

She breathed in his tangy masculine scent and her whole body relaxed. He was back and he didn't seem upset or angry. She couldn't believe how much she'd missed him and how much pleasure he brought her just by being so compassionate and caring. He understood her in ways no one else did.

"Sure. I was just telling my crew about her."

Beau walked in and looked into the bassinet. "May I hold her?"

"Okay, but wash your hands first. At this stage she's susceptible to so many things." She had no qualms about letting Beau hold Zoë. He was around Jake's kids all the time.

Beau headed for the kitchen and did as she asked, then he lifted Zoë into his arms as if it were something he did every day. He sat on the sofa and Macy thought how right he looked with a baby cradled in his arms. Ben and Katie loved him because he was so good with them. He deserved his own kids. She felt a catch in her throat and realized even with Beau's kindness her decision hadn't changed.

"She feels as light as a feather and…" His voice trailed away as Zoë's little fingers curled around one of his. "Oh, my."

Macy sat beside them. "Isn't she adorable? Look at that bow of a mouth, those sweet cheeks and those big blue eyes."

Beau looked at her, his eyes soft.

"Don't say it," she said.

"I wasn't going to say one word of caution. I've held her for five minutes and I'm already attached to her." He glanced back at Zoë. "Have you heard from Delia?"

"No, and my mother hasn't, either."

"Do you have any idea where she was living?"

"She called me one time from Las Vegas asking for money. I know because I had to pay for the call."

Zoë squirmed and they both focused their attention on her. After a second she went back to sleep. A tense silence followed.

"Her wheezing is very noticeable," he remarked, listening to Zoë breathe.

"Yes. It's stridor, which I've seen before in newborns. It's an abnormality of the larynx. We just have to give her some time to outgrow this. I had to make sure it wasn't her heart."

Beau looked at her again. "How are you?"

"I'm fine." She was lying.

"No, you're not."

Looking into those dark eyes she wanted to say so many things. But she didn't. Instead she got to her feet and straightened the blanket in the bassinet.

Beau laid Zoë in her bed and pulled the blanket over her. He glanced at Macy. "I might be out of line, but I have to say this. It's not your fault your baby died. That would be like blaming your mother because she passed the gene to you. And it was wrong of Allen to blame you."

"This is not a comfortable subject for me."

"I know. I'm next door if you need anything." With that he walked out.

Macy stared after him with her mouth open. She quickly closed it. He was such an exceptional man and she couldn't have loved him more than she did at that moment. But she still had a lot of fears to conquer. She was so glad Beau wasn't angry with her anymore.

He hadn't said a word about the job offer. She wanted to ask but felt she didn't have that right. Was he leaving?

She sank down by Zoë. "It's just you and me, kiddo." Lefty barked. "And you, too."

But she needed more. She needed Beau. Would she ever feel she had the right to tell him?

BEAU VISITED Zoë every day and he and Macy resumed their easy, comfortable relationship. He told her he wasn't taking the offer in Dallas and she seemed relieved. But there was an underlying tension that they both could feel. Beau ignored it, intending to break through Macy's defenses. It might take time, but he could wait. But he wondered just how long.

Caleb turned up a lot on Allen Graves. He was a pharmaceutical salesman in Dallas and he'd remarried. He now had a son and was knee deep in debt. He had no criminal history—just a couple of traffic tickets. Being a big spender seemed to be his only crime.

He felt guilt about spying on Macy's past. At the time he thought Allen might have been abusing her and Beau was looking for answers. He now had those answers.

On Delia, Caleb had very little. She had a Las Vegas address, but had moved out months ago. After that there was no trace of her. Where was Delia? And when did she plan to come back?

The brothers had their monthly meeting at the same café where Beau and Tuck had met. It was the midway point for all of them.

After ordering, they discussed family matters. "Beau's having a midlife crisis," Jake said, squeezing lemon into his tea.

"You want to talk about what's going on with you?" Caleb asked.

Beau shifted in his chair. "I'm not moving to Dallas," he told them as the waitress served steaks all around.

"Hear, hear," Jake said. "Now we can stop worrying about you."

"Have you told Mom and Dad?" Caleb asked.

"No. I wanted to do that in person, but they're visiting Gertie in Austin at the moment. I'll let them know as soon as they return."

"Beau," Eli asked, "how do you think this family would survive without you?"

"You'd manage."

"But who'd bug the crap out of us?"

Beau cut into his steak with a grin. "I'm not the only one with that kind of talent."

"But you do it so well, and what about our brother get-togethers?" Eli continued. "I like our basketball time where we can get down and dirty and I can kick your asses."

"Yeah, right." Jake laughed. "We just enjoy showing that we're middle-age crazy."

"It took us a long time to become a family and we all want it to stay that way," Caleb said.

"That's for sure," Jake agreed.

Caleb looked at Beau. "How are things with Macy?"

"I told her how I feel and I'm optimistic about the future."

Dead silence followed his words.

"You told her how you feel?" Eli asked, shock on his face.

"Yes. After seven years I thought it was time."

"Evidently she didn't respond in kind."

"It's complicated," Beau said, not ready to share Macy's secret.

"Hell, man, just telling a woman those words takes a lot of guts, and believe me I know. I almost lost Caroline because I couldn't." They all knew Eli's story and his problems with the "I love you" factor. Seems all the McCain brothers suffered similar maladies.

Eli looked at his watch.

"Will you stop that." Tuck glared at him.

"I don't want to leave Caroline too long."

"She's two months pregnant and not even showing. Her sister, Grace, is with her, so relax."

Eli shook his head. "Man, this is the hardest thing I've ever done."

The brothers laughed.

"It's not funny. It's scary as hell. We're bringing this small life into the world and we're totally responsible for it."

"It comes easy," Jake said. "Trust me, and there's not another feeling in the world like it."

Eli nodded. "I'm looking forward to being a father."

"If Caroline doesn't kill you first." Tuck smiled slightly.

"I know I'm driving her crazy."

Tuck patted him on the back. "Relax, have a beer and let Caroline enjoy her evening with her sister."

The easy camaraderie between the brothers helped Beau to unwind. He would have missed their meetings, but love makes a man do crazy things. He'd told them that he was optimistic and he was. Other than that he wasn't ready to share anything else.

He stood. "Tuck and I have a pool game to finish."

"Great. I'll play the winner." Eli also got to his feet.

"What do you think, little brother?" Jake asked Caleb. "Want to try to beat me in a game of pool?"

"You're on," Caleb replied, glancing at his watch. "But I want to get home to Josie pretty soon."

Tuck grinned. "You married guys are pathetic."

Eli slapped him on the back. "Your day is coming. You may not believe that, but it is."

"Yeah," Jake said, getting to his feet. "We all like our freedom until the right woman comes along. And come to think of it I have a wife at home who won't go to bed without me, so let's get this pool game started."

It was after ten when Beau pulled into his garage. Macy's light was on and he wanted to go over and see Zoë. He wasn't sure Macy was getting much sleep since she watched Zoë constantly. He knew she was worried about Zoë's breathing. After what had happened to her baby, she had a reason to be. Having total responsibility for a child had to be scary, like Eli had said. And for Macy it was even worse.

He decided not to go over. It was late and he had to be in court early. Besides, he knew Macy had already put Zoë down for the night. He could say he'd forgotten just to get to see Macy, to make sure she was okay. He didn't do that, either. Instead he went to bed.

ZOË HAD BEEN FUSSY all day and Macy had spent a lot of time holding her. The noisy inspiratory breathing was more prominent when Macy was feeding her. A lot of the milk ran out of her mouth and Macy was worried about how much milk she was actually taking in.

When Macy laid her down, she seemed to gulp for air. Macy immediately picked her up. It was a pattern she'd followed all day and she was exhausted. After feeding Zoë one more time, she held her until she fell asleep, then gently placed her in the bassinet next to Macy's bed.

Hurriedly she took a shower and slipped into an oversized T-shirt. She turned off the lights, leaving on a night-light. Lucky and Lefty were in their beds in the kitchen. Freckles rested on the sofa in the living room, her favorite spot. Sometimes the pets slept in her room, but she had to stop that now with a baby in the house, just in case Zoë had allergies.

Macy watched Zoë closely. Her features were serene and peaceful. So tiny, so fragile and so very precious. How could Delia leave her? When Delia was born, Macy was the happiest ten-year-old on the planet. She'd always wanted a sister and having one was better than she'd ever imagined.

Irene complained that Delia didn't know who her mother was because Delia would rather be with Macy than anyone. Delia cried a lot as a baby and she always needed attention. Then began the unruly years of running, jumping, screaming and talking incessantly. Her parents knew Delia had problems.

Several doctor visits proved them right and thus began many years of trying to manage Delia and her medication. Her temper tantrums were common and seemed to get worse as she got older. She'd throw them in the supermarket, at the movies and in church, anywhere to get her way. The adults usually gave in. Her parents fought about disciplining Delia all the time. But Macy always felt Delia had a good heart and that would win out.

Then Macy went away to college and her parents started having problems in their marriage. The divorce hit them all hard and neither Irene nor Macy could control Delia. She was resentful, bitter and started skipping classes. When Delia ran away the first time, it was a wake-up call, but nothing Irene nor Macy said got through to Delia. And Ted, their father, was nowhere to be found.

Macy had no answers as to why Delia would abandon her baby, but she had some pretty good guesses. Delia was overwhelmed, confused and scared. Macy just wanted her to call so they could work this out.

Her eyes grew heavy and she wondered why Beau hadn't come by tonight. Then she remembered it was the last Friday of the month—the brothers' meeting. She'd see him tomorrow.

She didn't know how long she was asleep when she

stirred with an uneasy feeling. Opening one eye, she peeped at Zoë, who was so still and her face was...*blue*. Ohmygod! Macy leaped from the bed, grabbed her and shook her gently. Zoë gulped and began crying at the top of her lungs.

Macy's heart was beating so fast that she couldn't think, but one thing blared like a siren in her mind. *Zoë wasn't breathing! Zoë wasn't breathing!* If she hadn't woken up, the baby would have died. In the morning... Macy trembled from head to toe. With a shaky hand, she reached for the phone, carefully balancing wailing Zoë on her shoulder.

As soon as she heard the click of the receiver, she breathed, "Beau...Beau..." then her vocal cords closed up.

CHAPTER SEVEN

AT THE SOUND OF TERROR in Macy's voice, Beau sprang from the bed and was at her door in less than fifteen seconds. Macy stood in the open doorway, her hair in disarray, gently cuddling a screaming Zoë. Tears streamed down Macy's face and his gut twisted into a hard, painful knot.

"What's wrong?"

"She…she…"

Beau closed the door and took Zoë from her. "What's the matter, little angel?" Beau laid Zoë on his shoulder, patting her back and she quieted down. He looked at Macy's pale features. "What happened?"

"I…ah…"

"Take a deep breath," he instructed.

She drew in deeply and let out a ragged breath. "I…I woke up and took a peep at her and she was…was blue." She pushed her hair away from her face. "Zoë wasn't breathing. After I picked her up, she started screaming and breathing again." She paused and took another deep breath. "Something is wrong, Beau. Something…if I hadn't woken up…"

"But you did and I think we better get her to the emergency room."

"Yes, yes. I'll put on a pair of jeans."

Beau realized all he had on was pajama bottoms. He handed Macy the baby. "I'll grab some clothes and get the car."

A look of fright crossed Macy face as she held Zoë.

"It'll be okay," he told her.

"I don't know."

"Get dressed. I'll be out front in less than two minutes. We'll talk later."

In exactly two minutes Beau was in front of Macy's condo. She came out with Zoë and a diaper bag. In ten minutes they were in the emergency room. Macy filled out papers and the doctor on duty took a look at Zoë. She slept peacefully and the doctor could find nothing wrong.

"When I woke up, she wasn't breathing and her face was blue," Macy told him. "Something caused that."

"Ma'am, the baby is fine now. She has inspiratory stridor, which is very evident. Color change is a part of that and you should see your doctor to talk further with him. Try laying her on a pillow or at a thirty-degree angle. Other than that, ma'am, there's nothing else we can do."

"Don't call me ma'am and don't patronize me. I want Dr. Pender to look at her."

"Ma…ah…Dr. Pender isn't on-call and we can't call him unless it's an emergency."

"It's an emergency to me."

"I'm sorry. I don't see this as an emergency."

Macy was about to lose it, so Beau stepped in. The doctor was a pompous ass and too young and arrogant for his own good. "Are you willing to take responsibility for this baby if something happens to her during the night?"

The doctor looked at him as if he'd just crawled out from beneath a rock. "Listen…"

Beau didn't give him a chance to vent his opinion. "The hospital would be liable. I know. I'm a lawyer. Do you want to take that risk?"

That seemed to do the trick. His expression changed completely. "I'll call Dr. Pender."

"Thanks," Macy said as the doctor walked out. "I was losing my temper and about ready to hit him."

"I could see that," he replied, staring at Zoë who was asleep in her arms. "By looking at her, you wouldn't think anything was wrong with her."

"I know. That's what's so scary."

The young doctor came back into the small room. "Dr. Pender wants to speak with you," he said to Macy.

"Sure." She rose from her chair and handed Beau the baby. "I'll be right back. Don't take your eyes off her."

Beau took Zoë and sat in Macy's chair. As he looked at her, she squirmed and blinked, then opened her eyes. Two orbs of dazzling blue seemed to peer at him and he wondered how far babies could see at this age.

"Hi, little angel. Feeling better?"

Zoë stretched and made a face. "Okay. I won't ask questions. But I'm a lawyer and I'm used to doing that. Annoying, huh?"

Her head titled to one side and she once again drifted into blissful sleep. Beau placed his hand over her small chest. He immediately felt the thud of her little heart. And it was strong. "What's wrong, angel?" he whispered. "Is everything inside working the way it should? Your aunt fears it's not, but don't worry, we'll both be here to make it better."

As he said the words he knew they were true. He'd warned Macy about getting emotionally involved, but he should have warned himself.

He babysat Ben and Katie all the time. He'd had a car seat in his car until Katie got too big for it. At least once a month he took them to the movies and he enjoyed their excitement over the kiddie films. Sitting in the ice-cream shop with the two of them, he often wondered what it would be like to be a father.

Holding Zoë, he had an overwhelming feeling of love and protection, much like what a father would experience. Did he want to be a father? In his thirties he would have said "yes" immediately. But he was forty-two now and he realized it was possible it would never happen. He thought about that for just a minute.

As he sat there holding Zoë, he also realized it didn't matter. Loving Macy was more important to him. If he had to give up fatherhood to have Macy in his life, then he would. For the first time he acknowledged how deeply he loved her, and to him, that was all that mattered.

Macy came back and Beau glanced up. He stared at the freckles scattered across her nose and her curly hair sticking out in all directions. Why did he love her so much? He couldn't answer that question. He just knew that he did.

Clearing his throat, he asked, "What did he say?"

"Dr. Pender has called an ear, nose and throat doctor

and wants me take Zoë to see him at eight in the morning to check if something is obstructing her breathing. His name is Dr. Jim Fletcher."

"And in the meantime?"

"He said to watch her closely and to lay her on her stomach in a tilted position to sleep. Also, to hold her in an upright position for thirty minutes after feeding her."

"We can handle that," he said, getting to his feet.

"Beau…"

"Let's go home."

Macy didn't protest and soon they were back at the condo.

"You want the first or second shift?" Beau asked.

Macy looked up from placing Zoë on a pillow in the bassinet. "What are you talking about?"

"We have about five hours until morning. We'll take turns watching her because I know that's what you're going to do."

"Yes. I'll be afraid to take my eyes off her."

"I don't blame you, that's why I'm offering to help."

Her eyes caught his, concerned but relieved. "You don't have to do that."

"You can't go on no sleep."

She brushed her hair from her face. "I need very little sleep."

"I'm aware of that, but humor me." He picked up the bassinet. "You get a couple of hours sleep and I'll keep the little angel in the living room with me."

"Beau…"

"Macy…"

"Okay." She gave in. She put the formula and a bottle on the kitchen counter and scribbled a note. "Instructions in case she gets hungry."

"Got it. Now go to sleep." He closed her door to make sure she'd have no distractions.

MACY SLIPPED OUT of her jeans and curled beneath the sheets. She didn't worry about Zoë. She trusted Beau completely.

As she waited for sleep to claim her, thoughts tormented her. Was something wrong with Zoë's heart? Had Dr. Pender missed something? There could be so many things and fear once again took control. She couldn't handle losing another child. And this wasn't her child. Deep inside, though, in secret places, Zoë was becoming hers.

She threw back the covers and tiptoed to the door. Opening it a crack, she saw Beau sitting on the sofa, a cup of coffee on the end table, the TV humming senseless chatter and Zoë asleep on his chest. Everything was fine and she went back to bed, knowing she could sleep with Beau here.

What would she do without Beau? Once again she was leaning on him. But for now she could do nothing else.

WHEN MACY WOKE UP, she glanced at the clock. Six thirty! She jumped out of bed and ran into the living room. The bassinet and sofa were empty. For a minute her heart threatened to pound out of her chest, then she saw Beau in the kitchen with Zoë on his shoulder. She smelled food. Was he cooking?

"I'm sorry I overslept," she said, taking Zoë out of his arms. Her hand brushed his cheek and she just wanted to lay her hand against his bare skin to feel his warmth, his strength and to let him soothe away all her worries.

"You needed the rest."

"But you have to work today."

He brushed that off with a wave of his hand. "Doesn't matter. How about French toast?"

"I love your French toast."

He cocked an eyebrow. "All the women say that."

"Well, it's true." Macy pulled the bassinet to the table, avoiding a personal comment. "You're a good cook."

"I've lived on my own for a long time and takeout gets monotonous after a while." He placed toast and coffee in front of her.

"Thanks. How did Zoë do last night?"

"No problems. I fed her about five and I followed your instructions to the letter on how to mix the formula. After I changed her diaper, she went back to sleep. She does seem to sleep better laying at an angle." He refilled his coffee cup. "She took the bottle, but she doesn't take the nipple very well. Some of the milk runs out of mouth and she pushes the nipple away, then she's searching for it again."

"I know. That's part of stridor, but there might be something more wrong with her throat. She hasn't sucked very well from birth and she's not gaining weight like she should."

"Maybe we'll find some answers this morning." He

straddled a chair, sipping his coffee. His hair was tousled and he had a growth of beard. Her senses stirred with forbidden desires and she quickly dived into her toast.

"Mmm. This is good." She took a swallow of coffee. "I hate to ask another favor, but could you please watch Zoë while I take a quick shower?"

"Sure, but make it fast. I have to shower and shave."

She looked up. "You're not going to work, are you?"

"No. I'm going with you. I had a hearing this morning, but one of my lawyers is filling in for me. I called him at five after I changed Zoë."

"Beau." He didn't want him to put his life on hold for her.

"Go take a shower."

She hurried away because time was getting short and a part of her needed someone with her today.

THE MORNING PROVED to be stressful. Dr. Fletcher and his assistant passed a thin, flexible tube that housed a light and a scope through Zoë's nose. She squirmed and cried, not liking the procedure at all. It took Beau and Macy to hold her down and Macy cringed at the pain the procedure was causing Zoë. But it had to be done, she kept telling herself. She was so grateful Beau was with her.

After they calmed Zoë down, they met in Dr. Fletcher's office. He laid the pictures in front of them. "As you can see, there are no tumors or blockage in her throat."

"So why did she stop breathing?"

"She has laryngomalacia, which Dr. Pender has told you. It's commonly known as stridor or noisy breathing. It's a sound produced by turbulent flow of air through a narrowed segment of the respiratory tract. As a nurse, Ms. Randall, I'm sure you've seen this before."

"When I trained in Dallas, I saw several cases. I've only seen very minor cases here."

Dr. Fletcher pointed to one of the pictures. "She was early, so her esophageal rings haven't fully developed. That's part of her problem. Laryngomalacia is usually a self-limited process that the infant will outgrow between twelve and eighteen months of age. Zoë just needs some time."

"Dr. Pender did inform you of my family's medical history?" Macy asked.

"Yes. Dr. Pender did a full work-up in the hospital and he faxed over the results. Rest assured there is nothing wrong with Zoë's heart. Just watch her closely, keep her tilted and in an upright position most of the time, especially after feeding, and if anything else happens just call me."

"If she had died in her crib last night, it would have been called a crib death," Macy murmured.

"Possibly."

"That's not acceptable to me," Macy said. "Something is wrong."

Dr. Fletcher sighed. "I just told you what's wrong. If there is another problem, it may take time to manifest other symptoms. Let's give her time and I'll check her again in a week."

Macy gathered Zoë and the diaper bag and they left, but Beau knew she was upset.

"Everything he said sounded reasonable," Beau told her. "Zoë just needs to grow and get stronger."

"I know, but why can't I lose this feeling that something else is wrong?"

He glanced at her. "It probably has to do with your own personal experience."

Her eyes caught his. "Do you think I'm paranoid?"

"I think you're just worried." He maneuvered into traffic. "Try to relax. We'll watch her closely and keep her tilted and follow the doctor's instructions. I'll drop you at the condo and I'll be back later. I have to check in at the office just for a little while."

As she got out, she said, "We've taken up enough of your time. We'll be fine. Take all the time you need."

He lifted an eyebrow. "I'll see you later."

She nodded, but didn't say anything else as she went inside.

Beau hurried to his office. Going through the reception area, he said, "In my office, Liz."

Liz was a step behind him.

"How did it go this morning?"

"Jon did great. Judge Wimple granted full custody of the two minor children to their mother, Mira Hodges."

"Great. I would have hated to see them go back to their father." When the kids returned from visiting their father, they always had bruises. Mira finally got the younger girl to admit their father was hitting them. She contacted Beau and he'd worked for three months to get the hearing pushed through. He'd laid the case out for the judge and his decision was all they needed. He hated to miss it, but he had no choice. Early this morning he'd called Mira and she'd understood.

This was one of those cases Beau didn't fight to keep the family together. He recognized the abusive pattern in the father. The same pattern he saw in his own father. After Joe would hit Althea he'd apologize profusely and promise never to do it again. But he always did.

"Mr. Hodges can only see the kids with supervision."

"That's even better."

"The judge did query your absence," Liz added. "Said you never miss a trial or a hearing and he wondered if you were ill."

Beau stopped looking through his messages. "What did Jon say?"

"What you told him. That you had a family emergency." Liz waited a moment, then her curiosity got the best of her. "So which family member is in a crisis now?"

"Don't pry, Liz." He didn't feel he needed to explain himself.

"I take care of your affairs so I need to know what's going on."

"Yes, you do." He agreed with that part. "I have an announcement to make."

"Oh, mercy. Not today. I have a corn that's killing me and I've had a headache since I woke up this morning. I don't need any bad news."

"I'm not taking the offer in Dallas."

"Oh." Liz's eyes brightened. "My headache just left."

"But there will be some changes around here."

Her eyes narrowed. "Like what?"

"I won't be spending so much time in the office and I won't be taking on any more cases right now. I will speak to Jon, Natalie, Jeff and Gayle. They will be taking on a bigger load."

"So what's my job?"

"You will keep me posted on all cases and make sure this office runs smoothly, as always. I'll be dropping in from time to time, but you can always reach me on my cell. It's business as usual except I won't be here as much."

She lifted an arched eyebrow. "And where will you be?"

He walked around his desk and leaned against it, feeling a need to get everything out into the open. "I'll be helping Macy take care of a little girl who's going to need a lot of attention."

Liz placed her hands on her hips. "Beau McCain, I was hoping you were taking a cruise."

He winked. "Now do I look like a cruise type of guy?"

"No. You have the biggest, softest heart of anyone I know. I wish I had a daughter to marry you off to." She shook her head. "But someone has your heart and has for a long time."

Beau folded his arms. "Yeah." He saw no need to be secretive about his feelings.

Liz hugged him. "Good luck. And don't worry about this office. I'll make sure everyone stays in line." She turned, then glanced back. "I'm really glad you're staying."

"Thanks, Liz."

ON HIS WAY HOME he realized his parents were back and he needed to tell them he was staying in Waco. He didn't have time for a visit so a phone call would have to do. He immediately poked out the number.

"Hi, Mom."

"Beau, dear. It's good to hear from you." There was a chill in her words. "Since we're home, I was hoping you'd come by for a visit."

"Sorry, Mom, I'm busy."

"You work too hard."

"I have good news."

"Oh?"

"I'm not taking the offer in Dallas."

"Oh, Beau. I'm so happy."

"I thought you would be."

There was silence for a moment, then, "I'm sorry I overreacted. I lean on you too much, I know, but…"

"It's okay, Mom. I understand. You don't have to worry about the family falling apart again. We're rock solid now. Not one of us would let that happen."

"Why don't you come for dinner. I'll fix anything you want."

"Thanks, but I have other plans." To keep from hurting her feelings he told her about Macy and Zoë.

"Oh, my. Delia left the baby?"

"Yes, and Macy's going to need a lot of help."

"You'll help her all you can. I know you will. You're a good son."

Beau smiled. "Thanks, Mom. Tell Dad I said hi." Clicking off, he kept smiling. Everything was better now. It felt pretty damn good to be loved so much. Getting Macy to love him was another matter.

He hadn't planned to take any time off, but as he walked into his office, his concentration wasn't there. His thoughts were with Macy and Zoë.

He was thinking of making Jon a partner and Beau's absence would be good for him, too. It would show Beau if Jon could handle the office while he was away. And Liz. If he didn't allow her to intimidate him, that would be a plus in Jon's favor.

He threw his jacket and tie over the sofa and stretched his tired shoulders. He wasn't sure how Macy was going to take his decision to help her. Probably not well. But then again, Macy was afraid. He saw it in her eyes and heard in her voice, so she might be more agreeable in accepting his help. All he knew was that he couldn't let her face this alone.

Falling across his bed, he was instantly asleep.

THE DAYS THAT FOLLOWED weren't easy. Macy was against him taking time away from his work, but she didn't object too strongly. She clearly saw that she couldn't do this alone. While she slept, he watched Zoë and vice versa. They made several trips to the ENT doctor with no change. He inserted the scope in Zoë's nose again and that was stressful for all of them, especially when it showed the same results. The doctor ordered a short course of steroids, but it didn't change her breathing abnormality. Nothing seemed to change and Zoë was still turning blue and wasn't gaining as much weight as she should.

They seemed to be in a vicious cycle with no

improvement. Two months had passed and Zoë was still the same. Beau and Macy had very little time together, but they shared breakfast every morning. He enjoyed those times, but the stress was wearing them both down.

He missed the brothers' meeting and the McCains found they could go on without his supervision. They all wanted to help, but for now Beau felt he and Macy had to do this.

Every day he was falling more and more in love with the little girl. Like her aunt, she held his heart in the palm of her tiny hand.

They hadn't heard a word from Delia, but Caleb had found out the name of the man she was involved with—Keith Wallston, who'd been stabbed and killed outside a Las Vegas casino. He was a big-time gambler and known for his many women, but his parents were outstanding members of the community. His mother was into charitable works and they owned a string of small hotels throughout the country. They had homes in Florida, New York and Nevada. The son seemed to have strayed from the family and gotten in with a bad crowd. Delia was in the middle of it all.

She'd come to Macy as she always had when she was in trouble. Beau wondered what Delia was into and what her plans were for Zoë. Most of all he wondered when she'd return for her baby.

He just wished they could locate her. But he wasn't sure what that would solve except to put their minds at rest. With Delia, it was a game of wait and see. Beau had a surprise for her, though. He wasn't letting her take Zoë. Not in the baby's present state of health.

He sat on the sofa, Zoë on his chest, her tiny heart beating against his.

Maybe never.

CHAPTER EIGHT

MACY DIDN'T KNOW how much longer they could go on like this. Dana offered to help and Irene also volunteered. Although Dana was a nurse, Macy knew it would be devastating if something happened to Zoë while she was watching her. And her mother would bring her husband. Macy couldn't deal with that right now.

She hated pulling Beau more and more into her life, her problems, but was powerless to change the situation. She couldn't stay awake twenty-four hours a day, and she needed someone to lean on. Macy hated herself for that weakness.

Beau's extraordinary qualities became more and more apparent as each day passed. He had Caleb searching for Delia, but so far there was no sign of her. Even if she did return, there was no way she could care for Zoë in the baby's present condition. More to the point, there was no way Macy would allow this. Zoë needed special attention and until her health problems were resolved, she was staying with Macy.

She and Beau spent a lot of time holding and rocking Zoë. Being held all the time was spoiling her, but for now keeping Zoë breathing comfortably was more important.

Right before she turned three months of age, Zoë developed bronchitis and her condition worsened. Following another round of doctor visits, they got the same answers—lung infections were typical for preemies with stridor and to keep her on medication. Macy was nearly at her wit's end.

After a horrendous day in Dr. Fletcher's office, she'd had enough. Zoë was getting older and it took both of them to hold her down so Dr. Fletcher could insert the scope through her nose to check her throat. The struggle and Zoë's pitiful cries broke Macy's heart. She just couldn't take anymore.

That evening, holding a fussy Zoë, Macy knew she had reached the end of her patience. "I can't do this anymore," she told Beau.

"What do you mean?"

"I can't take Zoë back to Dr. Fletcher and put her through that torture again. It's not helping."

"I know." He ran a hand through his tousled hair. "What do you want to do?"

"Get her to a specialist."

"Fine. Who?"

"I'll have to get a referral from Dr. Pender. I think he'll give it to me. As a nurse, I know we left normal a long time ago. This is not typical stridor."

"Okay. I'm going to my office for a while then catch a few hours sleep. Find out if he'll see her tomorrow. Let's get this done as soon as we can. Pressure him if you have to."

Macy glanced at the clock. It was a little after four

in the afternoon. She slept during the day and Beau slept at night. "I'll call now."

Dr. Pender called back a little after six. After Macy told him how upset she was he agreed to see them in the morning.

She, Beau and Zoë were in his office the next day at nine. The baby was congested and fussy, but he was able to examine her. Zoë quieted down on Beau's shoulders, her little face pressed against his neck. Beau was becoming as attached to her as she was to him. That was something Macy felt powerless to change, too.

"It's very evident the noisy breathing is typical inspiratory stridor," Dr. Pender said. "But looking through the records from Dr. Fletcher, her esophageal rings have matured with no improvement with her breathing. Her weight and growth is still a problem." He took a deep breath. "I agree a specialist should look at her. We've missed something."

"Do you have any suggestions?" Macy asked, feeling a small measure of vindication.

"Texas Children's is the best. Eileen Cravey is a pediatric otolaryngologist and I've sent babies to her before. I've always been pleased with the results."

"Could you please get us an appointment as soon as possible?"

Dr. Pender nodded. "I'll get my secretary on it and she'll be in touch." He closed Zoë's file. "I'm sorry, Macy. I know this has been hard on you and Mr. McCain. I really thought time would help Zoë, but it hasn't. Eileen is very good and I feel certain she can find whatever Dr. Fletcher and I have missed."

"Thank you, Dr. Pender."

Macy was on pins and needles waiting for the call. She was relieved when it finally came. The nurse asked a lot of questions and said that Dr. Cravey had spoken with Dr. Pender, who confirmed that a barium swallow hadn't been done on Zoë. The doctors had done X-rays and scans, but this procedure would be the first she would do. Zoë was not to have a bottle after midnight on the day of the visit so her throat and stomach would be clear. The appointment was in two days. She didn't even question Beau going with her or try to dissuade him.

Macy left her pets at the kennel and they headed for Houston. Zoë's bronchitis was much better and she took the trip well, except she woke up a couple of times obviously hungry. The movement of the car lulled her back to sleep. The appointment was early and Macy was grateful for that. She had to fill out a lot of paperwork and was glad Beau was there to watch and pacify Zoë.

She went over the baby's case history with Dr. Cravey, who was a friendly, middle-aged woman with short brown hair.

After reviewing Zoë's records, Dr. Cravey glanced at Macy. "Dr. Pender said Zoë has never had a barium swallow."

"No."

"I see Fletcher was your ENT doctor. He did his residence here. I'm surprised he didn't order one first thing."

"He just kept running the scope through her nose and stuck with his diagnosis of stridor. He said her esopha-geal rings hadn't fully developed and with age she would improve. It's getting very exhausting to watch her every minute. But now I can almost detect when she's going to turn blue. That bothers me, too, because of the loss of oxygen to her brain. That's why we watch her constantly. When she starts to breathe heavily, we immediately pick her up. When we rock her, she seems to breathe almost normally."

"Mmm." Dr. Cravey scribbled in a chart. "I see from these papers that you are not Zoë's mother."

"No." Macy swallowed, but knew she had to tell Dr. Cravey everything. "My sister abandoned her and I am her legal guardian. The guardianship papers are enclosed." Macy made sure she had everything the doctor would need to treat Zoë.

"Yes. I see. Zoë is lucky to have a loving aunt and uncle."

"Oh." Macy realized the doctor thought she and Beau were married. A slight flush stained her cheeks and she couldn't stop it. "Beau and I aren't married. We're just very good friends."

"Mmm." The doctor seemed amused. "Every woman should have a friend like that."

Macy didn't know what to say so she said nothing. Their relationship had gone beyond friendship. Beau had told her how he felt, but she couldn't dwell on that right now.

"I'll examine her first then run the barium swallow test," Dr. Cravey said as she stood.

While Zoë was being examined, she and Beau sat in the waiting room.

"I like Dr. Cravey, don't you?" Beau asked.

"Yes, and she's very knowledgeable. I hope she finds something. I have to go back to work soon. My pay has stopped and we're living off my savings. I'm not sure how I'm going to pay for all this. I put in for a loan at the bank and I'm keeping my fingers crossed that it goes through."

"If you need any…"

"No." She stopped him. "I can handle it."

"Macy…"

"Let's don't talk about this now. I'm too nervous." She tucked a stray hair behind her ear. "Thank you for being here."

Her eyes held his and she knew her eyes were saying a lot more than she wanted them to. But sometimes those feelings were hard to hide.

"Dr. Cravey will see you now," a nurse said, and Macy immediately got to her feet.

Down the hall another nurse was walking toward them with a crying Zoë. Macy gathered her out of her arms and kissed Zoë's flushed cheeks.

"She wasn't happy with our poking and prodding," the nurse said. "She mainly just wants something to eat."

Macy cradled the baby against her. "It's okay. I'm here," she cooed.

The nurse led the way into a room and handed Macy a bottle. "We need her to drink this so Dr. Cravey can take a good look at her throat."

Zoë took the bottle with gusto, but she spit it out after a couple of swallows. Macy kept giving her the nipple and Zoë kept taking it as if she were hoping for decent milk soon.

Dr. Cravey and a group of students walked in and Macy and Beau made to leave. "You and Mr. McCain can stay if you like."

"Yes, please."

They laid Zoë on a table and strapped her down, Beau and Macy on one side, Dr. Cravey and an assistant on the other. Several students stood in the background, observing.

Dr. Cravey ran a scope through Zoë's nose. She struggled and cried like in Dr. Fletcher's office. Macy cringed. They had done this so many times. She fervently hoped this was the very last.

They could see Zoë's throat on a screen as the scope went down. Almost instantly Dr. Cravey said, "Aha, there it is." She pointed to a mass on the screen.

"What is it?" Macy asked, her voice hoarse.

"Very significant laryngomalacia. Totally treatable. We'll talk in my office."

Dr. Cravey spoke to the students. "My examination today revealed her ear canals are normal and her nasal passages are clear. There is no evidence of infection. The oral cavity is likewise normal. An endoscopy revealed significant laryngomalacia, larger than normal. Everyone take a good look at the mass so you'll know what to look for if you ever have a similar case. And remember a barium swallow is a must to distinguish this. Otherwise the scope won't detect it."

Everything else went over Macy's head. Treatable. She clung to those words. The nurse handed her Zoë and Macy immediately fixed her a bottle, then they waited in Dr. Cravey's office.

Dr. Cravey smiled at Zoë as she came in. "She's happy now that she's back with you."

"What does Zoë have?" Macy asked anxiously.

"Laryngomalacia, just as Dr. Fletcher diagnosed, except it's much more severe than he surmised. And I will be sending him a letter on this. In short, it's an excess of fatty tissue of the epiglottis, which is the flap of tissue that closes off the windpipe when you swallow. The tissue blocks her breathing at times and that's why she breathes noisily and turns blue. That's why rocking helps. It moves the tissue and she can breathe."

"How do we correct this?"

"Surgery."

Macy paled, remembering another surgery that was supposed to correct the problem. But it hadn't. She held Zoë a little tighter.

"In the operating room we will use a laser to trim this excess fold of tissue. There is always some risk with surgery, but the procedure is relatively safe. She would have to spend one to three days in the hospital then she can go home."

It sounded simple, but Macy wasn't so sure.

"If she doesn't have the surgery, what could happen?" Beau asked.

"The tissue could obstruct her breathing and cause asphyxiation and death."

Macy gasped. She couldn't help it. The fear was just so real.

She felt Beau's eyes on her. "Macy, I don't think you have much of a choice. Zoë needs the surgery."

She swallowed the bile in her throat and forced

herself to do what was best for Zoë. "When can you do the procedure?"

"Usually you'd have to wait until an operating room is open, but I have a little boy who was supposed to have surgery in the morning. He's running a high temperature and we've postponed it. Since you're in Houston and I consider this an emergency, I can schedule it for tomorrow. That is, if you can stay."

Macy took several deep breaths. "Schedule it."

After that everything went smoothly and quickly. They admitted Zoë to the hospital. With all of their concern for Zoë, they'd neglected to pack an overnight bag. They hadn't planned on staying. Beau went out in search of clothes and she stayed with the baby.

The room wasn't private, but for tonight they were the only occupants. The recliner was also a rocker and she sat rocking the baby. Zoë awoke and looked at her with big blue eyes, waving her fists around. The wheezing was very evident.

"I hope I'm doing the right thing, kiddo," she said. "But I can't let you go on like this."

Zoë kicked against her. "I wish your mother was here." She wasn't sure why she wished that, other than it would take some of the responsibility off of her. Responsibility never frightened her before, but when it came to the life of a child, fear was her constant companion.

A sweet smile tilted Zoë's mouth. "You have Beau wrapped around your little finger with that smile." Zoë's breathing became labored and Macy lifted her to her shoulder. "What am I going to do about Beau?"

Sweet, caring Beau. How many men would put up

with her paranoia and fears? She felt a crack in her defenses and for the first time she let herself consider a life with him.

It was everything that was wonderful. Everything that was good. But… No. Tonight she wouldn't listen to the buts.

BEAU SHOPPED as quickly as he could, but he got caught up in the moment. He'd never bought women's clothing before, not even for his mother. Macy had given him her sizes and said to buy something practical.

So he bought practical slacks and tops. Luxurious, sexy lingerie held his attention and the saleslady was only too eager to show him a variety of items. But he settled on blue silk pajamas because he knew Macy would love them.

As he carried the bags into their room, Macy was laying Zoë in the crib on a pillow. She turned and smiled at him, making him feel ten feet tall.

"Did you get everything?"

"Yes. All the essentials, including toothbrush and paste, deodorant and shaving stuff." He set the bags in a chair. "You didn't tell me what kind of night clothes you wanted."

She arched an eyebrow. "You see me every day and you see my laundry so you know what I sleep in."

"Yes, but…"

She pulled out the blue silk pajamas and her eyes grew wide. "Beau McCain." Her voice rose, but there was a hint of laughter in every syllable.

"I thought you might like something more than a

T-shirt, especially in the hospital." He tried very hard to explain, but he felt his face grow warm. "There's a robe, too."

"I see." She held it up.

"And underwear's in the bag."

"I'm almost afraid to look."

"Don't worry—they're practical. There are slacks and blouses in the clothes bag."

"What did you buy for yourself?"

"Slacks, shirts, socks, pajamas and underwear."

"Cotton," she said, her eyes sparkling. "And do you know how I know that?"

"You've seen my laundry." He smiled.

"Yes, and I really thought you were more observant."

"Men don't notice things like that."

"Oh, please." She rolled her eyes.

The easy banter released some of the tension and she seemed to relax. He glanced at Zoë. "How is she?" The whole time they'd be talking neither had taken their eyes off of her for more than five seconds.

"Sleeping peacefully, but she'll be awake soon. It's almost time for a feeding."

Beau walked over and looked down at the sleeping baby. "This could be over tomorrow. Zoë will be able to breathe like a normal child."

"Yes. We should have come to Houston sooner, but I was trying not to be paranoid. I wanted to trust the doctors at home."

He looked at her. "Try not to worry about the surgery. Dr. Cravey is very competent."

"I'll try." She looked away. "We better get some sleep. You could go to a hotel. You'd rest better there."

"No way. I've come this far and I'm not leaving now."

She didn't try to talk him out of it. She would need him tomorrow. Macy took the bathroom first, staring a moment at the cobalt-blue silk pajamas and robe. She'd never bought anything like this for herself before. For her honeymoon years ago, she bought a white silk gown and robe. She'd packed it in with other clothes for the poor when she cleaned out the house she'd shared with Allen. All the memories from that life, she'd left behind. Only one memory remained—her baby.

These days she didn't need lingerie like this. Cotton was her fabric of choice, but the silk felt wonderful.

When she came out of the bathroom, Beau just stared at her, his dark eyes melting like the sweetest chocolate. She could almost taste the sweetness, the decadent…

"I'm done in there," she said to hide her nervousness.

"Oh. Yeah." Beau seemed distracted, then grabbed a bag and went into the bathroom.

For years she'd avoided looking for those signals from Beau. Signals that told her he saw her as an attractive woman—a woman he desired. She blew out a hot breath. She could always control her feelings, but tonight they were tempting her like a ripe strawberry sliding through rich cream. She allowed herself a moment of pure indulgence and the moment dragged on as the fantasy of Beau loving her captured her completely.

The nurse came in with a bottle for Zoë and she came back to reality with a thud. But she didn't regret the lapse. She actually enjoyed it—maybe a little too much.

BEAU TOOK A COLD SHOWER. When he'd bought the blue silk, he knew it would be gorgeous on her. More to the point, she'd look gorgeous in it. And did she. His pulse still hammered loudly in his ears.

It was an impulse buy, which was something he'd heard women talk about. He wasn't a fan of shopping. He bought what he had to and that was it. But today he'd enjoyed buying clothes for her and imagining her in them. It kept his mind off of what they had to face tomorrow.

The doctor had said the procedure was safe and he had to believe her. At the back of his mind, he was worried about Macy handling surgery of another child. But this one would have a happy ending. It had to.

When he walked into the room in his navy cotton pajamas and robe, Macy was feeding Zoë. She stood and placed the baby in the crib.

Beau reached over and kissed Zoë. "'Night, little angel."

"That was the last bottle before the surgery," Macy said. "Let's hope she doesn't wake up wanting another. We better get some rest. You can have the recliner and I'll sit by her bedside." As he started to complain, she held up a hand. "You sleep first then I'll sleep a couple of hours."

Beau didn't argue as he flipped off the light and slipped into the recliner. "This might be our last night doing this," he murmured.

"I hope so."

The room became quiet. A night-light illuminated the small space, making shadows dance on the wall.

Noises from the hall sounded like thunder, magnified by the visions in their heads.

"Are you thinking about your daughter?" He broached the subject with a bit of trepidation.

"Some," she whispered.

Relieved at her answer, he asked, "What was her name?"

"Hope."

"That's pretty. I like it." He paused. "Did she have fuzzy strawberry-blond hair?"

"No. It was more blond, like Allen, but she looked a lot like Zoë, except she weighed seven pounds at birth."

"I'm so sorry you lost her."

He heard a hiccup. "She never had a chance."

"You can't keep blaming yourself for that."

There was a long pause. "I don't want to talk about it."

"Macy, it was wrong for Allen to blame you," he said, ignoring that warning in her voice.

"He never came out and said it was my fault." The words seemed to come from deep within her. "We couldn't talk anymore and we both were so sad. It was just something in the way he looked at me."

"He was hurting, Macy."

"I know. He wanted me to go to counseling, but I couldn't share that pain. It's so deep and private. I'll never get over it."

Silence filled the room and Beau could almost read her thoughts. *It's happening again.*

"Tomorrow will be different," he said. "Zoë is older, stronger and her heart is fine."

"Maybe."

"Macy, I will be here for you and Zoë. You know that, don't you?"

"Yes, and you shouldn't. You shouldn't even be here with me. You should be taking care of a family of your own, having your own kids."

"Maybe, but first I need to find a mother for them."

The silence this time was long and awkward. "Beau…"

"Good night, Macy." He didn't want to hear what she had to say. He'd heard it before and he was sick of it. Tonight he'd rather go to sleep with the fantasy of her in his head.

CHAPTER NINE

THE NEXT MORNING, Beau was barely through shaving when the nurse came for Zoë. Macy held her, kissing her cheeks, her forehead. Zoë was hungry and wanting her bottle so she was more than fussy. She was irritable.

Beau took her, cradling the baby against him and patting her back. "This is it, little one. Today the doctor is going to make it all better." He kissed her head, hoping and praying his words were true as he handed her to the nurse.

They followed the crib as far as they could. Zoë looked at them with big blue eyes and they stood holding hands as the nurse took her away.

Beau watched Macy pace. She kept trying to sit but was up and down like a yo-yo. They didn't talk much. The time seemed to drag.

"Try to relax," he finally said.

"I can't. I'm so worried."

"Macy…"

He stopped as Dr. Cravey came into the waiting room and motioned to them. They hurried to meet her in the hall.

"How did it go?" Macy asked in a rush.

"Fine. Zoë is in recovery and you can see her in a few minutes. She'll sleep for a while. Everything went as planned. I removed the excess tissue with a laser and Zoë is now breathing normally."

"Oh, that's wonderful." Macy held her hands against her face in relief.

"Will it grow back?" Beau asked.

"No. It's just excess benign tissue."

"When can we take her home?"

"I'd like to keep her a couple of days to ensure there is no bleeding. They'll put her in a room later today, but you don't have to watch her all the time now. You'll realize that when you see her."

"Thank you, Dr. Cravey," Macy said. "Thank you."

"Yes," Beau added. "Thank you for everything."

Dr. Cravey nodded. "Now you can all breathe normally again."

As Dr. Cravey walked away, Macy turned to him. "Thank you for being here."

He shrugged. "No problem."

They stared at each other for endless seconds, then Macy threw her arms around his neck and hugged him. He felt her tremble. She didn't let go as he expected her to. Her hands cupped the back of his head and her soft body pressed into his. His heart skipped a beat. She kissed the side of his neck and her lips trailed to his cheek. He turned his head and their lips met in a blending of pure need, fueled by the years of friendship, sadness and joy. And much more. She opened her mouth and he kissed her like he'd been dreaming about. They were lost in the moment, the undeniable feelings they couldn't ignore. Neither seemed inclined to stop.

As people started coming down the hall, they slowly drew apart. "Thank you," she whispered again, stepping back, her eyes dark with emotion.

He nodded, unable to speak. But those two little words meant as a courtesy didn't sit well with him. He didn't want politeness or good manners from her. He wanted passion, as hot as possible. The spark was there. He'd just felt it. He just had to work on igniting it.

They made their way to the recovery room. It was full of cribs partitioned off with long curtains. A nurse took them to Zoë. Another nurse was removing her IV. Zoë lay on her back, sleeping peacefully. And breathing without a problem. No noises. Macy caught her breath at the wonderful sound.

Beau reached for her hand and held it. She squeezed until his fingers were numb.

"Can you hear it?" she whispered.

"Yes. It's unbelievable."

The nurse looked puzzled. "I don't hear a thing," she said.

"That's what we hear, too," he told her. "She's been wheezing almost from the moment she was born."

"Oh."

"It's over. I can't believe it's finally over. Zoë is okay. I…" Tears trailed down Macy's cheeks and she ran from the room.

The nurse looked even more puzzled.

"It's been an emotional time," he explained.

The nurse nodded and Beau quickly went after Macy.

FINDING AN EMPTY WAITING ROOM, Macy sank into a chair. Seeing Zoë breathing so naturally caused all the pent-up emotions she'd been feeling in the past three months to come to the surface. Months of hell were now over. Months of praying that they didn't slip up and let Zoë die. Zoë was going to be fine. That was an incredible gift.

She wiped away tears with a shaky hand and realized she was an emotional wreck. She had to pull herself together. Taking a couple of deep breaths, she allowed herself to relax. As she did other feelings surfaced. Her forefinger touched her lips. She'd kissed Beau—something she'd wanted to do for years. She hadn't even thought about it. After all they'd been through, she wanted to be as close to him as possible. It was everything she knew it would be. Tender, sensual and toes-curled-into-her-shoes good.

What was she going to do about Beau?

Love him. Have a life with him. The answer was so simple, yet she couldn't do it. Beau loved kids and he deserved his own. She couldn't give him that. Yesterday she let herself entertain the idea of a life with him. But today her defenses were back and she couldn't think beyond that one little, but big, obstacle.

Her heart felt heavy and she curled her hands into fists. A part of her wanted to be selfish and take what he was offering. But she couldn't do that to Beau. She loved him too much.

"Macy."

She looked up to see Beau staring at her with a worried expression.

"Are you okay?"

She inhaled a deep breath. "Yes. I am now. It's just been an emotional time. Seeing Zoë breathing so normally was just overwhelming."

"I know. We did the right thing in coming here. Zoë's better. I'm just a little upset that the doctors at home couldn't have figured this out. Dr. Cravey found it almost instantly."

"I don't have any strength left to be angry. Dr. Cravey said she would be writing Dr. Fletcher a letter. At least he'll be aware of the problem and maybe someone else won't have to go through this." She brushed away an errant tear. The tears weren't only for Zoë. They were for the man standing in front of her, who she'd soon have to let go.

"Let's have some breakfast," he suggested. "The nurse said we have a little while before Zoë wakes up."

"Okay." She stood. "I could use a cup of coffee and some food."

"They just might have donuts," he teased.

"Mmm. Sounds good."

They started toward the cafeteria. "Macy," someone shouted.

She turned to see her father strolling toward them. Tall with graying brown hair, he was noticeably thin. Years ago, he'd been heavier. Delia had said that the new wife had him on a strict diet and exercise program. At fifty-six the years were beginning to show around his eyes and mouth.

"Macy, I've been looking all over for you," he said as he reached her.

She frowned. "Dad, what are you doing here?"

"I called your condo but you never answered, so I phoned your mother and she said Delia had left the baby and the baby was having surgery here in Houston. I'm surprised you didn't call me. I don't live that far away."

"Excuse me?" she said, trying to control her temper. "I did call you and you wanted nothing to do with Delia or her baby."

"Beau McCain, isn't it?" Her father glanced at Beau with a gleam of recognition, totally ignoring her words.

Beau shook his hand. "Yes. How are you, Ted?"

"Fine."

Beau looked from one to the other. "I'll check on Zoë."

"No." Macy stopped him. "There's no need for you to leave. I have nothing to say to my father."

"I would like to talk to you, Macy," Ted said.

She hadn't seen her father in ten years. They talked on the phone but that was it. She avoided all his attempts to see her. Now he wanted to talk. The man who she'd thought could do no wrong had done the unforgivable— walked out on his family. There was nothing left to be said.

She caught that look in Beau's eyes and she knew what he was trying to tell her—talk to your father. Beau believed in families working their problems out, but there was nothing that could fix the Randall family. Then why was she hesitating? Why didn't she walk off and leave her father standing there? Just as he'd left them.

Because Beau was watching her, expecting her to do the right thing. Damn you, Beau. Without a word she turned and walked back into the waiting room. Her father followed.

Ted sat beside her. "I know you've been angry with me for a long time."

"Yes." There was no reason to deny it.

"Sometimes things happen between a man and a woman that their kids don't understand."

She glared at him. "I wasn't a kid, I was a grown woman. An explanation would have helped."

"Some things are private," he replied, not batting an eye.

"Oh, please." She folded her arms around her waist. "You gave me this spiel when I was twenty-four. I didn't understand it then and I don't understand it now. Why can't you just be honest and say you fell in love with someone else? Why can't you admit that you cheated on Mom?"

"Because I didn't."

For a moment she was stunned. He was telling her the truth. She knew her father's voice very well. "Then why?" was all she could say.

"Just accept that my leaving had nothing to do with the way that I feel about you and Delia. You're my girls. I love you."

She tried to stop the words, but she couldn't. "Is that why you never visited? Is that why you missed our birthdays, the holidays? The card with the money in it was always a loving sentiment."

He sighed. "I was going through a rough time, but my behavior to my children was unforgivable."

That took the wind right out of her lungs. He was talking like the father she'd loved and that brought back so many memories. She quickly pushed them away.

"I have tried to see you in the last few years and you've refused."

"Yes. Can you blame me?"

"No, not really." There was an awkward moment, then he asked, "How's the baby?"

Now they were on safer ground. She told him about Zoë and her health problems.

"But she's fine now?"

"The doctor says she will be."

He shook his head. "You're the kindest, most loving person I've ever known. Not many sisters would do what you've done."

She twisted her fingers together. "Zoë needed someone."

"Like every abused animal?"

She had to force herself not to smile. As a child, they had that conversation many times. *Macy, you can't help every animal. Macy, no more animals in this house. I love you, Macy.*

Forgotten words that she needed to remember. Or maybe not. They made her weak and she couldn't let her father get to her.

"Have you heard from Delia?" Ted asked after a minute.

"No, but Caleb McCain is looking for her."

"Still have a crush on Beau?"

Her eyes flew to his.

He lifted an eyebrow. "Guess I'm still not supposed to say that."

"Beau and I are very good friends," she said in her most serious voice.

"If you say so."

Her father knew everything about her and that was a bit daunting. Some girls kept diaries, but she'd told her father her secrets and her dreams. And he had crushed them all without a second thought.

She stood. "I have to get back to Zoë."

"Do you mind if I see my granddaughter?"

Macy was taken aback. Why was he showing interest after ten years? Why now? Something in her wouldn't allow her to say no and she hoped she didn't live to regret it. She nodded and he followed her down the hall.

Ted could only see Zoë for a few minutes, but he said he'd be back tomorrow. That surprised her even more.

She didn't have long to ponder what had happened with her father. Zoë woke up crying and it took all of Macy and Beau's efforts to calm her down. Finally Macy rocked her and that did the trick. The bottle helped, too. Zoë was hungry, but she didn't take it as well as Macy thought she would. Then she realized her throat was probably sore. The baby fell asleep again and they soon moved her to a private room.

Macy looked around. "This has to be a mistake. I didn't ask for a private room. I can't afford this." She glanced at Beau. "Please watch Zoë while I get this straightened out."

Beau caught her arm. "It's fine, Macy. Don't worry about the room."

Her eyes narrowed. "Did you ask for a private room?"

"Yes. It's the only way you're going to get any rest."

Anger simmered inside her. "I didn't ask you to do that."

"I know, but I felt…"

"It's not up to you," she said, her voice rising. "I can't afford this and I don't need you paying my bills."

"Don't overreact."

"And don't tell me how to act," she shouted, waking Zoë, who began to cry.

Macy immediately lifted her out of the crib, cooing to her.

"Okay," Beau said, watching them. "I overstepped, but privacy would help you and Zoë. If you insist, you can pay me back."

Macy sank into a rocker and Zoë curled up against her. Her anger dissipated as quickly as it had flared. Why did the men in her life have to be so difficult? And why did Beau have to be so nice?

After that things were strained between them and Macy thought that was just as well. They were getting too comfortable together. But the room was nice, furnished with a cot and a rocker-recliner that made into a bed. Even though the doctor said Zoë was fine, they were both up during the night checking on her.

The next morning, feeling rested for the first time in months, Macy wanted to thank Beau for the room. But thanking Beau led to other things and she had to steer clear of intimate moments.

Dr. Cravey checked Zoë once again and released her, saying she wanted to see Zoë in a week.

Her father stopped by. Macy told him everything was fine and they were headed back to Waco. He held Zoë for the first time and Macy wasn't sure what to think anymore. Ted seemed so sincere. As he left, he said he'd be in touch and they left it at that. Macy didn't know if he'd see him again or not. By late afternoon she, Beau and Zoë were on the road headed home.

They didn't talk much on the drive, then Beau suddenly asked, "How do feel about seeing your father?"

As always with Beau, words spilled out. "I have all this resentment for what he did, but seeing him and talking to him I was remembering the good father that he was. I wanted to say so many things, but mostly I just listened. He says he wasn't having an affair so I'm more confused than ever."

"You were very close to Ted," Beau remarked. "I remember he coached your soccer and Little League teams. And he made all kinds of pens for your animals in the backyard."

"Mmm." Macy glanced back at Zoë who was sleeping in the car seat. On the way to Houston, Macy had sat in the back with her in case she'd stopped breathing. "I guess I was the boy he never had. Delia never liked sports of any kind and she hated my pets, including my turtle and fish. She especially hated my dogs and cats in her room."

"Not to mention the raccoon and possum," Beau teased.

"Grandma Jane lived on several acres and my friend Tanya and I always loved to explore. We found them caught in a neighbors trap in the woods. After the vet made sure they didn't have rabies, Dad and I kept them in a cage until we could let them back out into the wild."

"I remember thinking that no one had a raccoon or a possum for a pet but Macy Randall."

"Did you think I was nuts?"

He screwed up his face in thought.

She slapped at his shoulder playfully. "Don't answer that." She relaxed in her seat. "Dad and I had a special connection, but he and Delia never seemed to connect on any level."

"Few people connect with Delia. And I'm one of those people who tried."

Beau had had his run-ins with Delia. She'd been told repeatedly that she couldn't ride her bike in the street. One day Beau turned the corner and almost ran into her. He gave her a good scolding and told Irene and Ted. Delia, in retaliation, threw mud at Beau's car. Andrew had seen her from his study so she couldn't lie her way out of it. Ted had paid to have the car cleaned, but he could never get Delia to apologize.

"I don't believe Delia is ever going to change," Macy admitted. "And I'm worried about her caring for Zoë."

"You might prepare for the long haul."

"No." She shook her head. "This is only temporary. Zoë is Delia's child, not mine."

Beau gave her a puzzled glance as he negotiated traffic, but he didn't say anything.

That was just as well. She wasn't sure why she was so adamant, but it had something to do with protecting her heart. As long as the arrangement was temporary she could deal with losing Zoë. Once she let herself believe that Zoë could be hers, the parting would devastate her. She'd lost one child and she couldn't recover from that kind of loss again.

They rode in comfortable silence for a while. "I'm sorry I upset you about the room," Beau said.

"I'm sorry I overreacted. But, please, don't do that again. Don't try to take care of me. I can take care of myself."

"But…"

"No buts." She turned in the seat to face him. "The extra expense is going to put an even bigger strain on my finances—something I didn't need right now."

"It was a gift, Macy. Look at it that way."

"I will pay you back."

"Did anyone ever tell you that you don't accept gifts graciously?"

"You can't fix everyone's problems," she told him. "You're a perpetual caregiver to your family, to me. It's time you started thinking about yourself."

"I have, but I hit a brick wall."

The words hung between them and she refused to answer him. He was referring to his declaration of love that she couldn't accept.

They passed the rest of the trip in silence and Macy was glad to see the cul-de-sac. She carried Zoë inside while Beau grabbed the rest of their things.

She saw the bag of clothes Beau had bought her. Her first instinct was to give them back, but that would hurt him and she found she couldn't do it. She would accept this gift graciously.

Laying Zoë in the bassinet, she turned to Beau. "Do you mind staying with Zoë while I go to the kennel to collect my pets?" She hated to ask a favor, but she knew her guys were anxious to come home and she didn't want them to think she'd deserted them.

"Sure. Take your time."

Macy flew out the door and Beau sat on the sofa, pulling the bassinet closer.

"Hey there, little angel," he said to Zoë. "Glad to be home?"

Zoë kicked her feet and waved her hands in response.

"I screwed up big time with your aunt. I take one step forward and about ten backward. Not sure about much of anything anymore, but I'm glad you're going to be okay."

Zoë started to cry.

"You hear my voice and you want to be held, don't you?"

She cried louder and he immediately picked her up, not wanting any damage to be done to her throat. As soon as he laid Zoë on his shoulder, she stopped crying.

"Oh, yeah, you've become a rotten egg." He patted her back. "Little angel, disciplining you will be about the hardest thing I've ever had to do."

Except walking away from Macy.

That was still in the cards. She hadn't relented in her stance on their relationship, but she had kissed him. A kiss that he could still taste and feel. He wasn't walking away until he knew for certain there was no future for them.

CHAPTER TEN

THE NEXT COUPLE OF DAYS were awkward and Macy seemed not to want Beau around. So he gave her her space for now. He had dinner with his parents and went to one of Ben's games. With Zoë needing his attention, he'd only been able to make a couple. Ben didn't get to play much, but he was happy to have a uniform and to be with the other kids.

Beau called a brothers' meeting.

"Here's to us all back together again," Jake said, raising his beer bottle.

They clicked their bottles together.

"I'm here under protest," Eli said. "Caroline basically kicked me out of the house."

"She did not," Tuck said. "She thought you needed to get out."

"Same thing."

"Eli's having birthing pains a little early." Tuck took a swig from the bottle.

"Wait until she's in labor screaming her head off," Jake said. "You'll…"

"Don't tell him." Tuck stopped Jake. "He's paranoid enough."

"How's Zoë?" Caleb asked, wisely steering the conversation in another direction.

"Much better," Beau replied. "Breathing like an angel, but we've spoiled her and now she just wants to be held."

"Are you still helping Macy?"

"Now that's a loaded question," Jake said.

"I'm giving her her space at the moment." He looked at Caleb. "Anything new on Delia?"

"Delia's worked on and off as a waitress in one of the casino's restaurants. The manager said when she's short of money or looking for a new boyfriend, she'll come in wanting a job. I told him to give me a call if she ever showed up. In case he forgets, I'll keep calling him so he knows I mean business. But other than that, I don't have a thing."

"Thanks, Caleb. Let's hope the guy calls."

Eli stood. "I really have to get going."

"Me, too," Caleb said. "Josie's home by now."

"Good to have you back, little brother." Jake patted his back. "I've got to go, too."

That left Tuck and Beau, the two bachelors. Tuck eyed him. "If you want to go, you can. I know you're thinking about her."

"Nah. How about a game of pool?"

"Sure."

As they walked toward the poolroom, Beau wondered if he and Tuck were destined to be lonely forever.

It was almost eleven when he drove into his garage. Macy's light was on, but he didn't go over. Absence might make the heart grow fonder—or at least become more understanding.

BEAU STILL HADN'T gone back to work. He kept tabs on the office through Liz and he checked in from time to time to go over cases with his colleagues. Although he enjoyed his work, he also enjoyed this time away. But he'd have to return soon.

He decided to cook dinner for Macy. He'd grilled chicken breasts and vegetables, then made a salad because he knew that's what she liked. Donuts were on the counter for dessert. That was the extent of his culinary skills in the dessert department.

At five he went over to Macy's. It was the beginning of June and the weather was warm so he wore denim shorts, a T-shirt and flip-flops.

Macy opened the door. "Beau." She seemed surprised.

He walked in and picked up Zoë who was in a playpen—a new purchase, as was the crib in Macy's bedroom. Zoë had outgrown the bassinet.

"Hey, munchkin." Lucky and Lefty came to investigate.

Zoë held her head up very well now and she smiled a toothless grin, her hands slapping at his face.

"How's she doing?" he asked.

"Great. No problem with her breathing and she's taking the bottle better. She actually slept for six hours last night."

"Wow. That calls for a celebration."

Macy's eyes narrowed. "What do you mean?"

"You ladies, pets included, are invited for dinner. All I have to do is put the chicken breasts on the grill."

"Beau…"

"I won't take no for an answer." He handed her Zoë

and began to fold up the playpen. Lucky and Lu. licked his hands and he bent down to pat them.

"I need to change."

She was wearing white shorts and a light blue tank top. It had rained earlier and the humidity had turned her hair into frizzy curls. She looked wonderful, though. Her skin glowed, her eyes sparkled and she looked rested. "Why? We're just going next door."

Before she could protest further, he headed them toward his place. The dogs were excited to be there, yelping for treats. Freckles curled up in the windowsill.

Macy watched Beau giving the dogs treats and realized she should have said no more strongly, but she'd missed him so much. She hadn't seen him in two days. She missed everything about him—his kindness, his gentleness, his sense of humor and his presence in her life. She was trying very hard to be strong, but lately she could feel herself weakening.

Beau knew everything about her, the good and the bad. But did he love her enough to live without children? That one thing kept her backing off.

Beau brought her a glass of wine. "Sit down and relax. Zoë's occupying herself." Zoë was enthralled with the patterns on the quilt at the bottom of the playpen. "The dogs are fed and dinner will be ready in about twenty minutes."

She curled her feet beneath her on the sofa, sipping the wine. "Evidently you haven't gone back to work."

"No. Probably next week," he replied.

"I talked to my supervisor and I go back to work next Monday. My mother said she'd come and watch Zoë

Monday, Tuesday and Wednesday, the days that I work. But that doesn't solve the problem of a babysitter for later. Mrs. Pruett, across the street, said she'd love to keep Zoë."

His eyebrows lifted. "Mrs. Pruett is seventy-five years old."

"She can still take care of a baby."

He shook his head. "No, no. I'll take care of Zoë. She's used to me."

"You have to go back to work," she reminded him.

His lips twitched. "I'm the boss. I can work around your schedule."

"Beau…"

A timer went off in the kitchen. "Dinner's ready."

Macy let the issue slide for now. She was tired of always being the bad person. The wine relaxed her and she didn't allow other thoughts to intrude. They laughed and talked like they usually did.

"So you're getting along better with your mom?" he asked, pouring her more wine with dinner.

"At first she didn't seem too concerned about Delia or the baby, but now she does."

"And your father. Have you heard any more from him?"

"He's called several times. He wants me to meet his wife."

Beau stopped in the process of serving the chicken breasts and vegetables. "You've never met his wife?"

"No. Delia has, but I just couldn't meet this woman who I thought had broken up our home."

"What do you think now?"

She wiped her mouth with a napkin. "I think I'm

getting too old to be petulant about the breakup. It happened and I need to get over it."

"And not blame yourself."

Her head jerked up. "How do you know that?"

"Because I know you. Also, I've had similar feelings."

"About your father?" Macy knew about his issues with Joe McCain. They'd talked about it many times.

Beau took a swallow of wine. "Yeah. I felt it was my fault Jake chose to stay with our father when our parents divorced. I should have tried to talk him out of it, but I was eight years old and scared to death of my father. As I watched my mother grieve for her eldest son, I knew it was all my fault. I felt like the bad son my father called me. Maybe that's why I try so hard at family unity, in my job and in my life. Maybe I need to prove over and over that I am good."

She placed a hand over her heart, her eyes soft. "You never have to try to be good. It's in here and it goes all the way down to your soul."

"Thanks." He felt warm all over from her sincere words. "Sometimes, though, it's hard to forget his words and I think I subconsciously overcompensate the nice-guy role."

"Oh, please." She rolled her eyes. "Good is who you are, Beau. Don't you know that by now? Joe McCain didn't deserve a son like you."

He toyed with his glass. "You could be prejudiced."

She held up her glass, her eyes glowing. "Nope. It's the absolute truth."

The warmth in her eyes let him believe. "Maybe," he conceded. "In my teens, Mom told me the whole story and I knew I wasn't the reason for her heartache, or the divorce, or for Jake staying with Joe."

"Did you work so hard to get Jake back into the family because you felt guilty?"

"Partly. I definitely wanted my brother back in my life. It took years because he's stubborn as an ox, but we're finally a family—even Eli is now one of us."

"Only a very good person would keep trying."

He looked into her eyes and knew that was true.

"No more talk about the bad son," she said, and got to her feet. She took her plate to the sink. "The Randalls will never be a family again because my parents aren't willing to share what really happened. So be happy about your role in getting the McCains back together."

Beau met her at the sink with his plate. "Talking always helps."

Unable to resist, she touched the lean lines of his face. "You believe in talking. I could see it in your eyes when we were in Houston and my father wanted to see me. That look made me give in."

"I'm glad. You needed to talk to him." He caught her hand and held it. "And we need to talk, too."

A wail pierced the pregnant pause. Macy pulled away to go to Zoë. Perfect timing, she thought. There was nothing to talk about. He thought one way and she another. But could there be a compromise?

She fed Zoë while Beau puts dishes in the dishwasher. Repleted, the baby fell asleep and Macy tucked her into the playpen.

"Dessert," Beau said, setting donuts on the coffee table.

"Beau…"

He handed her another glass of wine. Why not, she thought. She curled her feet beneath her and ate to her heart's content.

"Delicious." She licked her fingers and reached for the wine. Feeling warm inside, she smiled at Beau. His eyes were dark and sensuous, igniting a fluttering in her lower abdomen.

He sat beside her and removed a crumb of icing from the corner of her mouth. At his touch, the warmth turned into a wildfire blazing through her veins. How many times had she fantasized about Beau looking at her like this? Too many to count.

His hair, which was always neatly combed, was tousled across his forehead giving him a sexy, hunky look. All she wanted to do was kiss him, hold him and not worry about tomorrow. Or the future.

As if reading her mind, his eyes on her lips, he said, "You haven't mentioned the kiss in the hospital."

Her pulse raced and she twirled the remaining wine in her glass. "I was excited and very grateful."

"I don't want gratitude from you." His voice was soft, tempting like a haunting chord of music.

She looked into the wine and wondered if she was just plain nuts. Why was she depriving herself of something she wanted so badly? Because she cared too much. That was her biggest problem.

Her eyes caught his. "What do you want?"

He took the glass from her and set it on the table. "This," he said, cupping her face and touching her lips in the most gentle and explosive kiss she'd ever experienced. She felt it all the way to her soul, in those places locked in pain. He didn't take the kiss further. He was leaving that up to her.

Without thinking, without analyzing the moment, she wrapped her arms around his neck and returned the kiss.

He groaned and pulled her to him. The kiss deepened to a level they both needed. She opened her mouth and gave herself up to Beau, tasting, feeling and discovering all those intimate treasures about him.

His hand slipped beneath her top, caressing her skin, her breasts. At his intimate touch her nipples hardened and her senses spun, then soared. A physical need welled up in her—a need for Beau. A woman's need. She wanted to ignore it and ask him to stop, but she wanted this as bad as he did.

He drew back and gazed into her eyes. "Macy…" His voice was ragged.

She placed a finger over his lips. "Let's don't talk. Make love to me." She heard her words and wanted to snatch them back, but tonight the woman in her was in control.

His laden eyes held hers. "Are you sure? Be absolutely sure."

She nodded and kissed his chin, his neck, and trailed lingering kisses to his mouth. He captured her lips, swung her up in his arms and carried her into his bedroom. Laying her on the bed, he quickly followed, removing his T-shirt.

She ran her hands across his broad shoulders, then pulled his head down to hers. The room was in darkness but they didn't notice. Sensations, beautiful, spine-tingling sensations, carried them on a journey they'd both been waiting for.

Beau gently removed her clothes and the rest of his, then they were skin on skin, heart on heart, as their hands and lips discovered new and stimulating places. She moaned as Beau's tongue lavished her breasts and lingered lower. She'd forgotten this. She'd forgotten what it was like to just feel—to feel like a woman.

But she couldn't be careless.

"Beau, I'm not on the pill."

He paused for a second, his breath warm against her skin. "Don't worry. I have condoms—somewhere." He rolled away and she felt bereft without his body on hers.

Rummaging through the nightstand, he found them. "Got it."

Through the dim light she watched as he sheathed himself then, unable to wait any longer, her hands eagerly sought his body, trailing through his chest hair to touch him completely, intimately. He groaned and rolled atop her and she spread her legs as excitement mounted in her. Taking her lips, he thrust deep inside her. She gripped his shoulders, his back, and accepted him with an urgency like she'd never felt before. Her hips moved in rhythm with his until the crescendo built to an orgasmic explosion of sheer pleasure. Her body shuttered in release and a moment later she felt Beau tremble in her arms.

"I love you," he breathed. "Oh, God. I love you."

She wanted to say the words back, but they were stuck in her throat. She clung to him that much tighter and the room became quiet with just the two of them savoring this moment. This time out of time.

Beau gulped in air, hardly believing that after all this time Macy was finally his. Loving Macy was everything he knew it would be, electrifying, fulfilling and better than anything he'd ever imagined. She hadn't said she loved him, but for now he wouldn't worry about that.

He pulled the sheet over them and she settled into his arms as if she belonged there. Kissing her forehead, he asked, "Comfy?"

"Mmm." She ran her toes up his shin. "You have hairy legs. Nice. Sexy." She kissed his chest. "I like that."

She was half laying on him and he trailed his fingers down her smooth back. "Soft, soft skin. Kissable. Delectable." He rested his face in the crook of her neck breathing in the scent of her. "Heavenly."

"Mmm," she murmured drowsily as they drifted into sleep.

A WAIL WOKE THEM instantly. Macy made to get up, but Beau pushed her back down. "I'll take care of Zoë." He grabbed his robe and headed for the living room.

Macy could hear him clearly. "What's the matter, little angel? Did you miss us? Oh, a wet diaper. Let's take care of that, then I'll give you a bottle. Will that make you happy?"

Macy turned over, doubts and insecurities crowding back into her mind. *No, don't listen.* But she did. Beau was so good with children. He was a natural father. Pleasure mingled with pain. *No.* She tried not to think about it, didn't want to think about it, but the same old fear, the monster, was creeping out into the open again.

Fear that she couldn't give Beau what he wanted—children. Could she take that from him?

Beau slipped in bed beside her and gathered her into his arms. "Miss me?"

For the first time in her life she did something she wouldn't normally do. She took the initiative and straddled him, sliding her body down his and instantly feeling his reaction. Tonight was hers and she loved him as if it were their last time.

Because it was.

Afterward, their sweat-bathed bodies lay entwined. When Beau fell asleep, Macy gently kissed his lips, watching him for a long time. She lightly ran her hands over his face, feeling his stubble, his straight nose, lean cheeks and wide forehead. Imprinting his features to memory. But she didn't have to do that. She knew every inch of him. One last kiss and she slipped from the bed and dressed.

In the living room she sat on the sofa, tears streaming down her face. She had to do this. There was no future for her and Beau. Lucky and Lefty crawled into her lap and she took comfort from them.

BEAU WOKE UP to a lethargic feeling and a smile spread across his face as he remembered last night. He reached for Macy, but the bed was empty. Grabbing his robe, he headed for the living room. The lights were out and Macy was sitting on the sofa.

He walked to her and he could see her face clearly from the light streaming through the window. She was crying. His gut tightened.

"Macy, what's wrong?"

She brushed away tears. "I've been waiting for you to wake up."

"Why?"

"Because…because I have to tell you something. Last…last night was a mistake. It should never have happened."

His heart slammed into his chest. "Last night was wonderful. What are you talking about?"

She looked up at him. "My redemption, so to speak, is caring for other people's children. I will never care for a child of my own. I've resigned myself to that, but you should have your own kids. I can't give you that."

"I don't need kids. I just need you." He had to make her understand that.

"You say that now, but years down the road you'll feel differently. And you'll look at me differently. You'll grow to hate me."

"You can't presume to know how I will feel later."

"I guess not." She stood. "But I know how I feel now. You love kids. Look how wonderful you are with Zoë. Not to mention Ben and Katie. You deserve a whole woman."

He jammed his hands through his hair. "I don't understand this. If we want children, we can adopt."

"But you don't need to do that. You can have your own."

He fought back in the only way he knew how—with facts. "So can you. You can still have a healthy baby."

"I can also have one with a heart defect. I can't live through that again. Not even for you."

"Macy…"

"Please, Beau. It's the way I feel and I can't change that. I've tried but…"

He took a sharp breath that burned his throat. "I wish you could see yourself the way I see you—whole, complete and perfect in every way. And you don't need a child to be whole. You just need to be a woman who can give and accept love—like you did last night."

Lifting Zoë out of the playpen, she grabbed the diaper bag. "I'll pick up the playpen later."

She wasn't even listening to him. Her mind was made up, but he couldn't accept it.

When he had sat in the emergency room with Zoë, he knew he loved Macy but couldn't explain why. He could now. He saw all the way to her heart and knew that it tore her up that she had in some way hurt her child. And she was trying to protect him from getting hurt. Her caring, loving nature had always attracted him.

Although he understood that, it also angered him. That was the dark side of him, the bad son part. And he gave into every emotion that drove those feelings.

He caught her arm. "Can you forget last night? Wipe it from your mind as if it never happened?"

"Beau, please."

"You say I deserve so much. Well, I deserve more than this."

She didn't respond, just settled Zoë in her arms.

"It's not me that needs a child, Macy. It's you. That's why your life revolves around babies. Somehow you've equated femininity with motherhood. You can't love me because you can't have children. That's absurd.

You're punishing yourself for the loss of your daughter. Don't punish me, too."

She walked to the door just as she did before—as if she hadn't heard a word he'd said. That fueled his anger.

"If you walk out that door, its over for us. Don't call me or contact me in any way."

She turned and looked at him and he felt her pain as if it were his own. But he was powerless to help her. Powerless to stop the emotions that were tearing them apart.

"Goodbye, Beau," she murmured, and disappeared into the morning light with her animals behind her.

He fell to the sofa and buried his face in his hands. He hadn't cried in years, but the urge to cry was strong. For a brief moment he had everything he'd ever wanted. In the blink of an eye it was gone and he never felt so alone or empty in his life.

He went into the kitchen and found a bottle of bourbon. He filled a shot glass. "Here's to lonely, Beau McCain. Get used to it." He downed the drink and poured another. By the third drink he realized he'd sunk to his lowest depth—giving in to self-pity.

Giving in to his darker side.

Grabbing the coffeepot, he put on coffee, then went to take a shower. When he came back his head wasn't so fuzzy, but the pain was like an open wound. Pouring a cup of coffee, he forced himself to face facts. He had to move on. He couldn't keep doing this to himself.

Life after Macy. Surely there was one. But for the life of him he couldn't fathom it.

CHAPTER ELEVEN

BEAU DRESSED FOR WORK. That was all he could do now, throw himself back into his routine, his life. Before he left, he folded the playpen and placed it at Macy's front door. He didn't pause or contemplate what could have been. It was over and he didn't have the strength or energy to keep fighting a losing battle. He finally admitted defeat. If he didn't, it would cripple him.

Everyone at the office was surprised to see him. He called a meeting and announced he'd returned for good. Faces stared back at him, stunned, and he knew what they were thinking—they'd been expecting a wedding announcement. He quickly doused their hopes, going over recent cases that met with his disapproval. He was now back in command and it would stay that way.

After the meeting, he sat in his office and realized he'd been harsh with his colleagues. Not like himself at all. Maybe that was a sign of rejection and unrequited love—becoming a bitter and frustrated man. Like his father.

Liz walked in. "You were a bit rough on Natalie," she said.

He didn't look up from a file. "She should have won

the Hardy case. Evidently she didn't do her homework. The father should have won custody."

"Beau, you know as well as I do that a judge always tries to place the kids with the mother."

Beau laid down his pen. "The mother is a drug addict."

"She's been clean for six months."

"And while she was sobering up, the father had the kids, caring for them and loving them. It's not right that we didn't fight hard enough to make sure it stayed that way."

"It was temporary and he knew it. The mother wanted the kids and she has a right to have them as long as she stays clean. The judge believed her sincerity and commitment."

"What gives a woman so much right?" He sprung from his chair and walked to the window, looking at the gently rolling hills of Waco, but not really seeing anything at all. Now that he and Macy were over, Zoë would no longer be in his life. She'd become a part of him and losing her, too, was a hard blow to take.

"When did you become so judgmental and critical?"

When he had his heart ripped out. In that moment he knew he was losing his perspective, his sense of right and wrong. That was detrimental to him as a lawyer and as a man. All his life he had a clear perception of right and wrong. It's how he lived his life. Macy had crippled him in more ways than one and he was angry. This was a bad son's reaction and he didn't push it away. He needed to feel it.

"Did the father take it hard?" His emotions were tainted by what had happened to him. He didn't even know the man involved. He just felt his pain.

"Not really," Liz replied. "He's remarried and from what Natalie said, the new wife isn't all that thrilled about raising three kids. He has visitation and CPS is keeping a close eye on the mother."

"Good."

"Beau?"

"Hmm?"

"Are you all right?"

He turned around. "I'm fine. I'll apologize to Natalie." But he knew he was far from fine. That would take time.

Liz nodded and left.

He needed physical exercise. With everything that had been going on with Zoë, he'd missed his running. There was a gym on the bottom floor of his building. He grabbed his bag out of a closet and headed downstairs.

Keeping pace with the treadmill, thoughts of Macy plagued him. Tomorrow was Zoë's appointment in Houston for a checkup. He'd planned to go with them. He turned up the speed. But outrunning thoughts of Macy was like trying to outrun the treadmill.

MACY FORCED HERSELF not to cry. At the oddest moment, though, she'd find tears rolling down her cheeks. She'd done the right thing for Beau, but then why did she feel so bad? She had to stop thinking about it or she'd go crazy.

The playpen was still at Beau's and she didn't have the strength to go and get it. If she saw him, she'd weaken. She could still feel his touch on her skin, his lips on her body. She jumped up, needing to do something.

She slipped into running shorts and a top, and gathered Zoë and the diaper bag. It was time to check out Mrs. Pruett's babysitting skills. Opening the door, she stopped short. The playpen leaned against the jamb. Unable to stop them, tears filled her eyes. Dear, sweet, kind Beau. With one hand she pulled it inside. *Don't think*, she kept repeating to herself.

She walked across the street, Lucky and Lefty following her, to Mrs. Pruett's condo and rang the bell.

"Macy," Mrs. Pruett said as she opened the door. Her gray hair was tightly permed and a housedress covered her ample body. "You brought the baby."

"Yes. I was hoping you'd watch her for a few minutes while I take the dogs to the park for a run."

"Oh, I'd love to." Macy handed Zoë to her. "She's growing. Look at those big blue eyes."

"A bottle and diapers are in the bag, but I won't be gone that long."

"Take your time."

"Come on, guys," she said to the dogs, and started running down the sidewalk to the small park. Once they reached it, Lucky and Lefty lay down, breathing heavily. She continued to jog and the dogs barked at her every time she passed them. She ran until she couldn't think and breathing became difficult.

Flopping to the ground, she lay prone in the grass. The hot sun beat down on her sweat-soaked skin and still she didn't move. There was something therapeutic about the rays of the sun seeping into her, searing all those crazy dreams in her head. She should never have let last night get out of control. It was her fault and she'd hurt Beau. The sun couldn't scorch away that memory.

Lucky and Lefty licked her face. She raised herself to a sitting position and started the trek home.

She didn't feel any better, but now she could cope. Or at least make a very good attempt at coping. But the restless frustration in her was gone. Now she had to face the rest of her life without Beau in it. Was she strong enough for that?

THE WEEK PASSED slowly for Beau. He counted the days off in his head and he wondered how long it would take before he stopped thinking about her every waking minute. Throwing himself into his work hadn't helped. Everyone tended to avoid him and his moodiness unless it was absolutely necessary.

He wondered how Zoë's appointment in Houston had gone. But he didn't call or go over and ask. He was sure everything was fine. Being on the outside was hell.

He was pondering going to the gym when Caleb breezed in.

"Hey, brother, want to go out for a cup of coffee?"

His eyes narrowed. "Did Liz call you?" Beau thought it strange that Caleb would show up out of the blue.

Caleb frowned. "No. Should she…?" Caleb zeroed in on his face. "What's wrong?"

"Nothing." He didn't feel like talking, not even to Caleb.

Caleb removed his hat and took a seat. "Really? You look a little peaked. Are you ill?"

Beau sighed. "What are you doing here?"

"Had a deposition of a witness in Dallas this morning, so I stopped by Mom and Dad's for a visit on the way home. They said they haven't seen you in a while and they're worried. What's going on?"

"I've been busy and I wished everyone would stop worrying about me. I'm a grown man—I do not require constant supervision."

"Whoa. That bad, huh?"

"Go home, Caleb."

Caleb made a church steeple with his fingers, eyeing Beau. "Let's go over to the park and throw some hoops."

"I'm busy."

"Mmm. You can either come or I'm going to sit here and bug the crap out of you. Your choice."

"I'm not in the mood."

"Get in the mood." Caleb stood. "Remember when I was a kid and something bad would happen and I'd clam up?"

"Yeah. You kept everything inside."

"And you're doing that now."

"Go home, Caleb."

"You're a firm believer in talking. There were times, like when Josie was engaged to someone else, when you made me talk and all I wanted to do was smack you in the face."

"So?" Beau knew exactly were this was leading.

Caleb placed his palms on the desk and leaned in close. "We're going to shoot some hoops and you're going to talk or I'm going to smack you. Either way I'm not leaving you here looking as if you've lost everything that matters to you."

Ten minutes later Beau found himself sitting on the asphalt looking up at the basketball hoop. The park wasn't far from where they grew up and they'd come here many times as kids to play.

"You know, Caleb," Beau said, staring at the hoop, "we need a ball to shoot hoops."

"Yeah." Caleb grinned. "Minor detail, but I've taken care of it."

Beau didn't ask how. He really didn't care.

"The park seems the same, doesn't it?" Caleb mused.

Beau looked around. The basketball and tennis courts were the same, except there was new asphalt. The pool house farther to the right had been completely redone, as had the baseball field that could be seen through the trees. The park benches and swings seemed untouched.

"A part of our childhood," he murmured. "I can't remember all the times I had to come and get you because you weren't supposed to be in the park after dark."

"Yeah, then we'd shoot some hoops before going home to a home-cooked meal."

"Mmm. We had a good life," Beau said, feeling some of the tension in him easing.

"Even if Joe McCain was our father."

Beau glanced at his brother. "Because we're survivors."

"Yeah." Caleb nodded. "So what's wrong?"

Beau removed his tie and jacket, laying them beside him. He stared at his cowboy boots. Caleb got him to wearing the boots and he liked them. They were comfortable. Some days he wore suits to work, but most of the time he wore jeans, shirt and tie, boots and a jacket, like today. He brushed a speck of dust from the toes.

"Do you think I'm bad?"

"What?"

"Joe called me the bad son. I think about that a lot."

He could feel Caleb's eyes on him. "If there was a book with people's names in it, beside Beau McCain would be the word *good*—good to the core." Caleb paused. "Why would you even think that?"

"Because sometimes I feel bad." He swallowed hard. "Macy and I are over—for good this time." There, he'd said it out loud and it hurt just like he knew it would. "I want to go to her and shake her and when I have those feelings I…"

"Beau, that's because you're hurt. You would never hurt Macy or anyone, and I speak from experience. I gave you plenty of opportunities as a kid. Not once have you ever hit me in anger. We horsed around a lot."

"Yeah." Beau felt more tension ease inside him. "I don't know why I'm feeling this way."

"Because you're Beau, trying to make life better for everyone."

"But I can't seem to do that for myself."

There was silence for a moment.

"What happened with Macy?" Caleb finally asked.

Beau told him about Macy's baby and all the heartache.

"Damn. I never knew she had a child, but I remember her sister dying. I must have been around five or six. I remember Mom helping all she could and I remember Macy crying and crying."

"The sister had a heart defect just like Macy's daughter. It's genetic and Macy blames herself for the death of her daughter. She had to watch her die and evidently the baby suffered."

"And now Macy won't allow herself to love again?"

"That's about it. I tried to tell her that I don't need kids, but she can't seem to hear me."

"When Macy and I were kids, she always made me play dolls before we could play cops and robbers or race cars. She'd put dresses on her dogs, too. She always wanted lots of kids."

"Yeah." Beau gazed at a mother pushing a stroller to the swing set. Another little boy was already on the swings. "You and Macy played together a lot as kids," he said. "I'm surprised you didn't fall for each other."

"Nah. Macy and I were always friends. The chemistry wasn't there."

"Funny how that works."

"Mmm. I though Josie would fall for Eli since he was the Ranger who rescued her, but she said she never saw Eli in that way. And boy, am I grateful."

Beau smiled, but it didn't reach his heart. It seemed to be frozen.

After a moment, Caleb said, "I'm sorry, Beau. For you and Macy."

"I know, and thanks for dragging me…" His voice trailed away as he saw Jake's truck pull up to the curb. He got out with a basketball in his hand. He now knew how Caleb had taken care of the ball problem. His gaze swung to Caleb. "Reinforcements, huh?"

Caleb only grinned.

Jake bounced the ball to Beau. "Get off your asses, little brothers. Let's play ball."

Beau caught the ball and leaped to his feet, the quick movement releasing the rest of the pent-up tension. Caleb removed his hat, gun and badge. Jake sailed his hat into the grass and caught the ball as Beau threw it to him. He jumped and made a basket. They shuffled around the court, laughed and tried to outdo each other.

Beau leaped and made a basket.

"Damn, Beau. You've been practicing?"

Beau swung around to see Eli and Tuck standing there. Caleb had called all the brothers. They must have been in the area to have gotten here so quickly.

"And you've beefed up," Eli added, removing his hat and gun, as did Tuck. Beau threw him the ball and Eli jumped and made a three-pointer.

Beau caught the rebound and bounced the ball. "You think you're the only one who can do that? Watch." He turned, sending the ball sailing through the hoop. "Bam. Three points," he yelled. "Oh, yeah."

They horsed around until they all had trouble breathing and their feet ached from playing in their cowboy boots. Sinking to the asphalt they sat in a circle. Beau told them the story he'd told Caleb, and it felt good to talk.

"That's rough," Jake said. "Having kids, I can see her point of view."

Beau wiped sweat from his forehead. "I can, too. I just wished she'd believe me when I say I don't need kids."

There was a long pause.

"Are you sure about that?" Jake asked.

"Yes. I'm sure. Without Macy, I don't have much of a life."

"Give it time," Eli suggested.

"I'm forty-two and I've given it more time than I care to remember."

"Then start dating other women. It will give you a different perspective." Eli thought for a minute. "And I have the perfect woman. There's a sister who spends entirely too much time at my house. Ask Grace out. She's an attorney. You're an attorney, so you have a lot in common."

"Now why would you inflict cruel and unusual punishment on him?" Tuck asked.

They all laughed.

"I like Grace," Beau said. "But I'm just not ready." And he didn't know if he ever would be. That was the problem.

The sun sank slowly in the western sky, blanketing the park in a yellow glow. Sitting there with his brothers around him Beau knew he was going to be okay. He was a survivor, as he'd told Caleb, and he had great family support. He'd survive Macy. He just wasn't sure how yet.

MACY'S DAYS PASSED in a steady blur. She kept busy. The trip to Houston went very well. Zoë was doing better every day and Macy wanted to share the news with Beau, but refrained from calling him. She thought about him constantly. She probably would never be able to stop that. She'd adjust.

Zoë had gained two pounds and was taking her bottle without a problem. Macy's thoughts were now on going back to work. She hadn't heard from her mother so she assumed she wasn't coming for a visit. Mrs. Pruett was all set to care for Zoë at night.

She'd hoped to have heard from Delia by now. But there'd been no word—not even a postcard. As the days stretched on, Macy wondered if she planned to come back at all.

The doorbell rang and she went to answer it. Zoë was awake and staring transfixed at the mobile in the playpen. She yanked open the door and her mouth fell open. Her mother stood there with her husband—a mother she hardly recognized.

In tight stretch capris, a halter top and high heel shoes, Irene's reddish-blonde hair was piled atop her head and long earrings dangled from her ears.

"Mom?"

"It's me. Hi, sugar."

Sugar? Her mother never called her sugar.

Irene hugged her in a cloud of expensive perfume. She waved a hand filled with rings and a dangly bracelet. "You remember Perry."

"Yes," she replied in a daze. "How are you?"

"Super peachy." Perry winked. With blond hair, blue eyes, bulging muscles and a killer tan he reminded her of a pampered trainer somewhere on the California coast.

Perry set down a suitcase and Macy wondered if they planned to stay with her. Having her mother and her boy toy in the upstairs bedroom was not appealing.

"Where's that baby?" Irene asked, and Macy noticed she didn't say grandbaby.

Zoë was in plain sight so she didn't think she needed to point her out.

"There she is." Her mother gazed at Zoë. "My, my, Macy. She looks just like you did as a baby."

"You think so?"

"Yes. Definitely."

"I really must be going," Perry said.

"Oh, darlin'." Her mother tottered over and wrapped her arms around him. "I'll miss you."

"If you need to go, Mom, I have a neighbor who will watch Zoë."

"No, sugar. I'm staying. You've had to deal with this all alone. I can help for a couple of days." She kissed Perry. "Perry's going to visit his brother in Fort Worth." Wiping lipstick from his mouth, Irene added, "You be good now."

After Perry left, her mother kicked off her shoes and removed her jewelry.

Macy watched this stranger who was her mother. "Who are you?"

Irene flopped onto the sofa. "Don't be silly. I'm your mother."

"Not the mother I remember. She wore loose-fitting slacks and blouses and hardly any makeup or jewelry. Now you have your body on display and your breasts are about to kiss sunshine."

"I'm young and happy."

"You're fifty-five years old."

Irene got up. "I don't want to argue with you. I want to hold this gorgeous baby."

Macy let it go, knowing Ted had hurt Irene terribly.

If Perry made her happy then Macy would keep her mouth shut. She just hated her mother looking like a tramp.

As they were getting ready for bed, Macy realized that she hadn't spent any time alone with her mother in years. With Zoë asleep in her crib, they sat on the sofa drinking tea. Macy noticed her mother putting something in hers and she didn't pry. But the last time she'd visited her mother she saw that she was drinking more than usual. Staying young came at a price.

"Have you heard from Delia?" Irene asked.

"No. Have you?"

Irene shook her head. "I thought she would have come back by now."

"Me, too."

Irene took a swallow of the tea. "Who knows what goes through her mind? I certainly never did."

"You and Dad argued a lot about Delia."

"Oh, yeah. He wanted to discipline her and I wouldn't let him."

"Why?"

"It's hard to explain. Discipline never seemed to help. Delia just needed to stay on her meds." Irene took the clip out of her hair and ran her fingers through it. Macy noticed there was no gray and the red was brighter.

She brought her thoughts back to what Irene had said. Macy had certainly heard that before. "I saw Dad."

Irene's head jerked toward her. "Really? How is he with the new Mrs. Randall?"

"He looks lean and fit." It was the truth.

Irene took a big gulp of tea. "He was always a good-looking man."

"Yeah," Macy agreed. "We talked some and he said he wasn't having an affair with Nina when he left."

"And you believed him?"

Macy looked directly at her. "Yes."

Irene turned away.

"Mom, what happened to end your marriage? I was already out of college and working so I don't know all the details."

Irene walked into the kitchen to refill her glass. "It happened so long ago and I don't want to talk about it anymore." With the glass in her hand, she came back. "I'm a little tired after the long drive. Think I'll have an early night."

"I'm staying up. I'll sleep some in the morning so I can get back into my routine of working nights."

"If you're asleep, I'll take care of Zoë."

"Thanks, Mom."

Irene took a couple of steps and stopped. "Where's Beau?"

"What?"

"Beau. He was helping you with Zoë. Where is he?"

"He's not helping me anymore."

"Why?"

Macy picked up the remote control and realized her hand was shaking. "I'd rather not talk about it."

Irene shrugged and went to bed.

Where was Beau? She didn't have a clue. She hadn't

seen him in days, not even a glimpse. She missed him more than she thought possible. Why was this so hard? She kept telling herself that she'd done the right thing, but deep inside the pain was about to kill her.

How much more could she take?

CHAPTER TWELVE

MACY SLEPT UNTIL NOON, and Irene and Zoë were getting to know each other. Lucky and Lefty stayed in her room, wary of the new visitor.

She dressed and took the dogs for a walk. Freckles lay on the step waiting for them. When she returned, her mother had lunch waiting. It was nice to be pampered, but she noticed her mother ate very little.

"How about ice cream for dessert?" she asked. "I have rocky road and pecan praline."

"Please! It goes straight to my hips. At my age I have to watch what I eat."

"Why? You've never been overweight."

"I have a very young husband and if I want to keep him, I have to watch my diet and stay in shape."

Macy watched her mother for a moment. "Why did you marry Perry?"

"For the sex."

Macy gasped and couldn't stop the stain that colored her cheeks. She didn't expect her mother to be so honest or blunt.

"And of course the companionship. It's hell being alone."

She regained her composure. "But you have nothing in common. He rebuilds motors and is into motorcycle racing. You have a degree in business and worked in a bank for a number of years."

"That's what makes the relationship exciting. He's good to me and we have fun. He makes me feel young."

She kept watching her mother and noticed the lines on her face weren't so pronounced. Had she had something done? "Your face looks different."

"BOTOX, sugar."

"I never realized that getting older bothered you so much."

"It didn't until your father walked out, then I felt like a used-up hag."

"Mom."

Irene carried dishes to the sink. "Don't lecture me. I should be lecturing you. Where's Beau? You two were inseparable."

The doorbell rang, preventing her from answering. She opened the door to a man she'd never seen before.

"Macy Randall," he asked.

"Yes."

He handed her some papers and quickly left.

"Who was that?" her mother called.

"I don't know." She ripped open the envelope and scanned the document. "Oh, no."

"What is it?"

"It's a court order for a DNA test on Zoë."

"What?"

"That's what it says."

Her mother came to look over her shoulder. "That's odd. Who wants the test done?"

Macy read the names and they meant nothing to her. "Clifford and Myrna Wallston."

"Do you have any idea who they might be?"

"No, but evidently someone who thinks they're related to Zoë." She thought for a minute. "Caleb was doing some investigating and found Delia was involved with a married man. This must be him and his wife. No. Wait. I thought Beau said he was killed or murdered or something. I wish I could remember his name."

"Call Beau. He can tell you how to deal with this."

She whirled around. "I'm not calling Beau."

"Macy, don't be stubborn. He can help."

"Beau doesn't need to be involved. I can hire another attorney to take care of this matter."

"But why, when you have a very competent one next door?"

"Mom, please, don't pressure me." She paced back and forth wondering what this meant. That wasn't too difficult to figure out. Someone wanted Zoë and it wasn't Delia. That left the father.

She picked up Zoë and held her tight. It was one thing to say the arrangement was temporary and one day she'd have to let Zoë go, but it was an entirely different matter to actually be able to do it. She'd lost Beau. She couldn't lose Zoë. She recognized the thought for what it was—good old fear again. That fear of being alone. But it was more. She enjoyed that feeling of being a mother.

It's not me that needs a child, Macy. It's you. That's why your life revolves around babies.

Beau was right. She needed to be a mother—to Zoë. She took a couple of deep breaths, trying to stop the panic in her, trying not to fall apart at this revelation.

She quickly made an appointment with a lawyer. He agreed to see her before she went to work. Her mother took care of Zoë and she was glad she was there.

The lawyer didn't have much advice, just to take the test and contact him if anything arose from the result. He was an inept idiot and he wasn't Beau. But she couldn't call Beau. She remembered his words vividly. *Don't call or contact me in any way.*

She hurried to work and it felt exhilarating to be back in the swing of things. There were only two births so the night was quiet. She sat holding a newborn, getting ready to carry her to her mother for a feeding. Newborns were so fragile, sweet and irresistible. And they had a smell all their own—a delicate scent that wrapped around your heart. The little girl was perfectly healthy, with red cheeks, a button nose and a bald head. She was adorable.

I'll never have my own child. Never experience these feelings again. The thoughts surprised her as it slipped from her subconscious.

Somehow you equate motherhood with femininity. Beau was right. She was a natural mother. Even when she was small she always said she wanted lots of children. Now that was over and it motivated everything she did, even her rejection of Beau.

She allowed herself to feel like a woman in his arms and the pain wasn't so bad. Reality intruded quickly and she was still struggling to justify her actions so that she could understand them herself.

On the way home, she got a call from the animal shelter. They had an abused dog that needed some extra attention. Macy said she'd be right there, then she called her mom to say she was running late.

The little dog was a Chihuahua and he had burns on his body. Judy said they were cigarette burns. The police made a call to an apartment where a man was beating his girlfriend. After breaking up the fight and arresting the man, the police found the dog and took him to the shelter.

"The little thing is scared to death and he obviously hates men," Judy said. "His wounds have healed and now he just needs some love and attention so he can trust people again."

A helper brought the dog out in a cage. He cowered in a corner.

"What's his name?" Macy asked.

"The girlfriend said the man called him Dog."

"That won't do." Macy peered into the cage. "Hi there, little fellow." The dog whined and curled into a ball and she could see the charred spots on his body. Anger welled inside her.

The dog was a light brownish-tan that reminded Macy of a peanut. "I'll call him Peanut."

"Fits him perfectly," Judy said.

Macy carried the cage to her car, placing Peanut in the passenger seat and heading home. "Don't worry, I won't hurt you," she told Peanut. "I have some playmates for you at home. You'll like it there. I'll be very good to you and maybe soon you'll trust me."

When Macy carried the cage in, Irene sighed.

"Macy, for heaven sakes, you can't have another animal in this place."

Irene was holding Zoë, who whined for Macy to take her. "Hey, kiddo." She kissed her fat cheek and took her. "Missed me?"

Zoë smiled, then laid her head on Macy's shoulder and Macy's heart melted. How was she going to let her go?

Lucky and Lefty ran into the room and barked at the newcomer. Freckles hissed and disappeared.

Macy sank to the floor with Zoë in front of her. She clapped her hands. "Listen up, guys. You, too, Freckles. Come out." Freckles slinked from the kitchen. "We have a new member in the family. His name is Peanut and we're going to treat him real nice, aren't we?"

Lucky and Lefty sniffed the cage. Freckles walked by it, drank from her water bowl and curled up, watching the new dog.

She pointed to the cage. "See, Zoë, puppy."

Zoë waved her hands, made a noise and turned into Macy's arms. She just wanted to be held.

"How was she?" Macy asked, getting to her feet.

"Fine. She slept all night. But I don't think she liked waking up without you here. She's been fussing ever since."

"We had to rock her so much when she was born that she's a little spoiled. I'm working on unspoiling her."

"Yeah, right."

Macy glanced at her mother who wore a skimpy, lacy negligé.

Macy frowned. "Do you sleep in that?"

"Well, I don't go dancing in it." She smiled. "Although Perry might like that. I'll have to suggest it."

"You've changed," Macy said. "You used to wear an old ratty robe. Delia and I bought you a new one for Christmas and you still wore the ratty robe."

"It was comfortable."

"Like Dad?" The words slipped out before Macy could stop them.

"Yeah. Like your father." She brushed back her hair. "But sometimes comfortable gets boring."

"Mom…"

"What did you find out about the DNA test?"

Just like her father, her mother wasn't going to talk about what had happened in their marriage. So it was time to just move on. Her parents certainly had.

"The lawyer said it was a court order and I have to take Zoë in to be tested or I could be held in contempt of court. He said if anything arises from the test, to contact him."

"That doesn't sound like very good advice."

Macy shrugged. "After I sleep a few hours, I'll take her in."

"You know what this means, don't you, Macy?"

Macy bit her lip and her arms tightened around Zoë.

"If Zoë's DNA turns out like these people suspect, they'll be filing for custody."

Her throat closed up and she took a deep breath. "I know."

"Then call Beau. Maybe he can step up the search for Delia. You have to do something. You can't let these people take her."

"I…I can't call Beau." She put Zoë in her playpen

and watched her kick and play for a moment before sitting on the sofa.

Irene sat down beside her. "Since the divorce, you and I haven't been close. I was dealing with my own pain and you were grown, living your own life. I guess that happens in families. They grow apart."

Macy didn't respond.

"But you really had a rapport with your father. He could get you to do anything. You were his little girl."

"Yes."

"And you're like him. You feel things deeply and hold them in until you just burst from the emotional buildup. Sometimes it helps to talk."

Somewhere in the corner of her soul where she'd banished all those painful emotions, she felt a sliver of hope. *Hope!* Her little girl. In that moment she knew she had to tell her mother.

"My baby died." The words came out low and hoarse, but they were audible.

"What?"

"My baby girl died." The words were much clearer.

"Macy, what are talking about?"

And just like that, emotions she thought she would never share with her mother came spilling out—all the pain, heartache and suffering.

"Oh, Macy. I'm so sorry." Irene held her as if she were five years old. "Why did you never call me? Never let me know?"

"I just didn't think you'd care, you or Dad. Neither of you called or seemed interested in my life. Allen was my life and we were so looking forward to our baby's birth."

Irene drew back. "Hope had the same genetic heart defect as Sabrina?"

"Yes. They operated, but she wasn't strong enough to survive."

Irene tucked Macy's hair behind her ears. "You've asked what happened in our marriage. It started when we lost Sabrina. It devastated both of us and we never completely recovered. I wanted more children. Ted didn't. He said he couldn't go through that again. So you see, you're just like your father."

Through a cloud of tears, she said, "But you had Delia."

"Yes." A shadow crossed her mother's face. "It was stressful from the moment I found out I was pregnant and it didn't change after Delia's birth. Your father felt I'd tricked him. Delia was healthy when she was born, but later we found she had problems. Your father and I disagreed on how to help her and that caused more problems. Finally the marriage just fell apart, but I couldn't believe he'd walk away from all those years of marriage. That hurt."

"It hurt us all," Macy murmured, hardly believing her mother was opening up and talking to her. Looking back, Macy remembered the strain in her parents' relationship—how they'd stopped smiling and laughing. But she never thought they'd separate.

There was silence for a moment.

"So why won't you call Beau?" Irene asked.

She told Irene about their relationship. It was easy to share her pain because she'd already opened up to Beau. Beau was… She shut her thoughts down immediately.

"Oh, Macy." Irene wiped away a tear. "Don't be afraid to take a risk. Your father was and we lost everything."

Macy twisted her hands. "I just can't have another child."

"But you can love a man and that's all Beau wants—your love."

"It's not that simple."

"Sometimes it is."

When she didn't answer, Irene added, "You're just like all these hurt and abused animals you take in. They need to heal with love. Let Beau help you heal."

Macy went to sleep with those words in her head. *Let Beau help you heal.* She slept better than she had in a long time. When she awoke, she got acquainted with Peanut. The little thing trembled violently when she held it, but she stroked and cuddled him, letting him know she wasn't going to hurt him.

Then she dressed Zoë and they took her for the DNA test. It didn't take long. Soon she dropped her mom and Zoë at home and went to work.

Now she waited.

THE DAYS PASSED SLOWLY and there was still no word from Delia. Perry picked up her mother and the condo was lonely without her new flamboyant personality. Macy was glad they had had this chance to talk. She still didn't understand clearly why her father had left, but she could accept it now. Her father was happy and her mother was happy. That's what mattered, but she knew they carried scars—just like she did.

Mrs. Pruett was now keeping Zoë while Macy

worked and the system was running smoothly. Peanut was also better and the other dogs had accepted him. Peanut was a puppy and sometimes he just wanted to play. Lucky and Lefty were older and enjoyed their naps, but they tolerated Peanut with a patience that amused Macy.

It was now the end of July and she still hadn't spoken to Beau. Every day she kept waiting for papers to arrive about the DNA test. When they didn't, she breathed a little easier.

She took Zoë for her last checkup with Dr. Cravey, who said Zoë was fine and completely healed. She'd gained five pounds and was filling out and getting chubby. Macy wondered how long she would have her.

Late one afternoon she decided to take Zoë and the dogs to the park. As she pushed the stroller out the front door, she saw Beau drive into his garage. She wanted to go over so he could see Zoë, but she turned toward the park. She missed everything about Beau, but she really missed talking to him, just seeing him every day. Was she afraid to take a risk on his love?

She thought about that all the way to the park and it was on her mind when they returned. She still didn't have an answer.

Peanut grew tired and Macy put him in the bottom of the stroller. Zoë kept trying to see him, almost leaning out of the stroller. Like Macy, she was going to love animals.

When they reached the condo, a man was standing on her doorstep. As she pushed the stroller up the sidewalk, he came toward her. "Ms. Macy Randall?"

"Yes."

He handed her a manila envelope and there was a lawyer's name on the return address. She hurried inside, put Zoë in the playpen and ripped open the envelope. *Oh my God!* Clifford and Myrna Wallston, parents of Keith Wallston, father of minor child, Zoë June Randall, had filed a motion to modify custody of the minor child. Her heart fell to the pit of her stomach.

She sank onto the sofa and tried to control her breathing, then she read the document more clearly. A custody hearing was set for two weeks from today. Two weeks! That wasn't enough time. What was she going to do?

She glanced toward Beau's condo. He was home and would know what to do. Without thinking, she picked up Zoë and headed over there.

"Stay," she said to the dogs. "I'll be right back." She didn't need any distractions.

Knocking on his door, she shifted Zoë to her other hip, clutching the papers in her hand.

Beau opened the door with a surprised look. "Macy."

"I hate to bother you, but I don't have any other choice." She walked in before he could say anything. Zoë, seeing Beau, smiled and leaned toward him, wanting him to take her.

As he scooped Zoë out of her arms, his hand brushed Macy's breast and her whole body tingled from the contact. "Hi, little angel. You're turning into a munchkin." Beau kissed Zoë's cheek. "She's getting fat."

"Yes. She takes her bottle without a problem now." Macy paused. "She misses you."

"I miss her, too." Their eyes clung for a minute, then he handed Zoë back to her. "Thanks for bringing her over, but I have to go. I have a date."

Date? For a moment she couldn't speak and she wanted to leave. But she remembered the papers in her hand. "It will only take a minute."

"Sorry, I don't have a minute." He turned toward his garage.

"Zoë's grandparents have filed a motion to modify custody of her," she blurted out before he could leave. "They're seeking custody of her. I need a lawyer."

He stopped and slowly turned to face her. The pain on his face cracked her strong resolve. "I'll give you a name of a competent lawyer."

"I'd rather that you handled it."

He shook his head. "No. I told you not to contact me for anything. I can't put myself through that again. You'll have to find someone else."

A pain shot right through her. Dependable, reliable Beau was saying no and she deserved it. But it didn't make that deep pain go away.

"I'm sorry I bothered you." She shifted Zoë on her hip and walked out the door. She kept waiting for him to call her back, but he didn't.

Entering her condo, she let the tears flow freely. What had she done to Beau? She'd made him into a monster. *The monster under her bed.* In a crystal clear moment she recognized that the monster was not the loss of her child. It was her love for Beau. That's what she was so afraid of—loving him and not being the woman he wanted.

What had she done? She drew a deep breath. Like her father she was afraid to take risks and now she'd lost everything.

CHAPTER THIRTEEN

BEAU DIDN'T HAVE a date. He'd lied, but helping Macy just wasn't on his schedule anymore. Every instinct in him wanted to help, to make everything right in her world. He couldn't, though. He'd been hurt too badly. She'd made the choice and now they both had to live with it.

For the first time he realized he was acting like the bad son, thinking only of himself and his pain. He'd been doing a lot of that lately.

What if she loses Zoë? The good son surfaced quickly and he had to force himself to stop thinking about it. He wasn't the only lawyer in town. He was the only one, though, who loved Zoë—and Macy.

No. He couldn't put himself through that kind of pain again. He not only missed Macy, but it had been hell not seeing Zoë, too. It was over.

He headed out to Jake's to play ball with Ben. Little League was over and considering Ben's coordination, he'd done very well. He never lost his enthusiasm and next year Ben wanted to make the all-star team. If he didn't, Ben would just keep trying. And Beau would be there to help him.

As Beau pulled up, Jake walked from the garage. He

was dressed in slacks, which meant he was going out for the evening. Beau should have called, but it didn't matter, he'd just play with the kids.

"Beau," Jake said in surprise.

"Hey, big brother."

"We've got plans to go out for the evening," Jake told him. "You're welcome to come with us."

"Nah. I'll just play with Ben and Katie." He wasn't in a mood to socialize.

"The kids are at Mom's and Aunt Vin is out for the evening."

"Oh." He should have guessed that.

"Eli, Caroline, Caleb and Josie will be here in a minute. We're going to a movie then dinner. It's a chick flick and we're protesting. Come on, it'll be fun. With you along we'll outnumber the ladies."

Beau shook his head, really not wanting to be a lonely seventh party, so to speak. Tuck was out of town and Beau didn't think he had enough strength to endure an evening with three happy couples even if they were his brothers and their wives.

Before he could respond, a Suburban drove up and Eli, Caroline, Caleb and Josie got out. He hadn't seen Caroline in a while and she was now showing and she glowed. Eli and Jake had both married gorgeous blondes. Josie was the only dark one and she was in a class all her own.

"I'm trying to talk Beau into going with us," Jake informed them. "But he's resisting."

"We'll do it another time," Beau said and quickly changed the subject. "You look wonderful, Caroline."

Caroline looped an arm around him. "Thank you. I needed to hear that. I'm beginning to feel like a blimp."

"Hey, I tell you every day how wonderful you look." Eli pretended to be offended.

"You have to tell me that, mister." Caroline smiled. "It's in our marriage contract."

Everyone laughed.

Talk of babies and marriage went over Beau's head. *What if she loses Zoë?* The question darted through his mind, looking for an escape, but there wasn't one. He had to acknowledge the truth. He couldn't live with himself if that happened. He might want to be the bad son his father had called him, but he couldn't pull it off. And what was a little more pain? He'd told Caleb they were survivors. Now he'd find out just how strong he was.

"Y'all come on in," Jake invited. "Elise is in the house."

"I'll catch y'all later," Beau said. "Have a fun evening."

Josie curled her arm through his. "Please come. You can sit by me and I'll hold your hand."

"I don't think so," Caleb said with a grin, pulling Josie away.

Beau grinned, too. "I'm leaving now and if anyone tries to stop me I'm going to kiss all your wives."

As he walked away, he heard, "What do you think, Josie?" That was Caroline.

"I have a jealous husband," Josie replied.

"So do I," Caroline added. "I guess we have to let him go."

But Caleb hurried after him. "All joking aside, are you sure? An evening out might be what you need."

"Thanks, but I really have something I need to do."
He climbed into his car. "I'm fine, so stop worrying."

He drove away and looked through his rearview
mirror. They were all waving. He didn't get to see the
kids, but he'd see them later. That was one thing that
was great about living in Waco—family was close.

Now his mind turned to the task ahead of him.

Seeing Macy.

MACY PUT ZOË DOWN for the night and read through the
papers once again—two weeks. That wasn't much time.
How did the Wallstons get it pushed through so quickly?
That didn't matter. She now had to deal with it.

Grabbing a phone book, she searched through lawyer's names. No one caught her eye. She could use the
same one she'd seen earlier, but she didn't like his
attitude. She wanted someone who would fight for her.

Beau would. But now that was out of the question.

She walked to Zoë's crib and watched her sleep.
Breathing perfectly, it was hard to imagine the first
weeks of her life had been so traumatic. She was
flipping over and soon she'd be sitting up. She was pro-
gressing like a normal child. The strawberry-blond hair
curled along her nape and Macy could now put a bow
on the top.

"I love you, little one," she whispered. "But I have
to do what's best for you." She couldn't pretend that Zoë
was her child. If she allowed herself to do that, parting
would be too painful.

Afraid to take a risk.

She pushed the thought away and wished Delia

would come back. That would solve all the problems. Or would it?

The doorbell rang and she hurried to answer it, hoping it was Delia. She swung the door open without looking through the peephole. Beau charged in. Her heart kicked against her ribs.

"Where's the papers?"

"What?"

"The custody papers, where are they?"

"Ah…on the kitchen table."

As Beau started toward the table, Peanut nipped at his jeans, shaking and growling in a menacing manner.

"What the…"

She grabbed Peanut and soothed him with a gentle hand. "I'm sorry. Peanut doesn't do well with men. He was abused, poor thing."

"How many animals are you going to fit into this condo?" he asked with a sarcastic tone so unlike the kind Beau she knew.

He didn't give her time to answer as he sat at the table and skimmed the papers. He stood quickly, papers in hand and headed for the door.

"Beau."

He turned. "What?"

"Are you taking the case?"

"Yes. But don't read anything into it. This is business. Strictly business."

She bit her lip. "I know you'd do it for anyone."

"Yes." His eyes held hers. "That's the only time you need me—when you need help. You wouldn't even allow me to pay for Zoë's medical bill at Texas

Children's. I called to get the amount and they said it had already been paid. You just had to do it before I could."

"What?" She blinked in confusion. "I called, too, and they said it would be weeks before I got a complete bill. So far nothing has come. I haven't paid the bill. I was hoping they'd allow me to make monthly payments."

"The bill's been paid, Macy."

"I don't understand, but I'll definitely call and find out what's going on."

Some of his anger seemed to leave him. "Evidently someone wanted to pay Zoë's bill."

"But who?" She thought for a minute. "Do you think it could have been Delia?"

"Where would she get that kind of money?"

"I don't know."

"I've got to go," he said abruptly.

"Beau?" He turned to look at her. "Thanks, and I will pay you."

"By all means. That will keep it from getting personal."

"Oh, Beau." Her heart crumbled at the pain in his eyes.

"I'll be in touch when I have any news." With that he was gone.

BEAU WENT HOME feeling worse than he ever had. It wasn't like him to be so sarcastic and resentful and it left him feeling rotten inside. Being bad was hell on his nerves. In a moment of clarity he acknowledged that loving Macy was a part of what made him good.

His goal now was to get past his hurt feelings and concentrate on Zoë's future. Being a lawyer—that's what he did best.

The next morning he called Caleb and told him what had happened.

"I really need you to find Delia."

"I'll call the restaurant manager and see what I can do."

"Thanks, Caleb."

"Is this what you had to do last night?"

"Yes."

"You're a glutton for punishment, but I know you're not going to let anyone take that baby from Macy."

"Mmm. Pitiful, aren't I?"

"No. You're just Beau."

"Yeah, can't escape that."

"I'll call you later."

Beau went to work and find out everything he could on the Wallstons. They'd had one son, Keith, and he had a wife and two children, who lived in Boston. The Wallstons had several homes, but Reno, Nevada, was listed as their residence. They had money and from the lawyer's name on the papers they were using it to procure permanent custody of Zoë.

He contacted Spencer Harcourt of Philadelphia, their attorney who was licensed to practice in Texas, and obtained a copy of the DNA test. Spencer basically told him not to fight it because the Wallstons intended to gain custody of their dead son's child, and Spencer was going to make sure it happened.

"A good fight makes my day," Beau told him.

"Looking forward to it, McCain, but take my advice

and don't waste too much time on it. That baby will be leaving for Nevada in two weeks. I don't lose."

"Neither do I, Mr. Harcourt."

Beau heard his derisive laugh as he hung up. That fueled his drive that much more. Nothing like pitting two successful lawyers with a need to win against each other. Testosterone levels would be very high at the hearing. Now Beau had to figure out a way to beat the odds.

While Jon and Liz worked on the details, Beau drove to Macy's. He needed to explain their course of action and make sure she agreed with it. This time he left his hurt feelings behind.

MACY CALLED HER MOTHER to let her know what was happening, then she called her father. They were both very understanding and for once she didn't feel all alone. Maybe, without knowing it, Delia had brought them all together again.

As she was talking to Ted, she thought of the hospital bill and asked if he would make a visit to Texas Children's and check out what had happened.

There was a long pause on the other end of the line, and Macy assumed it was something he didn't want to do.

"That's okay. I'll just make another phone call."

"You don't need to do that." Another pause. "I paid the bill."

Macy was taken aback. She never expected this.

"Please don't be angry. I have a good job and it was the least I could do."

Anger simmered just for a second, then she realized

how misplaced it was. She did need help and she was touched by his generosity.

"Why didn't you tell me?"

"I was afraid you'd turn it down."

He was probably right, so she curbed that reaction. "Thank you. I'd gotten a loan at the bank, but I guess I won't need it now."

"Just take care of my granddaughter."

"I will, Dad, and thanks again."

She sat there staring at the phone, realizing something was happening inside her. She was opening up and accepting, whereas before she'd shut down and refuse all offers of help. And she could also see her father still cared about her and Delia.

BEAU CAME OVER about noon and again he didn't seem so angry. She was so grateful he was helping and she wanted to throw her arms around him and hold on for dear life. But she didn't. She couldn't do that to him. For a split second she wondered why she was so stubborn, resisting a life that...

Maybe that would be the last metamorphosis inside her—accepting love totally and completely and feeling worthy of it.

She told Beau that her father had paid the hospital bill.

"That makes sense. Are you okay with that?"

She nodded. "Yes, I am."

He seemed relieved and showed her a copy of the DNA test. "No doubt Zoë's Keith Wallston's daughter," he said.

"Yes," she murmured, reading the paper. "Ninety-nine point nine—that's about as accurate as you can get."

"Mmm."

She looked up. "What should we do?"

"That's what I'm here to find out. Do you want permanent custody of Zoë?" His eyes held hers.

"She's Delia daughter." She glanced away, running her fingers through her hair, making it stand out.

"That's not an answer," he told her, taking a seat on the sofa. "Spencer Harcourt states in his motion that a change of circumstances has occurred, that being the knowledge that Zoë is the Wallstons' granddaughter. They have to prove Zoë will be better off with them. We have to prove that this disruption would be bad for Zoë."

Macy sat beside him, her arms around her waist. The thought of losing Zoë was tearing her apart. There was only one thing to do.

Peanut sniffed around Beau's shoes. "Don't even think about it," Beau said to the dog. Lucky and Lefty whined at his feet and he bent to pat them. "See, I'm not so bad," he said to Peanut and held out his hand.

Macy held her breath. Finally Peanut licked Beau's hand and Beau picked him up, stroking him. Beau was so gentle, so caring. That was one of the things she loved most about him.

He turned to Macy, still holding Peanut. "What's your answer?"

"Without Delia here, I don't have a choice. I have to fight for Zoë."

Beau nodded and placed Peanut on the floor. "Is Zoë sleeping?"

"Yes." She had the urge to wake her so Beau could see her.

"Are you off tonight?"

"Yes." They were talking again and it felt so wonderful.

"Maybe I can see her later."

"Sure. No problem."

He got to his feet. "I better go. I'll call you later." He stopped at the door with a frown.

She stood. "What?"

"It just hit me. How did the Wallstons find out about Zoë?"

She thought about it. "I don't know. Maybe they knew Delia was pregnant."

"Or maybe Delia told them."

"No." She felt a shiver of alarm.

"They found out some way and I intend to find out how. I'll be in touch."

Macy stared after him, wondering what all this meant. Delia couldn't have contacted the Wallstons, could she? And if she did, what was her motive? Zoë cried and she hurried to get her.

BEAU SPENT EVERY waking moment working on the case. The Wallstons never stayed in one place for more than a month, so why did they want custody of a baby? At least their marriage appeared stable. And there was Keith's wife. Cynthia Wallston was a pillar of the community involved in all sorts of charities. Her children were in boarding school. But he wondered about her relationship with the Wallstons.

Whenever he needed dirt on someone, he had a couple of P.I.s who were more than good at their jobs.

He didn't want Caleb involved in this part of the case because Caleb would never do anything to tarnish the Texas Ranger badge. And Beau wouldn't want him to. It didn't take the P.I. long to discover that Cynthia had been having an affair with a local art dealer for years. So the younger Wallstons' marriage hadn't been a stable one. Beau wondered how Cynthia felt about the senior Wallstons wanting Zoë. That could be the ace up his sleeve. He would definitely talk to Cynthia Wallston.

He called Caleb and talked to him about Delia's whereabouts. So far, the restaurant manager hadn't seen her.

Beau picked his brain about how the Wallstons could have found out about Zoë. "That's a puzzle," Caleb said. "Someone had to have alerted them." There was a pause. "You're thinking it's Delia?"

"Yes. The Wallstons have a residence in Reno. Delia could possibly be hiding there."

"That doesn't make any sense. If Delia wanted them to have Zoë, she could just come and get her and hand her over. She is Zoë's mother."

"But Macy has had Zoë for almost six months because Delia abandoned her. She might be worried about criminal charges. Hell, I don't know what Delia is thinking and a team of psychologists probably couldn't figure it out, either. But no one's taking that baby without a fight."

There was a pregnant pause.

"I'm emotionally involved and you don't have to remind me." Beau was the first to speak.

"I'm not. I was just going to say that you care for Zoë more than you want to admit."

"Yeah. That's another story. I'm too old for a lecture just in case you're thinking about it."

"Not me. I always say older brother knows best— most of the time."

"I'll remember that."

He heard a chuckle "I'll call when I have something."

Beau hung up with a determined expression. He'd stayed away from Zoë because it was too painful to be around Macy. That was going to change. He'd missed the little angel.

THAT NIGHT BEAU MADE sure he knocked on Macy's door early enough so Zoë wouldn't be asleep.

"Beau, come in," Macy invited. "Have you found out anything?"

Beau went straight to the playpen and picked up Zoë. She smiled at him and waved her hands at his face. He sat down on the sofa and marveled at how much she'd grown. Her arms and legs were pudgy and her cheeks had filled out. Those beautiful blue eyes scanned his face and she made cooing sounds. He was enthralled.

"Beau?"

"What?"

"Have you found out anything?"

Still watching Zoë, he told her all he'd found out about the Wallstons, Cynthia and the conversation he'd had with Caleb.

"So what does it all mean?" She curled up next to him and the smell of her did a number on his senses.

Suddenly a wave of memories washed over him, memories he'd kept at bay, of him touching her, kissing her and making love to her. Tonight he didn't push them away. Those memories meant something to him and probably always would. Pain or joy, his life was entwined with Macy's.

He bounced Zoë on his knee and she made a laughing sound. "Did you hear that?" he asked Macy, his voice excited.

"Yes. She's making a lot of sounds now."

"And slobbering." He reached for a towel to wipe her mouth.

"Beau?"

"What?"

"You didn't answer me. What does all this mean?"

"I don't know yet, but I know we're in for a fight. We really need Delia on our side."

"I keep waiting for her to call. I can't understand how she can go this long without checking on her baby."

He lifted an eyebrow. "Are we talking about the same Delia?"

"Okay." She rolled her eyes. "Delia's not the most responsible or caring person around."

"No."

She scooted to face him. She wore shorts and a sleeveless top. All he could see was smooth, silky skin—skin he wanted to touch and freckles he wanted to kiss.

"I had a long talk with my mother."

"Really." He caught Zoë's hands and wiggled his nose against hers. She cooed loudly.

"Yes, and it felt good."

"You haven't had much of a relationship with either of your parents since the divorce."

"No, and part of that is my fault. I should have made an effort, especially…especially when I was pregnant."

He shifted his gaze from Zoë to Macy. "You told your mother about Hope."

She nodded. "It wasn't as hard as I thought it would be. We share a lot of the same feelings."

"Because your mother lost a baby, too?"

"Mmm." She tucked hair behind her ears and lifted her eyes to his. "I'm sorry I hurt you."

"I'm sorry you hurt me, too."

She licked her lips. "I wish you could understand how I feel."

"And I wish you could understand how I feel."

She swallowed, but didn't respond.

"Love to me is unconditional. It doesn't come with a list—'must have babies, must be picture perfect.' Love is a feeling that overpowers all that. It just is and you can't change it. Lord knows, I have tried."

"Beau…"

He placed Zoë in her lap. "I can't stay angry at you. You're hurting and I was hoping I could ease that pain inside you. But I can't. I'm not sure if anything ever will."

She blinked back a tear. "It's worse when you're nice to me."

He wiped a tear from her cheek. "Be nice to yourself." He kissed Zoë on the head and stood. The dogs, including Peanut, sniffed at his feet. He bent to pat them. "Gotta go, boys."

"Beau."

He turned to stare into her sad eyes. The love she couldn't voice was there, burning bright. And there was nothing he could do about it. She had to heal on her own and accept love again—a man's love, hopefully his. But he wasn't holding his breath or beating himself up anymore.

"Thank you," she whispered.

He nodded and walked out before his courage gave way.

CHAPTER FOURTEEN

THE DAYS PASSED quickly and the hearing was upon them. Beau had his P.I. helping in the search for Delia, but there was still no sign of her. She seemed to have disappeared completely. The Wallstons were in town with Spencer Harcourt and Beau finally managed to get Cynthia Wallston on the phone. She'd been out of the country and Beau was about to give up hope.

"Mr. McCain, my secretary said you've been calling. What is this about?"

"It's about your husband, Keith."

"My husband is dead."

"I'm aware of that, but are you aware that your in-laws have filed for custody of minor child, Zoë Randall?"

"Randall? Does this have anything to do with that tramp Delia?"

Beau took a breath. "Yes, ma'am. Delia is Zoë's mother."

"I'm not following you. Why in the world would Cliff and Myrna want custody of that child?"

Beau didn't know how to soften the words, but he suspected that Cynthia already knew the answer. "They ordered a DNA test first," he replied.

"Oh my God. They don't think…"

"Yes, ma'am. You got it now. Keith is Zoë's biological father."

"That sorry bastard."

"Zoë is in the custody of her aunt, who wants to have permanent custody."

"Where is Delia?"

"We don't know. She abandoned the baby in the hospital."

"Keith always had a fetish for trash."

"That's beside the point. I felt you had a right to know since this affects your children."

"Mr. McCain, I'm not testifying for your client."

"That's your prerogative, especially if you feel the Wallstons are the best ones to raise the little girl."

"Oh, please. Cliff and Myrna didn't even raise their own son and he resented it every day of his life."

"Mrs. Wallston, the hearing is tomorrow at one o'clock at the McLennan County Courthouse in Waco, Texas. If you have any strong feelings about Zoë's custody, I suggest you attend."

"I'll give it some thought."

"Thank you."

When Beau hung up, his cell rang. It was Caleb.

"I found Delia, Beau."

He sat up straight. "Where?"

"In a motel in Reno. I remembered Irene saying when Delia ran away at fourteen that she used Irene's maiden name. That's why it was so hard to find her. It was a hunch, but it paid off. She's using Delia Gordon. I'm flying out to bring her back. Tuck's going with me.

Eli wanted to, but I told him there was no need and I know he doesn't want to get too far away from Caroline."

"That's above and beyond anything I expected."

"Let's hope she's still there when we arrive. I warned the motel manager about alerting her."

There was a long pause.

"Beau?"

"Yeah. I'm still here. I was just thinking that Delia is in Reno for a reason."

"Mmm. You better be prepared for that."

"I'm getting a real bad feeling."

"I'll get her back here as soon as I can, and hopefully she'll be on Macy's side."

"We don't have much time. The hearing is at one tomorrow and I need to speak with Delia an hour before that."

"I'll be in touch."

"Thanks, Caleb."

Beau clicked off and stood, needing to tell Macy. He didn't want to do that over the phone.

Liz walked in, eyeing him. "It's so good to have you back—the real you." There was a wealth of meaning in the last three words.

"Don't like a tyrant for a boss?"

"Absolutely not." She laid papers on his desk. "I'm getting too old to toe the line."

"Liz, you're ageless."

"Yeah. Tell that to my body." Her mouth twitched into a rare smile and she pointed at the files. "That's more financial records on the Wallstons."

"Thanks. I'll go over them later. Now I need to talk to Macy. If you need me, you can reach me on my cell." He headed for the door.

"Do you want Jon in court tomorrow?"

He stopped. "No. I want him here in case I need any last-minute detail."

"You got it."

Beau walked away, thinking that old saying, "You can catch more flies with honey than with vinegar" was very true. His office was in chaos when he was in a bad mood. Now it was running smoothly, like it always had. He had to remember to leave his heart-ache at home.

ZOË WAS CRYING and Macy let her, trying not to pick her up every time she whimpered. And the restraint was difficult. Zoë rolled onto her back, kicking and screaming, then flipped again to her stomach. She scooted to the edge of the playpen, her watery eyes searching for Macy. The dogs, all three of them, began to bark, alerting Macy that Zoë needed her. When Macy made no move toward the playpen, they trotted to it. As soon as Zoë saw the dogs, she quieted down, sticking her fingers to the netting trying to reach them.

Macy smiled. Oh, yes, someone was very spoiled. The doorbell rang. Macy clapped her hands. "It's your favorite person," she cooed to Zoë. "I bet he'll pick you up."

Captivated by the dogs, Zoë didn't pay her any attention, so Macy hurried to the door, knowing it had to be Beau.

But it was her father. "Dad, what are you doing here?" The words came out harshly, which is not how she meant them. "Come in."

Her father stepped into her home for the first time and it was a surreal moment. Lucky and Lefty barked at the stranger. Peanut ran to his bed. Freckles didn't move from her perch on the sofa.

"Hush," Macy said to the dogs, and they trotted back to Zoë, where their attention was appreciated.

"Still have a menagerie?"

"Yes. I don't think that's ever going to change."

He smiled slightly and she knew he was remembering all the years that he'd nurtured her love of animals. Spotting Zoë, he immediately went to her. "She's grown so much." He glanced at Macy. "Do you mind if I pick her up?"

"Oh, she'd loved that," she replied, unable to resist.

Her father held Zoë effortlessly. He was good with children. Macy had forgotten that. She remembered what her mother had said—that Ted didn't want any more kids. That was hard to believe and she knew she had to talk to her father.

After Ted visited with Zoë for a while, Macy fed her and put her down for a nap. Then she sat on the sofa next to him.

"I thought I'd come and offer my support for tomorrow."

"Thank you. I'd like that." She meant it, and that surprised her.

"Any word from Delia?"

"No."

He ran his hands over his face. "I failed both my girls and I'm so sorry for that."

"I wish I understood why."

He looked down at his hands. "Irene and I handled things badly."

"I talked to Mom."

His eyes swung to her. "What did she say?"

"Basically the same thing you did." She took a deep breath, needing to tell him, needing to open her soul one more time. "I have to tell you something."

"What?"

She swallowed. "I had a baby."

"Excuse me?"

"Allen and I had a baby girl. She lived four days. She was born with a congenital heart defect. They operated but she didn't survive."

"Oh no!"

"The defective gene came from me. After that Allen looked at me differently and he blamed me. Or I thought he blamed me. He never came out and said the words. But I'm the reason our baby girl died." As hard as she tried she couldn't stop the tears.

Ted took her in his arms. "Oh, Macy, honey. I'm so sorry." He drew back and lifted her chin with his forefinger. "Listen to me. You are *not* the reason your baby died."

"Then why do I feel like it?"

"Because you feel things deeply, just like me. Neither your mother nor I are the reason Sabrina died, either. It took a lot of years for me to admit that. It just happened. But at a time like that it's so easy to place and accept blame."

She felt a measure of peace in the arms of her father, a man who knew her better than anyone. She drew away, wiping away tears with the back of her hands.

"Does Irene know?" he asked.

"I told her for the first time when she visited Zoë."

"You've kept all this inside you?"

"Yes. My family had fallen apart and I felt you and Mom didn't care. I felt so alone."

He drew a sharp breath and stroked her hair.

"I came home to Waco, hoping to put it all behind me, but it haunts me every day."

"Macy." He pulled her to his shoulder. "I'm sorry, honey. I don't know what else to say."

"Just talk to me."

"When Sabrina died, it was the worst time of my life, except when I made the decision to leave your mother."

"Why did you do that?"

"I couldn't stay with her any longer. I…"

The doorbell rang.

No, Macy cried inwardly. She needed to hear his explanation, but she rose to get the door.

Beau came charging in. "Caleb found Delia."

"Oh. Where?"

"In Reno, Nevada. Caleb and Tuck are flying out to bring her back. Hopefully she'll be here in time for the hearing." Beau suddenly saw Ted. "Hi, Ted." They shook hands.

"Have you spoken to her?" Macy asked eagerly.

"No. I don't want to spook her at this late stage."

Ted stood. "I should go. Nina is waiting at the hotel."

"She came with you?" Macy shoved back her hair, feeling a taste of resentment returning.

"Yes. It's time she met my daughter." He kissed her cheek. "I'll see you tomorrow. Beau." He nodded and was gone.

"How do you feel about that?" Beau asked as the door closed.

"I can't think about it right now. I have to concentrate on tomorrow."

"Yeah."

He didn't push her and she was glad.

"Do you want to go over what's going to happen tomorrow?" he asked.

"No. I trust you."

"Macy…"

"Just do what you have to," she snapped, her nerves stretched beyond endurance. "But I want to speak with Delia as soon as she arrives."

"Okay. I'll be over in the morning, then I have a meeting with Harcourt and the judge."

She slumped onto the sofa. "This all hinges on Delia, doesn't it?"

"Yes. Even though she abandoned Zoë, Zoë is still her child." She could feel his warm eyes on her. "Try to get some rest. I'll be in touch."

So many emotions churned inside her and she couldn't make sense of any of them. But she was so afraid. That she could identify, but identifying what she was afraid of was more difficult.

THE MORNING DAWNED bright and sunny. It was early August and the heat was stifling. Macy quickly dressed and got ready for the day, trying to keep her anxieties at bay. As she was dressing Zoë, the doorbell rang.

"We're very popular these days," she said to Zoë, laying her in her crib with nothing on but a diaper.

Hurrying to the door, she opened it.

"Hi there, sugar," her mother said. "Thought I'd come and be with you today. There's no need for you to have to face this alone." She walked in and set down a suitcase.

Her mother was here! Her father was here! The last thing she needed today—her parents together after ten years.

"Mom, I wish you would have called."

"Why? You can't handle everything by yourself, Macy. Though Lord knows you try." Irene looked around. "Where's Zoë? Where's that beautiful baby?"

"In her crib. I was just getting her dressed. Mrs. Pruett is going to watch her while…"

The doorbell pealed again. Irene disappeared into the bedroom and Macy took a long breath. Please be Beau. Please be Beau, she prayed as she opened the door. Her prayer wasn't answered. Her father stood there.

"Thought I'd come by and see if you needed any help this morning."

Before she could find a suitable reply, Beau walked up. "Good morning, Ted."

The two men shook hands. "Beau. Any news about Delia?" Ted asked.

"I haven't heard from Caleb so I'm hoping that's good news."

They both stared at Macy and she didn't even realize that she had one hand on the open door and the other on the doorjamb, as if to block their entrance.

"Oh, oh, come in." She stepped back, knowing there was nothing she could do to stop this meeting.

"Macy, what do you want Zoë to wear? How about this pink-and-green sunsuit? It's so…" Her voice trailed away as she saw who was in the room.

Ted and Beau stared in puzzlement at the woman in tight capris, equally tight top with plunging neckline, flamboyant jewelry, dyed hair and high heels.

Finally, her dad said, "Irene?"

"Ted." For a moment Macy could see her mother was thrown, but she quickly recovered. "Don't tell me you didn't recognize me."

"No. I didn't."

Irene spun around. "I've changed—for the better."

"I'm not so sure."

Her mother's blue eyes flashed a warning and Beau stepped in. "I need to speak with Macy alone, so that will give you two time to get…reacquainted."

He pulled her into the bedroom before she could protest. "I don't think it's a good idea to leave them alone," Macy said.

"Trust me. Sometimes it helps divorced couples to talk in private."

At the sound of Beau's voice, Zoë kicked and made funny spluttering noises.

"Hey, munchkin." He tickled Zoë's stomach, then picked her up, kissing her cheek. "I love the way she smells."

"I just bathed her."

Beau stared at her, his eyes soft, and her heart flip-flopped. "Are you ready for today?"

She nodded and wanted to tell him about the talk with her father. But it wasn't the right time. She wanted to talk to Beau when they'd have no distractions.

He glanced at his watch and placed Zoë in her crib. "I really need to get going. I have a meeting with Harcourt and the judge. I just came by to tell you to be at the court-house by twelve. Judge Brampton is a stickler for punctuality and we don't want to start off on the wrong foot."

"I'll be there."

He glanced at his watch again. "I have to go, so I guess I'll brave the intrusion."

Opening the door a crack, Macy heard loud voices clearly and her first instinct was to shut it again. But a phrase held her attention.

"You destroyed our marriage without a second thought," her father screamed.

"That's a lie," her mother denied hotly. "I tried everything to save it."

"Yeah," Ted said, laughing bitterly. "Having an affair and a child by another man is not what I call trying to save it."

"You drove me to it!"

"You can blame me all you want, Irene, but it doesn't change the facts."

The words were like a blow to Macy's chest and she struggled to breathe. She backed into the solid wall of Beau's chest and his strength kept her from sinking to the floor.

He gripped her elbows. "Macy…"

"I'm fine," she murmured, and yanked opened the door, ready to face her parents—and the truth.

"Macy." Her mother stopped in the middle of her tirade. "I didn't realize…"

"Yes. I heard you." She walked closer. "How many times have I asked both of you what happened to break up our home? How many times have I begged and pleaded for some answers?"

"I'm sorry you heard that," her father said.

"Why?"

"It's between your mother and me."

"I'm tired of hearing that. You have two daughters who were affected and we deserve to know the truth. We deserve to know why our world was turned upside down."

Her mother twisted a ring on her finger and Ted looked away. "Or should I say one daughter. Evidently one of us is not yours. I'm assuming it's Delia."

"Yes," her father replied, still not looking at her.

Macy's gaze centered on her mother. "You had an affair?"

"It wasn't my fault," Irene mumbled.

A chill slide down Macy's back. "Were you raped?"

Irene clamped her lips together.

"Tell her, Irene. For heaven's sakes, it's time to tell her."

Her mother brushed away a tear. "After…after Sabrina died, Ted refused to have any more children. I wanted another child, but he said he couldn't go through that kind of pain again. We argued and argued and I could never make him understand that life didn't come with a pain-free guarantee. It came with risks, challenges, joys and, yes, pain. That's what life is all about. If I could have another baby, a healthy one, it would be worth the risk."

Irene gulped in a breath. "But Ted remained steadfast in his decision and I tried to accept it. We stopped having sex and I had to beg to sleep with my husband. I was angry and hurt. I didn't feel attractive anymore. That year we had a big argument right before the Christmas party at the bank and he refused to go with me, so I went alone. I started drinking and one thing led to another."

There was a long pause. "When I realized I was pregnant, I was excited and I did what any red-blooded woman in love with her husband would do. I passed the child off as his."

Macy's mind was a patchwork jumble of shredded emotions and it was an effort to just think. She realized Beau was still standing beside her and she wanted to tell him he could leave, but her vocal cords seemed broken. When she'd asked for the truth, she never dreamed it would be worse than not knowing. Pandora's box was wide open and she had to hear the rest of the story. "When did you find out differently?" she asked her father.

He swallowed visibly. "Remember when Delia was in that car accident with the Chandlers?"

"Yes." Macy remembered it very well. She'd hurried home from college to be with Delia. Mona Chandler was in a carpool with Irene and another lady. After Mona picked up the kids from school, a drunk driver hit the Chandlers' car causing a five-car pileup. Two of the girls had minor injuries but Delia's were severe. She was twelve and had a severe laceration on her head and a broken arm. She lost a lot of blood and stayed in the hospital for a week.

"Delia needed blood quickly and I offered mine. But it didn't match. That bothered me for a long time. Then I had a DNA test done for my own peace of mind." He took a deep breath. "Sometimes I wish I'd never done that. It didn't bring any peace—only more pain. Irene finally admitted the truth. That didn't make it better, either. I started drinking and Irene and I argued constantly. I didn't have any good feelings about my wife, my kids, my life or myself and I knew I had to get away. I couldn't stay in that situation any longer. So I did something I thought I would never do. I walked out."

He took a ragged breath. "I quit my job and went to Houston and stayed with my friend, Ed Holmes. I was drinking so heavily that he kicked me out after the first month. I gave Irene everything we had in the divorce so I had nothing. I stayed at a homeless shelter and drank myself into oblivion, then I had a mild heart attack and the doctor said if I didn't stop drinking and living the way I was I'd be dead in a year. Didn't matter to me, but eventually Ed saw to it that I got help. That's how I met Nina. She worked as a nutritionist in the rehab center I was in."

He looked at his daughter. "That's why you never heard from me. I wasn't in any shape to see anyone. Then when I was clean I didn't think you'd want to see me. I'm sorry for all the pain I've caused you and I'm extremely sorry I wasn't there when your daughter died."

Irene swung to look out the window.

Emotions were about to choke Macy, but she knew she couldn't deal with her parents right now. She had to know one thing, though.

"Does Delia know?"

Irene swung back around, her eyes clouded. "No, and I don't want her to ever know."

Macy shook her head. "I can't do this right now. My focus has to be on Zoë." She turned to Beau. "Go. What are you still doing here?"

"Macy…"

"Go or you're going to be late."

Beau hesitated for a second then headed for the door. In a numb state Macy went into the bedroom, dressed Zoë, grabbed the diaper bag and quickly hurried to Mrs. Pruett's. Her parents were gone when she entered the living room and that was just as well. She had to absorb everything they'd said and try to make sense of it all. And try to find a measure of understanding and forgiveness. That wouldn't come easy.

CHAPTER FIFTEEN

BEAU HURRIED TO THE courthouse and tried to put Macy and her parents out of his mind, though it seemed impossible. That family had been through so much heartache and the problems didn't seem to be getting any better.

Irene had said that Delia hadn't known about her paternity, but Beau doubted that. Delia's real problems started after the wreck. It was after that when she'd become defiant, angry and full of attitude. Ted said he and Irene argued all the time. Delia could have easily overheard them. And he was almost positive that was at the root of Delia's problems.

He pushed the thoughts away as a clerk showed him into Judge Brampton's chambers. Spencer Harcourt was already there. They shook hands and eyed each other. Tall and imposing, Harcourt epitomized an uptown lawyer from Philadelphia—from his coiffured silver hair to his tailored suit to his Italian shoes. Everything bespoke money and power.

"Welcome to Texas," Beau said.

"How do you stand this heat?" He had a northern accent.

"You get used to it."

"I don't plan to be here that long."

Judge Brampton entered, stopping conversation. After the introductions, the judge took his seat.

"Mr. Harcourt has brought this to my attention and, Mr. McCain, you have a right to see it before the hearing." Beau took a document from him "It will be a part of the pre-hearing evidence. Read it."

Beau scanned through the papers. *Son of a bitch.* The document was a notarized letter signed by Delia saying she wanted the Wallstons to have full custody of her daughter. Damn Delia. She'd had a plan all along. Now he had to find a way to undo the damage.

"You don't have a case, McCain." Harcourt looked at him over the steeple of his fingers, victory in his eyes.

Beau laid the papers on the judge's desk and he knew Brampton was waiting for him to withdraw his case. *No way in hell.*

"That's all very neat and tidy, but I'd rather hear Delia Randall say that in person. How do I know she wasn't coerced into signing that?"

"Mr. McCain, Ms. Randall wants the Wallstons to raise her daughter. It's plain and simple. And she wasn't coerced into anything."

"Well, Mr. Harcourt, there's the little matter of the abandonment. In my opinion, a mother who would abandon her baby doesn't have the right to negotiate custody of said child." He turned to the judge. "Your Honor, I'll have a motion on your desk within the hour to terminate Delia Randall's parental rights."

"Your Honor…" Harcourt was on his feet.

The judge held up a hand. "Enough. I don't take aban-donment lightly. I'm ordering Delia Randall to testify."

"Your Honor, that will push back the hearing," Harcourt complained.

"Not necessarily," Beau said. "My brother Caleb McCain is a Texas Ranger and has located her. I'm just waiting to hear from him."

"I take issue with that," Harcourt said. "Ranger McCain clearly has a vested interest in this case."

"Everyone here does, Mr. Harcount," the judge replied. "We want what's best for Zoë Randall and I trust Ranger McCain to do the job requested of him accord-ing to the laws of Texas. This hearing is going ahead. If Delia Randall is not present, I'll make a ruling on the evidence presented. The law will take care of Ms. Randall."

That was it. The judge walked out.

"You good ol' boys stick together down here," Harcourt remarked, reaching for his briefcase.

Beau eyed him for a moment. "I want what's best for Zoë Randall. What do you want, Mr. Harcourt?"

"Mr. McCain, I learned a long time ago to never get emotionally involved in a case."

"That's the difference between you and us good ol' boys. We fight from the heart." He picked up his brief-case. "See you at one."

WALKING DOWN THE HALL, Beau called his office.

"Liz, I need to speak with Jon."

Within five seconds, Jon was on the line. "Yes, sir."

"Jon, I need a termination of parental rights motion for Delia Randall done ASAP, like in an hour."

"Yes, sir."

"Get Natalie to help you go over the Wallstons' financial records. Look for a large transaction within the last two months."

"Yes, sir. I'm on it."

"I need something by one. All the details you can find."

"I'll do my best."

Beau clicked off, knowing the Wallstons had paid Delia to sign the paper. Now he had to prove it. Damn, where was Caleb? He tried his cell. Nothing. Time was running out.

MACY LEFT Zoë at Mrs. Pruett's and walked to the park. The hot sun bore down on her and she hardly noticed. *Delia was her half sister. Her mother had had an affair.* She sat on a park bench and let those two thoughts run through her mind. It explained so much. It was the reason her parents didn't get along after Delia's birth. Without knowing it her mother was instinctively protecting Delia from Ted. That's why she would never let Ted discipline her. Her mother's desire for a child had ruined her marriage, her life and now she was trying to recapture her youth.

She ran her hands over her face. *Her father*. When she thought of him now she felt so much pain—a different kind of pain. If she'd known, she could have helped him. Instead she'd been nurturing a hatred for a man who was hurting as bad as she was. How could her parents, who loved each other, do what they had done to themselves, to their children?

Through the massive heartache one thing became clear. She was doing the same thing. Like her father, she was afraid to take a risk, afraid of the pain, so she hurt the person she loved the most—Beau. By not accepting his love she told herself she was doing the right thing. Doing what was best for him. But she wasn't. It was never right when you hurt someone.

She glanced up at the bright sun, letting its rays burn through her defenses. For the first time in broad daylight she confronted the monster who controlled her life. And the monster wasn't the loss of her daughter, or Beau. It was herself. She was the one who nurtured the fear, kept it hidden, letting it affect her whole life. Letting it affect her relationship with Beau.

Like a spotlight, the sun opened up the avenues of her mind exposing reality in its truest form—the stark truth. If having children frightened her, Beau wouldn't pressure her, he wouldn't made her feel guilty. He would just love her. Why couldn't she have seen Beau for the wonderful man she knew him to be? Why did it take so much heartache for her to see that?

She brushed away an errant tear, knowing she had to prove to him that she could love him. Without guilt. Without fear. But first she had a hearing to go to. This time she was fighting for what she wanted.

BEAU GLANCED AT HIS WATCH and debated whether to go see Macy, to make sure she was okay, or go to the office.

He had to cut those ties to Macy. She'd made it clear that she didn't want him in her life, so the best course was to let her handle her parents on her own. But it didn't keep him from worrying about her.

He strolled down the hall to the parking area and stopped short. Caleb and Tuck came toward him. A black-haired woman in handcuffs walked between them. Could that be…? As they drew closer, he saw that it was her.

Caleb and Tuck wore frustrated expressions and Beau knew they hadn't had an easy time with Delia.

"You better tell them to get these damn handcuffs off me," Delia threatened as they reached Beau.

Beau shook his head and found a family meeting room so he could talk to Delia. Tuck stayed in the room with Delia while he talked to Caleb outside the door.

"Why haven't you called? I was getting worried."

"Hell, this turned into a nightmare. Delia did not want to come back. Somehow she found out someone was looking for her and she took off, but the manager knew what she was driving. A new red Corvette. I called the highway patrol and they called as soon as they stopped her. The moment she saw me she took off running, jumped the fence like a deer. Tuck was a step behind her. He tackled her and busted his cell. We finally got her in the car and headed for the airport. When I tried to call you, she grabbed my phone and threw it out the window. That's when I put the cuffs on her. She's not a happy camper, but I'll tell you, she can hold her own with any sailor."

"Talking to her is not going to be fun," Beau mused.

"I'll stick around just in case you need some help with her because if you take your eyes off her, she's gone."

"Did she say anything?"

"Nothing I'd like to repeat."

Beau glanced at the door. "She's changed her appearance."

"And she has money."

"Mmm. Don't have to guess where that came from." Beau thought for a minute. "I need to call my office."

He had Jon on the line in a second. "I have something else I need you to do. See if you can get bank records for a Delia Gordon in Reno or Vegas. Get Liz to help you. This might be tricky so use whatever means you can. Call Ric, the P.I., if you need help."

"Very wise," Caleb said as he clicked off.

Beau took a deep breath. "Now it's time to talk to Delia."

"I wouldn't take those handcuffs off if I were you. She's mad as hell."

Beau walked in and nodded to Tuck, who had scratches on his face and arms. "All yours," Tuck said as he closed the door and joined Caleb in the hall.

Beau sat across from Delia and stared into blue eyes as hot as coals. "You better take these freaking handcuffs off."

"I don't think you're in a position to be giving orders."

"Wanna bet?" She lifted a painted eyebrow.

Beau leaned back. "Aren't you going to ask how Zoë is?"

"No. Why should I?"

"She's your daughter."

The heat in her eyes turned up a notch, but there was not a flicker of heartfelt emotion. "Okay. I'll tell you about Zoë." He told her everything Zoë had been through—how he and Macy stayed up with her day and night, the surgery and Zoë return to good health. "She could have died if Macy hadn't been there to watch her twenty-four hours a day."

Delia shrugged. "So. That's why I left her with Macy. I knew she'd take good care of her."

"Until you were ready to sell her," Beau slipped in.

"That's ridiculous." Delia moved uneasily.

"Really? You have money now. Where did you get it?"

"I'm very good at slots."

"You're lying. You sold Zoë to the Wallstons."

Delia leaned forward, a gleam in her eyes. "Prove it."

His gaze didn't waver from hers. "You know how deeply Macy loves. She loves Zoë. Are you going to rip that baby right out of her arms?"

"If you're trying to reach my sensitive side, I don't have one."

"This is Macy, the person who is always there for you no matter what. The person you call when you're in trouble."

Delia shrugged. "Macy can have her own kids. She doesn't need to be saddled with one of mine."

Beau took a minute and knew he had to break a confidence. He didn't do that lightly.

"Macy won't have any children of her own."

"What?"

He told her about Hope. "She died the same way your sister Sabrina did, with a congenital heart defect. Macy feels responsible since the defective gene runs in your family and she will never have another child."

"You're lying. If Macy had a baby, I would know."

"Think back, Delia. You were constantly running away at that time and Macy was living in Dallas. How often did you see her?"

"She would have told me."

"Why? Would you have offered her sympathy? Comfort?"

"Shut up, man." She wiggled in the chair. "And get me out of these freaking handcuffs."

She wasn't going to break. Delia was tough as nails. But he knew her secret—a secret that had destroyed the Randall family just might save it.

He shoved his hands into his slacks, watching her closely. "Your mother and father are here."

"Whoop-de-do, bring out the wine."

"Macy's been talking to them."

"Well, pin a medal on her."

He waited a moment. "Macy knows."

There was complete silence and the come back wasn't so quick.

"Knows what?"

"The Randall family secret."

Delia jerked in her chair. "Go to hell, McCain. You don't know squat and you'd better undo these hand-cuffs."

"I know that lies and deceit have been like an acid in your system, eating away at you. Rebelling made them suffer so you just kept right on making them suffer."

"I don't know what the hell you're talking about."

He looked into her stormy eyes. "Don't do this to Macy. Don't do this to Zoë."

"The baby goes with the Wallstons." She didn't even blink and Beau left the room before he strangled her.

MACY FOUND A PARKING SPOT at the courthouse and hurried inside. She wanted to be early in case Caleb was back with Delia.

"Macy."

She turned and saw her mother walking toward her. She had on black slacks, a black-and-white pinstriped blouse and flats, no jewelry and very little makeup. She looked like the mother she had known, a mother who had lied to her for years. Resentment simmered inside her.

"I need to talk to you."

Macy sighed. "Could we do this later? I really need to see Beau to find out if Delia has arrived."

"Please, I…I…" Tears filled her mother's eyes.

Her resentment ebbed away. "Let's sit over here." She walked toward a bench and sat down. Her mother followed.

Irene put her purse on the floor. "I'm not sure where to start. I'm one of those women who has a need to have children. I miscarried a child between you and Sabrina and I was so happy to carry a baby to full term. Losing her was like having my heart ripped out. It was the same with Ted and we couldn't seem to get beyond all our pain. I desperately wanted to get pregnant again. Your father was adamantly against it. It was the first time we disagreed so vehemently. And well, you know the rest of the story."

"Did you love this other man?"

"Of course not. It was a one-night stand—a young guy who worked at the bank. Your father didn't seem to want me anymore and I felt unattractive and unwanted. I'm also one of those women who needs to feel wanted. Tony, that was his name, made me feel young and attractive and it went to my head. I made a colossal mistake. Afterward, I was so ashamed, but I couldn't go back and change it."

"What happened to Tony?"

"About a month later he transferred out of the bank to another city and I was glad about that. Every time I saw him it reminded me of what I'd done. With him gone I didn't have to think about it anymore. Then I discovered I was pregnant. Luckily I was feeling so guilty I pressured Ted into making love. So he naturally thought Delia was his." She took a breath. "When Delia was about four, I heard Tony was killed in a motorcycle accident."

"Did he know he had a child?"

"No," Irene replied with stubborn lift of her chin. "Delia was Ted's daughter in every way that counted."

Macy stared at her mother. "Then why did you shut Dad out? You wouldn't let him discipline her or connect with her on any level."

Irene swallowed. "When we found out about the ADHD I was so afraid he'd find out the truth—that Delia wasn't his."

Macy inhaled deeply. "It didn't work, did it?"

"No." Irene studied her long fingernails. "I never realized Ted suffered so much, but then I should have. I was married to him."

"It breaks my heart to think of him in a homeless shelter without anyone to care for him."

Irene brushed away a tear. "I thought he just didn't care about us anymore." She hiccuped. "I destroyed my family. I'm the one to blame. There, I've admitted it and it hurts like hell."

Somewhere in the conversation Macy knew she'd become the adult, the one to step forward and make everything right. "Maybe, but we have to get beyond that now and think about Delia. She's the one who has been hurt the most."

"I don't think there's any way to save Delia. She's been set on a course of self-destruction for a long time."

Macy grew thoughtful, and glanced at her mother. "Do you think she knows?"

Irene shook her head. "No. How could she? And I don't want her to ever know."

"Mom, I don't think that's going to be possible."

"She'll hate me."

"That's not anything new. Delia hates everyone and there has to be a reason for that." Macy stood. "I better go."

"I'm a pathetic woman trying to recapture her youth. You would think I'd have more sense."

"Is that why you changed your clothes?"

"Partly. This morning your father and I went for coffee and talked for a long time. We finally talked without the anger. I saw myself through his eyes and what I saw was a trampy woman. I didn't like that feeling."

"You and Dad went for coffee?"

"Yeah. Neither one of us like what we've done to our

children. Looking back together it was almost surreal as we could see our mistakes so clearly."

That shocked her. She never thought her parents would have a normal conversation. They were both still so angry. At the tone of her mother's voice she had to ask. "Do you still love him?"

Irene blinked and looked away. "Ted was my first true love and a part of me will always love him. That's just something you can't rip out of your heart, although I've tried."

Macy wished she had a magic wand she could wave and turn back the years, erase the heartache and have the young, happy parents she had known. But those days were gone. Now they had to deal with the broken hearts, broken trusts and broken faith. The only cure she knew was love and that was in short supply these days.

Her mother stood and picked up her purse. "After your father left, I'm sorry I wasn't there for you or Delia. All I could feel was my pain and I was just emotionally empty. Please forgive me."

"It was a hard time for all of us and it's not my place to judge you. You're my mother and I love you. That love is unconditional and…"

Her words trailed off as they rang a bell inside her head. Beau had said the same thing. *My love is unconditional. It doesn't come with a list, "must make babies, must be picture perfect."*

She was beginning to see what he'd meant. She was too blinded by the pain to recognize the real thing. Was she destined, like her parents, to destroy the good things in her life?

CHAPTER SIXTEEN

MACY HURRIED TO FIND Beau, though she knew she wouldn't have time to speak to him about anything personal. Still, just seeing him would help tremendously.

Down the hall she could see him talking to Caleb and Tuck. He looked worried. If Caleb and Tuck were here that meant Delia was, too. She wondered where she was and what kind of mood she was in. As much as she hated to admit it, the outcome of this day would depend on Delia's mood.

Beau saw her and came toward her. His warm, kind heart reminded her of everything that was good in this world and how lucky she'd been to have him in her life. Maybe soon she could tell him that. Of one thing she was certain—this day would not end until she did.

This is strictly business. That's what he'd said and at the time that was the way she wanted it. But now...

"Is Delia here?" she asked anxiously.

"Yes."

"Where? I want to speak with her."

A shadow crossed his face. "I need to speak with you first."

"What's wrong?"

He took her arm and led her down the hall to a couple of chairs. Once they were seated he said, "I've already spoken to Delia."

"And?"

"She's angry and not cooperative."

"Oh. Did she ask about Zoë?"

He shook his head. "No. She has no interest in keeping her baby." He drew in a breath. "She signed a document stating she wants the Wallstons to have full custody of Zoë."

"What?" She could feel the blood draining from her face.

"I feel she sold Zoë to the Wallstons, but I can't prove it yet."

"No. She wouldn't do that."

"Macy." He sighed. "You said she talked about a plan. I believe that plan was to get as much money as she could from the father's parents."

She remembered little things that Delia had said. *The father was out of the picture. She had a plan. A sick baby was no good to her.* Still she couldn't let herself believe it.

"Beau…"

"She was driving a new red Corvette."

"Oh, no!" The reality finally sunk in. She jumped to her feet. "I need to speak with her."

"Okay, but we don't have a lot of time. It's almost one and time for the hearing to start."

"I just need a few minutes."

They walked down the hall to Caleb and Tuck. She

spoke, but she wasn't sure what she said. Beau opened the door and they stepped in. Macy was taken aback for a second because she didn't recognize the woman at first. The black hair threw her.

"Go away, Macy. I don't want to talk to you."

That was definitely her sister's angry voice. She sat down and stared at this young girl who was filled with so much hate.

"Stop looking at me and tell your freaking boyfriend to get these cuffs off."

Macy frowned at Beau and he shook his head. "The judge has ordered her to testify and if we take the cuffs off she'll try to get away."

"Let me go because I won't testify in your favor."

"What?" Macy glanced at her sister.

"I want the Wallstons to have Zoë."

Macy was angered by the blunt response. "Why did you leave Zoë with me then? Why didn't you just take her?"

There was a noticeable pause.

"The kid had problems, and I couldn't take a sick kid with me, could I?"

Macy's eyes narrowed. "You're not that heartless. I know you're not."

"Oh, yeah," Delia screamed. "There's not any good left in me, Macy, so stop trying to find it. You're not getting my baby, so get over it."

Macy flinched.

"That a bit harsh for you? You were always the favorite one, the perfect daughter. Dad loved you and he never even noticed me. Well, I'm not giving you my daughter to make your life complete. Do that on your own and get out of my face."

"I never realized you hated me so much." She said it in a whisper, as if she didn't want to hear herself say the words.

Delia turned sideways in the chair. "Go away, Macy."

"It's time to go." She heard Beau's voice, rose to her feet as if in a trance and walked into the hall.

"Macy."

"I'm fine." She knew what he was going to ask.

"You have to be," he told her. "It's time for the hearing to start and you have to be in control."

"I will." But inside she felt raw and beaten. Her sister hated her.

"Delia knows," Beau said.

She blinked. "What?"

"Delia knows she's not Ted's daughter. That's why she's taking her anger out on you. You *are* his daughter."

"Yes. That makes sense." She glanced at the closed door. "I wish she'd talk to me."

"Let's concentrate on the hearing."

She nodded. "Delia's in no condition to raise Zoë and I don't feel the Wallstons are right for her, either." Her eyes held his. "Can we win this?"

"I'll give it my best."

As they took their seats in the courtroom, Macy knew that Beau's best was all she needed. But with Delia against her she wondered if it would be enough.

IRENE AND TED sat behind Beau and Macy, and Beau was glad they were there to offer their support. Macy would need them today. He watched as the Wallstons took their place next to Spencer Harcourt. They were exactly like he knew they would be—sophisticated, cultured. Mrs. Wallston's blond hair hung like a bell around her face and she wore a stylish suit. Mr. Wallston was also immaculately dressed, his brown hair without a speck of gray.

Harcourt presented his case stating a change of circumstance had occurred and that Zoë would be better off with her biological grandparents. Beau countered with the facts, starting with Zoë's birth, her health problems, Delia's disappearance and Macy's care of Zoë. He didn't leave out a thing, reiterating that a disruption in Zoë's routine could only harm her. Dr. Pender testified about Zoë's medical condition, the misdiagnosis. Dr. Cravey sent a statement to read concerning Zoë's surgery and how Macy was an exceptional mother to Zoë.

Macy took the stand and he went over it again. In the end he asked, "Ms. Randall, why do you want custody of Zoë?"

"Because I love her. I love her as if she were my own child."

Harcourt didn't question Macy. There wasn't much he could tear apart. He was basing his custody case on Delia.

Mrs. Wallston testified, saying how much they wanted Zoë, their dead son's child. Harcourt elicited a moving story from her about how much they loved their son and how much they wanted a part of him to live on with them.

"Why do you feel Zoë will be better off with you?" Harcourt asked.

"Because we're her grandparents and we want to give her a life that her father would have wanted for her. I always wanted a daughter, but I only had a son. I will shower her with love and attention and give her everything she needs. We're her family and—" she dabbed at her eyes with a tissue "—I have to do this for my son. I appreciate all that Ms. Randall has done for Zoë, and if we had known about Zoë's medical problems we would have been here to offer our support. We want what's best for our granddaughter and we believe that is with her grandparents."

"Thank you." Harcourt took his seat.

Beau stood for the cross-examination. "Mrs. Wallston, how old are you?"

"I beg your pardon?"

"Your Honor." Harcourt was immediately on his feet. "Her age is irrelevant."

"Your Honor, Mrs. Wallston is seeking custody of a baby. I think age is very relevant."

"I agree," the judge said. "State your age, Mrs. Wallston."

Her lips tightened. "I'm sixty-two."

"Will you be the primary caregiver for Zoë?"

"I don't understand the question."

"Will you be the one changing Zoë's diapers, feeding her, putting her to bed, reading her bedtime stories and performing all the tasks that taking care of a baby requires."

"Zoë will have a full-time nanny to attend to all her needs. She will want for nothing."

"Except maybe your love."

"Your Honor," Harcourt called. "I resent this type of questioning."

"Withdrawn," Beau said, and took a moment. "Mrs. Wallston, how many other grandchildren do you have?"

"Two. A boy and a girl."

"How often do you see them?"

"They're in boarding school so it's difficult to see them."

"Does the school not allow visits?" Beau asked.

"They do, but we'd rather not disrupt their schooling."

"So how often do you see your grandchildren?"

Mrs. Wallston cleared her throat. "We see them at Christmas and we make an effort on their birthdays."

"Twice a year?"

"Yes."

"You see your grandchildren twice a year. Do they know your name?"

"Your Honor," Harcourt objected.

"Mr. McCain…"

"Withdrawn, Your Honor."

Mr. Wallston testified next and Beau kept watching the door, hoping Jon would arrive with something. It was too late to call the office. It might be too late for anything.

Harcourt finished and Beau stood, praying for the door to open, but it didn't. He was hoping Cynthia Wallston would arrive, but that didn't happen, either. Now he had to go with a wing and a prayer.

"Mr. Wallston, do you know Delia Randall?"

"Not personally, no. Our son had an affair with her."

"How did you know Delia was pregnant with your son's child?"

"Delia called several times then she arrived at our home and said she gave birth to Keith's daughter and she wanted us to have custody."

"And you didn't believe her?"

"No. We had a DNA test done."

Beau went to his desk, pulled out the test, glanced at the door and walked back to Mr. Wallston. He laid it in front of him. He didn't need to do this. He was stalling for time.

"The test proves conclusively that Clifford Keith Wallston is the biological father of Zoë Jane Randall?"

"Yes."

He laid another piece of paper in front of him. "Can you tell us what that is?"

"Yes. It's a document that Delia Randall has signed stating that she wants us to raise her daughter."

"Mr. Wallston, why did Delia sign that document?"

"Because I told you she wants us to have custody."

"You're under oath, Mr. Wallston."

"I'm aware of that."

"Did you pay Delia Randall to sign that document?"

"Of course not."

Harcourt stood. "Your Honor, where is Mr. McCain going with this?"

"Mr. McCain…"

"That's all, Your Honor." Beau walked back to his seat cursing. Dammit. Dammit. Dammit. Delia was next. At this point, he didn't want Delia to be the deciding factor. But he didn't have much of a choice. The judge would have to decide, according to her testimony, whether to terminate her rights or give credence to her wishes. Now Beau would have to go after Delia. That was his only option.

"This isn't going well, is it?" Macy whispered.

"No." He didn't lie to her. "It doesn't help that Delia isn't on our side."

The bailiff brought Delia in without the handcuffs. Caleb and Tuck stood at the back of the room and Beau knew they were making sure that Delia didn't get away from them again.

She was sworn in and she told Harcourt the same story the Wallstons had. She felt Keith's parents were better for her child.

Beau walked to the witness stand. "Ms. Randall, are you aware there's a warrant out for your arrest?"

"I do now. Your Texas Ranger brother told me."

"Why is there a warrant for your arrest?"

"They say I abandoned my baby, but I didn't. I left her with my sister."

Beau laid the note Delia had left in the hospital in front of her. "Did you write that?"

Delia glanced at the note. "Yes."

"Would you please read it?"

She sighed. "'Macy, I can't do this. I can't deal with a sick baby. Take care of Zoë. Delia.'"

"You wanted your sister to take care of your daughter?"

"At the time, yes."

"What changed your mind?"

"The Wallstons have money and they can give Zoë a better life. Macy will just smother her to death like she did me and I don't want that for Zoë."

Beau saw Macy wince, but he turned his attention back to Delia. "By smother do you mean love?"

Delia's eyes narrowed. "Go to hell."

"Ms. Randall, I will not have that kind of language in this court." The judge reprimanded her.

"Yeah, okay."

The judge motioned for Beau to continue. He walked close and looked her in the eye. "Did you sell your baby to the Wallstons?"

"No." She didn't bat an eye.

"You just decided that Zoë would have a better life with them? These people who you don't even know. These people who have money." He was grasping at straws. He was debating his next move when Jon entered the courtroom. Relief sagged through him, but he didn't let it show.

"Your Honor, may I have a moment to speak with my assistant?"

"You have one minute, Mr. McCain."

Jon handed him several pieces of paper. "This might help. It's all I could dig up at such short notice."

"Thanks." Beau glanced at the papers and walked back to the judge, laying the papers in front of him. "You Honor, I'd like to enter these documents into evidence."

Spencer was immediately on his feet. He glanced at the documents. "Your Honor…"

"Save it, Mr. Harcourt," the judge replied. "I'll allow it, especially in light of your client's testimony."

Beau walked to Delia. "Ms. Randall, when the highway patrol stopped you, you were driving a red Corvette?"

"Yes."

"Where did you get it?"

"I won the money gambling. I'm very lucky."

He laid the two piece of paper in front of her. "Three weeks ago Clifford Wallston purchased a red Corvette."

"So?"

He pointed to the other piece of paper. "That same day the title was transferred into your name."

"So?"

"Mr. Wallston bought the car for you."

"Yeah. So what? I didn't have anything to drive."

He took a moment. "Delia, you sold your baby to the Wallstons."

"I did not."

He had to pull out all the stops. "How much did you get? A hundred thousand and a car?"

"I didn't sell my baby," Delia yelled.

"Two hundred thousand?" Beau kept on.

"Shut up."

"Your Honor, Mr. McCain is badgering the witness."

"Mr. McCain…"

But he wasn't listening. He kept pushing. "Four hundred thousand? Five hundred thousand?"

"Shut up! Shut up!"

"Mr. McCain…"

"Eight hundred thousand? A million dollars? Did the Wallstons offer you a million dollars for Zoë?"

"Yes, yes, yes and you're not taking it away from me."

The room became so quiet Beau could hear the ticking of his watch. Harcourt threw up his hands and slumped into his chair.

Before Beau could continue, Ted stood up. "Your Honor, I'm Ted Randall. May I speak to my daughter?"

"No." Delia rounded on the judge. "He's not my father and I'm not speaking to him."

"Young lady, you need to speak to someone," the judge said. "We'll take a thirty-minute recess."

MACY'S HEART WAS BEATING so fast that she had to take a deep breath. She couldn't believe the words coming out of Delia's mouth. She couldn't believe any of what was happening today, except for Beau. He was fighting for her like he always had. She wished she had a few minutes alone with him, but now she had to concentrate on her family.

Everyone cleared the room except for her mother, her father, Delia and Beau. Ted walked to the witness stand and took Delia's arm. She jerked away. Ted took it more firmly and pulled her to a chair, pushing her into in. He squatted in front of her.

"When did you find out I wasn't your real father?"

Delia clamped her lips together.

Ted took both her hands in his. "I love you. I have from the moment you were born."

"Yeah, right." Delia looked at the wall. Macy moved to stand behind her father.

Ted let that pass. "When did you find out?"

Delia licked her lips.

"Tell me."

"Shut up and leave me alone."

"Delia…"

"About a year after the accident, okay? Mom said I could go to the movies with my friend, Lisa. I ran out of the house before you could say no, but I forgot my purse and I hurried back to get it. You and Mom were arguing. You said my grades were down and I shouldn't be allowed privileges until I got them back up. One word led to another and Mom said for you to admit what was really bothering you—that you saw me differently since you found out I wasn't yours. Y'all said a lot of other things, but I just remembered that Mom said I wasn't your daughter."

"I'm sorry you heard that," Ted said. "I had a lot of anger when I found out, but it never changed the way I felt about you. I was your father in every way that counted, in every way that mattered."

Resentment burned in Delia's blue eyes. "Then why did you leave? You left because of me."

"No, baby, no." Ted reached up to smooth her hair. "I left because of your mother. I couldn't get over her betrayal."

Her mother whimpered and Macy took her hand and squeezed it. Even though the truth was hard to listen to, they all had to hear it.

"Why…why did you never come back?" Tears filled Delia's voice and Macy's throat closed up.

"I couldn't. When I left, I started drinking to forget and I didn't stop. I wound up in a homeless shelter drinking with the winos."

Delia gulped in a breath. "When I first ran away I went to find you, but I couldn't. I looked and looked and…"

"Oh, sweetheart. I'm so sorry your mother and I caused you so much pain." Ted took Delia in his arms and Delia didn't resist. He reached back for Macy, pulling her down beside them. "I have my girls back."

Macy swallowed the lump in her throat, wondering how their lives had gotten so out of control—and if they could ever put them back together again.

CHAPTER SEVENTEEN

TED DREW BACK. "Now I want you to do something for me."

"What?" Delia brushed away tears.

"I want you to get on the witness stand and tell the judge the truth. Do what's best for Zoë. Do what's best for yourself."

"I don't think I can."

"Yes, you can," Ted insisted. "Because I'll be right here waiting for you. Afterward I want you to come and live with Nina and me."

"What?"

"We have an extra bedroom with a private bath."

"But Nina doesn't like me."

"You've never given her a chance and you've always been very nasty to her."

"She's not my mother." Delia spat out the words.

"And she doesn't want to be."

Delia's eyes narrowed. "Why are you being so nice?"

"Because you're my daughter."

"Macy's your daughter. I'm just the result of Mom's affair." Delia glanced at Irene. "Where's your boy toy?"

Irene turned away.

"Stop it," Ted said, his voice stern.

Delia slumped back in the chair with a mutinous expression.

"Tantrums that you used to throw as a kid aren't going to work today. You're an adult now and you have a daughter. A daughter that your sister has taken very good care of."

"Perfect Macy," Delia derided. "I could never do anything as good as her. She was always your favorite."

"Is that why you're being so mean to her? You think I love her more?"

"You do." Delia stuck out her chin, her anger evident. "You always have."

"A father's love isn't like that. Macy's my strong, independent one with more energy than one person should have. She didn't start walking. She started running and Irene and I had a hard time keeping up with her. You were my fun and impulsive daughter, never afraid to take risks or chances. I always admired your courage. My love has no measurement. You are two different individuals and I love the differences in you and Macy."

"Yeah, right."

"It's true."

Delia looked down at her hands. "You're just saying that 'cause you want me to give Zoë to Macy."

"That's up to you. You know your sister, so do what's in your heart. I just want you to be able to live with yourself afterward."

Delia flipped back her hair. "Haven't you heard—
I don't have a conscience."

The bailiff came in. "Court is resuming. Take your
seats."

MACY TOOK HER SEAT by Beau. "She's not going to
change her mind. Beau…"

He looked into her troubled eyes. "Don't ask me to
go easy on her."

"She's just been through so much."

"Are you ready to let the Wallstons have custody?
Are you ready to let go of Zoë?"

She bit her lip. "No." Those motherly feelings she
had for Zoë were strong.

"Then let me handle this."

"Ms. Randall," the judge said. "You are still under
oath."

Delia nodded.

"Continue, Mr. McCain."

Beau walked forward. "Delia, did the Wallstons buy
you the Corvette?"

Delia looked at Ted, but she didn't respond.

"Ms. Randall, answer the question," the judge instructed.

"Would you like me to repeat it?" Beau asked.

"I'm not deaf," Delia snapped.

Beau took a patient breath. "Did the Wallstons buy
you the Corvette?"

"Yes." Delia looked straight at Ted.

"Why?"

Delia studied her hands that were clasped in her lap.

"I never wanted a child. It was an accident. Keith was angry at me for a long time, but I couldn't get rid of it like he wanted me to."

"You mean abort it?"

"Yes."

"Why?"

"It's hard to explain, but I have this sister who's perfect in every way. She'll even pick up a half-dead animal from the highway and nurse it back to health. Every time I thought about it, I'd see her face."

"This sister that you hate stopped you from having an abortion."

"You don't understand."

"Explain it to me," Beau suggested.

"That's what I meant by smothering a person to death. Macy just smothered me with all her caring, concerns and morals that I can't think straight. I don't want that for Zoë."

Beau shoved his hands into his pockets. "Delia, that's called love."

She chewed on her lip and didn't speak.

"When your parents were having difficulties, Macy was always there for you. She'd come home from college to spend a weekend with you, shopping and doing whatever you wanted. Yes, she might have imposed her morals and values on you, but that's because she cared so much."

"Your Honor," Harcourt objected. "Mr. McCain is getting sidetracked."

"I agree. Move on, Mr. McCain."

"Ms. Randall, did you sell your baby to the Wallstons?"

"Keith said they had money and I figured my child and I deserved some of it, so I called but they wouldn't talk to me. Then I had Zoë. Something was wrong with her and I was scared. Ever since I was little my mind goes a million miles an hour and I have trouble concentrating and sticking to anything. I knew I couldn't raise a kid. So I left and paid the Wallstons a visit in person. I told them about Keith's daughter. They didn't believe me and wanted a DNA test done. When the results came back, they said they wanted Zoë. I told them they could have her…for a price."

"What was the price?"

Delia looked at Ted and paused. For a moment Beau thought she wasn't going to answer, then her words came, very low, but clear. "A hundred thousand a year for ten years, and they bought me the car."

"I see." He stepped aside so Delia could see Macy. "Look at your sister and tell her what you want for Zoë. Can you do that? Can you rip Zoë from her arms? From this woman who gave you so much love that you thought twice about an abortion. From this woman who has always been there for you. Look at her and tell her what you want for Zoë."

Macy held her breath, not sure what Beau was trying to do.

"I'm sorry, Macy. I'm sorry," Delia cried.

Macy's heart sank. She made to get up and go to her sister, but Beau motioned her back down.

Delia wiped away tears, her eyes on Macy. "I do and say mean things to you and you still love me. I don't understand that. Sometimes I hate you because I'll never be as good as you. But most of the time I…"

"Delia, do you want custody of your child?" Beau asked, penetrating Macy's shaky emotions.

"Are you kidding?" Delia brushed away more tears. "I can't even take care of myself. I just don't have maternal feelings."

"Who do you want to have permanent custody of Zoë?"

Delia took a long breath, fighting tears. "Macy. I want Macy to raise Zoë." She jumped from the stand and ran into Macy's arms. "I'm sorry. I'm sorry."

Macy held her tight and Ted joined them. Out of the corner of her eye, Macy saw a woman come into the courtroom and speak to the Wallstons.

"Your Honor." Mr. Harcourt spoke to the judge. "The Wallstons withdraw their motion."

"Do they wish to seek visitation rights?"

Harcourt spoke to the couple and the other woman. "No, Your Honor," he replied.

"Bailiff, take Mr. Wallston into custody," the judge instructed.

"Your Honor," Harcourt objected.

"Mr. Harcourt, perjury is a crime in the state of Texas and I will not tolerate it in my courtroom. I'm sure you can have him out within the hour."

As the judge scribbled something in a file, he added, "I'm terminating Delia Randall's parental rights and granting full custody of minor child, Zoë Jane Randall, to Macy Randall."

"Thank you, Your Honor," Beau replied.

"Ranger McCain." The judge looked toward the back of the room and Caleb walked forward.

"Yes, Your Honor."

"I assume you are here to take Delia Randall into custody?"

"Yes, Your Honor. I promised the police chief I'd bring her in when the hearing was over."

The judge glanced toward Delia. "Ms. Randall, the DA may have more charges against you. Selling a baby is a crime, but I'll leave that up to the DA's office. You were lucky to have such caring people in your life. I hope you think twice before doing something like this again."

Delia nodded.

"This hearing is adjourned." The judge banged his gavel and stood, his eyes on Beau. "Always a pleasure, McCain."

"Thanks, judge."

Caleb snapped the handcuffs on Delia. "Daddy," she wailed.

"Don't worry, sweetheart," Ted replied. "I'm going with you and I'll have you out in no time."

Caleb, Tuck, Delia and Ted walked out.

"When did Ted become father of the year?" Irene asked with a touch of sarcasm.

"Mom." Macy shook her head. "Dad is what Delia needs now."

"I suppose, but I wish I didn't feel like the most evil person alive."

"It's going to take us a while to adjust, so just be patient."

"Mmm. The price of sin."

"If that's the way you want to look at it."

"Not really." Irene slipped her purse over her shoulder, her expression one of pain and regret. The secret was out and Macy knew her mother was feeling like the bad guy. It would take time for them all to heal and move on. "I'll meet you back at your place." Irene turned then stopped. "I'm glad everything turned out so well."

"Thanks, Mom."

"Do you want me to pick up Zoë?"

"No. I want to do that."

Irene walked off and complete joy filled Macy. Zoë was hers. She was a mother again. She swung to thank the man who had made it all happen. Beau was stuffing papers into his briefcase. They were the only two people left in the courtroom. Perfect.

"Thank you," she said, slipping her arms around his neck. The feel of his hair sensitized her fingers and his masculine scent stimulated her system like a glass of wine. She stood on tiptoes and kissed the corner of his mouth, then he caught her lips in an explosively charged kiss. His hands tightened around her waist and for a moment they were lost in the moment of mutual need.

When he rested his forehead against hers, she whispered, "I love you."

He stilled and removed her arms from around his neck. "Now that you have Zoë, a child, you can love me?"

"Beau…"

His eyes were dark, almost angry. "I've loved you

forever and all I wanted was for you to trust in that love. It didn't matter to me if you could have children or not. My love is unconditional. It's sharing a life together and working out the problems. You have to make up your mind what love means to you." With that he turned on his heel and left the courtroom.

"Beau..." she called out, but he was gone. She bit her hand to keep from crying out. She'd chosen the wrong moment to tell him how she felt. Now she'd lost him and for a moment she was paralyzed with a fear like she'd never known before—a fear of losing everything she'd ever wanted.

She grabbed her purse. For Zoë she had to be strong. As she walked from the courtroom, she thought this had to be the happiest and saddest day of her life. Losing her daughter had been traumatic and she'd survived. But could she survive without Beau's love?

SHE PICKED UP Zoë, who was always glad to see her. She rested her little face against Macy's neck. She did that whenever they'd been apart for any length of time.

Macy patted her diapered bottom as she walked across the street. "It's just you and me again, kiddo."

Zoë lifted her head and stared at her.

"I love you. I love you so much."

Zoë smiled, then rested her head on Macy's shoulder as if she understood every word Macy was saying.

As she opened her door, the dogs came running and Zoë struggled to get down to them. Macy placed her in her playpen and Zoë batted her hands against the netting, playing with the dogs.

Irene arrived and sat watching Zoë and the dogs. "Do you know if Ted and Delia are coming back here?"

Macy pushed back her hair, not knowing how much more she could take today. "I don't know. Dad didn't say."

Irene looked around. "Where's Beau?"

"I don't know that, either."

"Is he still at the courthouse?"

"Mom, I don't know where he is. Okay?" She was losing her temper, her cool.

She felt her mother's eyes on her. "Macy, don't lose something that could be so incredibly good for you."

Before Macy could answer, the doorbell rang and she hurried to the door. Her father, Delia and a pretty blond woman stood there. She had to be Nina, her father's wife.

For years Macy had hated this woman because she thought she'd taken her father away. Looking at her now, Macy felt no hate, just admiration for a woman who had been there when her father had needed someone.

Ted made the introductions. "It's nice to finally meet you," Nina said.

"Likewise, come on in," Macy said.

When Ted saw Irene he introduced her just as politely.

"Isn't this cozy?" was Irene's response.

Macy flashed her a warning glance and her mother immediately backed off.

Delia stood transfixed staring at Zoë playing with the dogs. "Is that her?" she asked quietly.

"Yes. That's Zoë," Macy replied.

"She's so big."

"She's almost six months old now. Would you like to hold her?"

Delia lifted an eyebrow. "Aren't you afraid I might want her back?"

Macy looked squarely at her. "Do you?"

In that instant Macy knew if Delia wanted to love and raise her daughter, she would find the strength to let her. She didn't need a baby to feel like a woman. All she needed was Beau. She could love him completely without the pain, just like she discovered when she'd sat in the park earlier. But it was too late.

Delia kept staring at the baby. "I don't feel any connection to her. What's wrong with me?"

"Nothing, sweetheart." Ted rubbed her shoulder. "You've just been through a great deal."

"I've done a lot of bad things."

"So have I. We'll get you back on your medication and get you some counseling. That will help you to understand your feelings."

"I don't want her to ever know who I am."

"No more secrets," Macy said. "Zoë will know who her mother is."

Delia frowned. "Why do you have to do that?"

"Think of all the pain you've suffered because a secret was kept from you. I don't want Zoë to go through that."

"She'll hate me."

"Like you hate Mom?" Macy didn't want to force the issue, but Delia had to confront her feelings about her mother.

Delia stared at Irene. Irene was the first to speak. "I made a mistake and if I could go back and change things, I would do it in a heartbeat. It would have saved my marriage, my sanity and the respect of my daughters."

"Did my biological father want me?"

"He died when you were four and he knew nothing about you. Ted is your father and that's the way I wanted it."

Delia chewed on her lip and didn't say anything.

Irene moved toward her. "Could we talk, please?"

Delia shrugged. "I suppose."

"Let's go for a walk," Irene suggested. They moved toward the door. "I really hate your hair that color."

"I knew you would."

As they walked out, Macy asked her father, "How did it go with the police?"

"She's out on bail and the hearing is in six weeks. I promised to make sure she shows up for court. There's still the matter of the car and money the Wallstons gave her, but we'll get it sorted out. In the meantime she's staying with Nina and me."

"That's very nice of you." She addressed her words to Nina.

"It's about time I got acquainted with Ted's daughters. I know Delia has problems and it won't be easy, but nothing in life worth anything is."

Macy had a feeling she was really going to like this woman.

Nina glanced at Zoë. "May I please hold her?"

"Of course."

While Nina was cuddling Zoë, Macy looked at her

father. They'd come a long way since that day in Houston when she was forced to speak to him.

She smiled. "You really came through for Delia."

"I'm glad it all worked out. You're going to be a great mother." He looked around. "Is Beau coming by later?"

"No." She swallowed hard. "Beau's not coming back."

"Macy." Hearing the anguish in her voice he took her in his arms and held her.

She gripped him tightly, holding on to a man who had meant the world to her. And still did. "I'm sorry for all the pain you've been through and I'm sorry for judging you without knowing the truth."

"It's okay, Macy." He smoothed her hair, then he drew back and looked into her eyes. "Don't be like me, afraid to take a risk, a chance at life. It may be the only chance you get for real happiness."

"I already know that." He didn't know that Beau had already rejected her vow of love. Not because he didn't love her, but because he thought she loved him for the wrong reason.

Soon everyone was gone. Her mother was the last to leave. She stood at the door, her suitcase at her feet.

"Did you and Delia have a good talk?" Macy asked.

"Mmm. We have a lot of things to work out. Forgiveness will take time."

"Yeah. We'll never be the family we once were, but now we know each other's faults and weaknesses and we can build a better relationship."

"You are so like your father, seeing the world through

rose-colored glasses. When the real world surfaced, or should I say the real me, he couldn't deal with it." She touched Macy's cheek. "Don't be afraid of the real world."

Macy swallowed, feeling as if her mother were looking into her soul. "I'll try."

"I guess I'll go home and see how Perry likes the real me."

"You're not turning back into the youthful Irene?"

"No." Suddenly she grabbed Macy and they hugged tightly. "Take care of yourself and that baby. Call if you need anything."

"You used to say that every time I went back to college."

Irene drew away. "That was your mother and she's back. 'Bye, Macy."

Her mother picked up her suitcase and ran to the rental car.

Macy closed the door and the condo seemed so quiet, but it wasn't empty. She had a baby, her animals. What else did she need?

Beau. She needed Beau.

That night she cried herself to sleep. She allowed herself that weakness. That was the woman in her. Tomorrow she'd be stronger and able to do what she had to. She refused to live a life without Beau. One way or the other she had to make him understand how much she loved him, which might prove to be the biggest challenge of her life.

CHAPTER EIGHTEEN

BEAU SAT IN THE BAR of the hotel, drinking straight bourbon. By midnight he was hoping he wouldn't remember his name. Or hers. By midnight he wouldn't care that Macy had said "I love you" at the wrong time, in the wrong place and for the wrong reason.

"Hey, Beau, need some company?"

He squinted at Tuck. "What the hell are you doing here?"

Tuck straddled the barstool next to his. "Having a very good evening. The question is, what are you doing here? Why aren't you out with Macy celebrating the victory?"

Beau swallowed the last of the bourbon in the glass and winced. "Don't say her name."

Tuck watched him for a moment. "Let's sit at a table and talk."

"Nope. I'm all through talking." He raised his glass to the bartender. "Another, please."

"Humor me," Tuck said, and walked to a table.

Beau took the glass from the bartender and followed Tuck. He'd rolled up his shirtsleeves earlier and he'd left his jacket and tie somewhere. He didn't bother to look because he didn't really care.

"What happened?" Tuck asked as Beau staggered to a seat.

"She said 'I love you.'"

Tuck removed his hat, laid it on the table and scratched his head. "Isn't that what you wanted?"

Beau took a swallow of the amber liquid. "Not that way."

"Beau, what are you talking about? You're not making any sense."

"She has Zoë, a baby. Now she can love me."

"And…that's wrong somehow?"

"Yes, dammit." He slammed his glass on the table, the liquid splashing onto his hand. But he didn't care. He didn't care about much of anything, but the pain driving him. "I needed her to trust in me and my love. I…I told her I didn't need a child. All I needed was her, but she didn't trust my feelings."

"Oh."

"Why do women have to ground you up into little bitty pieces and spit you out?"

"Is that how you're feeling?"

"Yep. Used up—emotionally." He downed another swallow. "This time Beau McCain is really moving on."

"How many times have you told yourself that?"

"Don't make me think, Tuck. Just go away and leave me to my misery."

"Sorry. I can't do that. You're the one who's big on talking, keeping the brothers together, keeping the family together through good times and bad. If I walked away and left you here, I wouldn't be much of a friend to you or the brothers."

Beau leaned across the table and whispered, "I'll never tell."

Tuck leaned closer, too. "You're drunk on your ass and about to fall out of that chair. C'mon, I'll take you home."

"Nope. Got a room here." Beau looked around the dimly lit bar. "This is a hotel, right?"

"Yeah. Where's your room key?"

"In my jacket."

"Where's your jacket?"

"Haven't got a clue." The room tilted and his head felt fuzzy and he recognized he'd reached his limit. He was stone drunk. But he remembered his name. And hers. Damn!

THE AUGUST MORNING dawned like a beacon pointed at Beau's skull. His head throbbed with a burning ache and the brightness of the day almost blinded him. For a moment he wondered where he was, then the evening came flooding back with painful clarity. He sat up, realizing he was still in his clothes and that someone was pounding at the door, making the ache in his head unbearable.

He quickly staggered to the door determined to stop the sound that was splitting open his head. Yanking the door wide with a frown, he saw Tuck holding a cup of coffee. He grabbed it immediately.

"Not feeling too good, huh?" Tuck asked.

Beau sat on the bed. "How did you know I was here?"

Tuck lifted an eyebrow. "You don't remember last night—in the bar?"

"Vaguely." He sipped the coffee. "Thought you were there, but again I could have imagined it."

Tuck pulled up a chair. "I was there."

"Didn't you and Caleb go home?"

"Caleb did. I stayed."

"Why? You don't have a vehicle here, do you?"

"No. It's at the Austin airport."

"So...? Don't make me ask questions because I'm not in a good mood."

"You weren't last night, either."

"I don't remember much about it. Just..." He took a quick swallow of coffee. "So why are you still in Waco?"

"When we were booking Delia yesterday, I met a police officer I worked a case with a couple of years ago. She said she'd take me to my car if I stayed over, so I did. We had dinner, talked and came back here—that's when I saw you."

Beau winced. "Damn. Sorry I ruined your evening."

Tuck grinned. "You didn't ruin my evening. I had a helluva of a good time."

"Here I was thinking you were pining for Grace."

"Grace?" Tuck frowned. "Are you still drunk?"

Beau nursed his coffee. "No, thank God, but every time Grace's name is mentioned you act like you've just received an electrical shock."

"That's true. The woman pushes every button I have."

"There has to be a reason for that."

"Oh, no, you're not turning the tables on me," Tuck said with a sly grin. "Before I left this morning I wanted to check and make sure that you were still alive."

"Barely, and speak softly, please."

"You were in pretty bad shape last night."

He stared into the black liquid. "I've never done anything like that before in my life."

"Mmm." Tuck leaned forward, his elbows on his knees. "I'm the last one to give advice on women, but you've loved Macy for a long time. I know you pretty well and I don't think that's ever going to change."

Beau didn't have a reply. He just stared into the coffee.

"Macy's been through a helluva lot, losing a father, a child, going through a divorce and then finding out her sister is a half sister. But she always finds comfort and strength in you. So she didn't say 'I love you' when you wanted her to. She finally said it. That's the main thing. Don't be pigheaded or you're going to lose what you've always wanted—a life with Macy."

Beau set his cup on the nightstand. "I didn't know you gave advice to the lovelorn."

"I don't." Tuck stood. "But I hate to see you in this much pain."

"Thanks, Tuck." Tuck was a good friend and Beau appreciated that. But he had to come to grips with what he was feeling on his own.

"I better go. A lady's waiting to drive me home."

"Love 'em and leave 'em, Tuck," Beau teased. "Maybe I need to take a lesson from you."

"There's no happiness in that, Beau. You've found the real thing so you better hold on for all it's worth. Go see Macy and make this right."

"Maybe."

Tuck stopped at the door. "Are you going to be okay?"

"Yeah." Beau nodded. "I'll survive."

He'd told Caleb they were survivors, but after Tuck left, Beau wondered how he was going to survive a broken heart—again.

BEAU WENT TO HIS CONDO, showered and changed, then he packed a bag. He was leaving. He wasn't sure where he was going, but he was leaving. He had to clear his head and think straight. There was no sign of Macy and he was glad. For the first time, he didn't want to see her.

He stopped at his office so Jon and Liz would know his plans. "You did a great job on the Randall case," he told Jon.

"Thank you, sir."

"I'm going to be gone for a while and I want you to look after the office."

"You got it."

After Jon left, Liz looked at him over the rim of her glasses. "What's going on with you?"

"It's personal."

"You're having a bad midlife crisis if you ask me. Take that cruise."

"I'm not asking," he replied, and to soften the words he kissed her cheek. "I'll be in touch."

Once in his car, he called his mom and dad and told them he was leaving town for a while.

"Okay, dear," Althea said. "When are you coming back?"

"I'm not sure, but I'll call."

"Is Macy going with you?"

He gripped the steering wheel until his knuckles were white. "No, Mom. I'm going alone."

"Beau…"

"'Bye, Mom." He clicked off because he didn't want to talk about Macy.

Next he headed for the McCain farm. Since school had started Elise and the kids wouldn't be there and that was okay. He needed to talk to Jake. He drove to the barns and found Jake in the equipment shed with Al, the mechanic.

"Hey, Beau," Jake said, wiping his hands on a grease rag, and walking toward him. "Congratulations on winning the case for Macy."

"Could we talk for a minute?"

"Sure."

They leaned on the wood fence and stared at rows and rows of cotton. Joe McCain had been a cotton farmer and Jake had taken over the farm.

"Every time I come here I have memories of him," Beau said. "I never thought I was much like him."

"You're not."

"Last night I got so drunk that I don't remember much of it. I guess Dad didn't remember much either after all those drinking binges."

"Probably not." Jake glanced at him. "Why were you drinking?"

Beau told him the truth because they were brothers and they shared a lot of pain when they were kids.

"Beau…"

"He called me the bad son so much that I had to prove that I wasn't. Maybe that's why I'm such a good guy, as people call me. I had to be."

"No. You're good because that's just the way you are. You don't even have to try. It's just natural." He paused. "When you were drunk, were you mean and abusive?"

"No."

"See. There's nothing bad about you."

"I'm beginning to see that."

"I'm sorry about Macy."

"Don't be. I have to sort this out on my own. I just came by to tell you I'll be gone for a while."

"Where you going?"

"I don't know."

"How long you plan on being gone?"

"Until…"

"Until you get over Macy," Jake finished for him.

Beau took a deep breath. "Yeah. That's about it."

"Do you think that's possible?"

"I don't know. That's what I have to find out for myself—just what the future holds."

He hugged Jake and headed for his car, finally letting go of the stigma of the bad son. Stopping for a moment, he stared at the rows of cotton and said goodbye to the kid and the man who always had to make everyone happy. It was time he made himself happy. Or as close as he could get.

MACY SPENT HER DAYS waiting for Beau. So far his place was deserted, no sign of life. Where was Beau?

She went to work, cleaned house, took care of Zoë and her animals, but her mind was on Beau. On the third day she broke down and called his office. Liz said he wasn't in. She didn't know if Beau had told her to say that, so she phoned Althea. Althea said Beau was out of town and she asked questions Macy couldn't answer. She finally had to admit that Beau had to get away from her. That hurt more than she ever thought possible. But she wasn't giving up.

That night as she was putting Zoë down, Beau's words came back to her. *You have to figure out what love means to you.* Up until a few days ago she thought she didn't have the right to love a man anymore. After hearing her parents' stories, she now saw how absurd that was. Love was a gift, without limits or conditions. That was the way Beau loved her—completely with all her faults. She'd been blinded by so much pain that she couldn't see that.

You have to figure out what does love mean to you. She sank onto her bed and thought about that for a moment. She turned around her and Beau's situation. If she wanted children, could she love Beau if he were sterile? Definitely. She didn't even have to think about it. She'd love him through the good and bad times, through any illness—no matter what, she would love him forever.

She had to take her feelings one step further. Did she love him enough to have another child? His child. Yes, she could. Just like that, the monster under her bed disappeared. As she had already begun to realize, she could do anything with Beau beside her. She felt liberated, free, and the only thing she needed now was for Beau to come home.

BEAU SPENT A COUPLE OF DAYS in San Antonio, strolling along the River Walk to the sounds of a mariachi band

and just enjoying the scenery. Lush green foliage grew along the banks of the river, which was shaded by towering cypresses, oaks and willows. Flowering gardens bordered the river. He ate at a Mexican restaurant and watched the boats with happy sightseers float down the river.

Later, he visited the Alamo, an eighteenth-century mission church where a group of courageous Texans made their last stand against the Mexican army for Texas independence. It was a Saturday, and everywhere he went he saw couples with children. Families. The way it was meant to be.

From there he headed for West Texas and the landscape was as lonely and desolate as he felt. Sand and cactus and more sand and cactus. He stopped in Marfa to view the mysterious Marfa lights and stayed a week in a primitive cabin communing with nature. To the north he could see the Davis Mountains, to the southeast the Chisos Mountains, and to the southwest the Chinati Mountains. The view was spectacular and the solitude, the isolation was what he needed to sort out what he was feeling. By the time he left, he still wasn't sure about anything, though. But he didn't need liquor to take away the pain. He wasn't following in his father's footsteps. He'd already put that idea to rest.

In the valley of South Texas on the Rio Grande River, he signed on to harvest an onion crop. It was late August and the sun was hot and the physical labor rejuvenated him in a way that he hadn't expected. He laughed with the Mexicans and they called him loco for working when he didn't have to.

The last day of the harvest the Mexicans had a party to celebrate. Beau drank tequila from a bottle and it heated his system, his thoughts. One of the Mexicans offered him a woman for the night and he politely declined. He finally could admit some hard truths. He was going to love Macy forever. Distance and time wasn't going to change that and he knew it was time to go home and face his life.

And face Macy.

THE FIRST THING he did when he reached Waco was contact a real estate agent. He had to get out of the condo. That was one thing he knew for sure. He had to make changes and that was a start.

He'd known Lois, the agent, for years. He'd handled her divorce. After showing him several houses on the computer, they went to look at several. Nothing suited him. Two hours later they were back in her office.

She flipped through several more houses. One caught his attention.

"Go back," he said.

"Which one?"

"It was a two-story."

"You don't want that one," Lois said.

"Why not?"

"It's right outside the city limits on fifty acres and it's a five-bedroom house."

"I want to see it."

Lois arched a fine eyebrow. "Do you have a secret family I don't know about?"

"No, but I have a niece and a nephew and another on the way. I'd like space for them when they stay with me."

She clicked her tongue. "Why hasn't some lucky woman taken you off the market, Beau McCain?"

"Guess I'm too hard to get along with."

"Oh, please. If I was twenty years younger…"

Beau laughed and he knew he was back to his old self. One look at the house and he made an offer on it. From there he went home to the condo.

MACY WATCHED Zoë in the playpen. She scooted all over the pen on her stomach. Raising to her knees, she'd rock back and forth. Soon she'd be crawling. She seemed to be growing by leaps and bounds. How she wished Beau could see her. She missed him and she knew Zoë did, too.

She heard a noise and swung around. Did that sound come from Beau's? She listened closely. Yes. Yes. He was home!

Grabbing Zoë, she headed for the door. The dogs ran ahead and she realized she should have brushed her hair, put on makeup or perfume, but she was too eager to see him. Shorts, a T-shirt and a clean face would have to do. The dogs scratched at the door and Macy took a deep breath before she rang the bell.

After a moment, Beau opened the door. She was expecting a haggard appearance, but he looked refreshed and even more handsome than she remembered. And he had a tan. Where had he been?

"Could I speak with you, please?"

He opened the door wider and she stepped inside, balancing Zoë on her hip. She came to a complete stop. There were boxes around the room, boxes that were being filled with his belongings.

"Are you moving?"

"Yes. I've made an offer on a house and I've started packing."

The old Macy would turn around and go home and not open herself up for any more pain. But she wasn't afraid anymore.

Her eyes held his. "Is there room in that house for Zoë and me?"

Zoë leaned toward Beau with her arms outstretched, whining for him to take her.

"Hey, little angel." He gathered her into his arms and held her close. Zoë rested her face against his neck.

Beau melted from the contact. God, how he loved this kid. He sat her on his knees. "She's growing. Her hair is longer and curly like yours."

"Yeah." Macy winced, and Beau knew there were days when she cursed her curly hair.

"She's scooting on her stomach so she'll probably be crawling before too much longer."

There was silence for a long moment.

"Are you still angry with me?" she asked.

He bounced Zoë until she giggled. "I wasn't angry. I was just hurt."

"I'm sorry I told you then. I was just so excited and grateful, but I already knew that I loved you. And it wasn't because I had a child." She paused. "You said for me to figure out what love means to me. I have."

He looked at her then. "What is it?"

"When Delia came by the house, she saw Zoë and said how pretty she was. I asked if she wanted to hold her. Delia asked if I was afraid that she might want Zoë back. I wasn't because if she wanted to raise her own child, I would have given Zoë to her. And I would still have loved you, wanted a life with you."

He started to speak, but she held up her hand. "Ever since I lost Hope, I've lived with this fear, especially at night. In my mind I called it the monster under my bed. For a long time I thought the fear of not being a complete woman was the monster, then I thought it was my love for you, but it's really me. I was afraid to live life. I'm not anymore. I'm not afraid to take a risk and I'm not afraid to love."

He swallowed. "How do you know that for sure?"

"Because I'm not afraid to have another child."

"I never asked that of you."

"I know, but now I can tell you what love is to me. It's loving you through sickness and health, through heartache, pain, suffering and happiness. It's being there for you no matter what. And it's letting go of the fear in me because I know I can face anything with you beside me. It's trusting and believing in that love always."

Beau carefully laid Zoë on the carpet on her stomach and watched her scoot to try to reach the dogs, who wisely stayed out of her reach. All the while Macy's words eased every doubt that may have lingered. He loved her and he finally believed she loved him, too.

He turned to gaze at her, unable to keep from

smiling. She was absolutely beautiful, with her frizzed hair sticking out and her face as fresh and innocent as Zoë's. "You ready to say that in front of a minister?"

"Oh, Beau." She threw herself into his arms and he held her as if she were the most precious thing on earth. To him she was. "Yes, yes." She kissed his neck, his chin and found his lips. He cupped her face and kissed her with all the love he'd ever felt for her.

For endless moments they were lost in the magic of that first kiss given with heartfelt love. She ran her fingers inside his shirt and his breathing became labored.

She drew back, her eyes heavy. "My place. Two minutes." One quick, lingering kiss and she picked up Zoë and disappeared out the door, her animals scurrying after her.

It didn't take him long to follow.

A LONG TIME LATER Macy laid curled up in Beau's arms with nothing, but nothing, between them. Zoë was asleep, her animals were, too. Everything was peaceful and quiet. Everything was perfect.

She kissed Beau's shoulder. "I love you."

"Mmm." He ran his hand up her smooth back. "I love you so much that the thought of living without you was killing me."

"Where have you been?"

"Everywhere, but you were always with me."

"I'm sorry I hurt you by blurting out my feelings."

He kissed the tip of her nose. "I know. I guess I was overly sensitive. I just wanted you to trust in my love."

She moved her leg over his and he smiled. "I do." She gently kissed his chest. "And I'm ready to face a future with you no matter what happens." She ran her hand down his body and he groaned.

"Macy…"

There were no more monsters under her bed—just an incredible, good man in it. For now and forever.

EPILOGUE

"COCK-A-DOODLE-DO."

Beau opened one eye, believing he was hearing things, then the rooster crowed again. "What the hell...."

He sat up and reached for his robe. Macy was at work and he hated those nights when she wasn't here. But she was giving her notice, so soon she'd be a full-time wife and mother. Though he knew she wouldn't entirely quit nursing. He went into Zoë's room and she was sleeping like the angel she was. He straightened her blanket and reached down to kiss her.

It was nearing the end of September and he and Macy had been married for almost a month. They'd had a simple ceremony with just family present and his parents hosted a reception in their home. Delia hadn't come to the wedding and Macy wasn't upset about that. Delia was in counseling and Ted said she was doing better than he or Nina had expected. Under her father's tutelage, Delia just might evolve into a decent person. Only time would tell. And Zoë was where she should be—with him and Macy, and they would love her beyond measure.

Delia was also making progress with Irene. They talked often and when she had all her legal problems settled, Delia planned to visit her in Colorado. Ted had made full restitution to the Wallstons and the Corvette had been returned.

Beau couldn't understand how the Wallstons could completely forget about Zoë, but he knew Cynthia Wallston had something to do with that and it was probably for the best. If Zoë ever asked about Keith's family, they would tell her the complete story—just as they would about Delia, her biological mother.

Keeping it a secret wasn't something they could do to Zoë. They wanted her to grow up healthy and happy without any skeletons in the family closet.

Macy had a new relationship with her mother and her father, and she talked to them often. Ted's oil company had offices and holdings in Alaska and he'd told Macy that Delia showed an interest in traveling and working there. Ted planned to take her as soon as Delia was allowed to leave the country.

Beau suspected Delia wanted to get away and start over, a new beginning. It might be the adventure she needed to find herself and to come to terms with her life. But Beau knew that Ted would never desert his daughters again. He was in their lives to stay.

Beau and Macy hadn't gone on a honeymoon yet. Instead they'd moved into their new house. Life was better than he'd ever dreamed. Beau McCain had definitely moved on to the best part of his life. He was in the process of adopting Zoë—the icing on the proverbial cake.

"Cock-a-doodle-do."

Dammit. Where was that sound coming from? Could someone's rooster have gotten loose? He went toward the kitchen to investigate. As he drew close, he heard Macy's voice and a warmth settled in his chest.

"Shh," she said. "I have to explain you to Beau first."

"What do you have to explain to Beau?" But it was pretty clear once he entered the kitchen. A red rooster was inside a cage.

The dogs charged into the kitchen, barking excitedly at the newcomer.

Macy clapped her hands. "Quiet."

He lifted an eyebrow. "A rooster?"

"The animal shelter called and I left work early to pick him up. The police broke up a cockfight and this bird is pretty beaten up. He's disturbing the other animals so I promised to find him a home."

Beau sank into a kitchen chair. "I'm in love with a crazy woman."

She curled into his lap and wrapped her arms around his neck. "She loves you, too." She kissed him briefly. "And I promise he won't be here long."

"Who are you kidding? You'll never get rid of that rooster."

"I know," she groaned. "Just look at him. His body has several deep pecked cuts and his foot is all chewed up. I'm not sure what to do with him."

"You do realize he's probably been trained to fight."

She nibbled on his ear. "But…"

"When you do that I can't think too clearly."

"I know." She laughed.

"Okay. I'll see if I can find someone to make him a

pen, and I was thinking about building a barn out back, maybe a stable. We have to have room for all these animals you keep bringing home."

"I knew I loved you for a reason." She kissed him deeply and her hands found their way inside his robe.

"Cock-a-doodle-do."

They broke apart laughing. "Good thing we don't have close neighbors," he said.

Zoë wailed from her room, the dogs barked loudly and the phone rang.

"I'll get Zoë." Macy hopped off his lap.

"I'll get the phone. Hush," he said to the dogs.

"Hey, Tuck," Beau said.

"Just wanted to let you know that Caroline just gave birth to a nine-pound boy. Eli wanted a girl, but he got a fullback."

"Whoa. Baby certainly takes after his father. How is everyone?"

"Mom and baby are fine. Eli's a wreck."

Beau laughed. "He'll recover."

"They named the baby Jesse."

"Are you okay with that?" Jesse was the name of Eli and Tuck's foster father.

"Sure. Eli and I talked about it and it's not like I'm ever going to use it. Pa would be proud."

Beau could hear someone in the background. "Who's that?"

"The drill sergeant."

"You mean Grace?"

"Yeah. I better go. She wants to use my cell phone. Why the woman doesn't have her own I don't know."

"Tell everyone 'hi' and we'll be over soon to see the baby."

"Cock-a-doodle-do."

"Beau…" He could hear the puzzlement in Tuck's voice.

"I'll explain later."

"Ah, Beau, it's good to know you're so happy."

"I am, Tuck. I really am."

Beau stared at the phone a minute after he hung up. He was happy, happier than he'd ever been in his life. Jon was now a partner in Beau's law firm and Beau had cut back on his workload. He was now a man with his own family who needed his time and attention.

The brothers' lives were changing. They had their own families and their meetings probably wouldn't be as often. They'd still be close, though. But he wouldn't feel the need to keep everyone together. Like his mom, subconsciously he was afraid of the family falling apart again. That's why he wanted everyone to talk, to get along. He now knew that love bound them together and he didn't have to worry.

There was just Tuck left, the lone bachelor, and he wondered if Tuck and Grace would ever find any common ground. The new nephew would be a start, except they'd probably argue over him, too.

Macy came back with a sleepy Zoë in her arms and he told her about the new baby.

"How wonderful. Nine pounds. Oh my goodness. Is everyone okay?"

"Yeah. Even Eli survived it—barely."

Zoë threw out her arms for Beau and he took her. She

nuzzled against him and went to sleep on his shoulder. "Bad old rooster woke Daddy's girl." He kissed her fat cheek. "I'll put her down." He and Macy had agreed that Zoë would call them Mommy and Daddy. They wanted to be a complete family.

Laying Zoë in her crib, he knew he couldn't love a child of his own any more.

He headed back to Macy. "I'll put the rooster in the garage and he can crow his head off out there."

When he returned to the kitchen, Macy was putting on coffee. She had a dreamy look on her face. He wrapped his arms around her waist from behind.

"What are you thinking?" He kissed the side of her face.

"How wonderful you are."

"Oh."

She leaned against him. "You were right. You love me with all my faults."

"And always will."

She turned in his arms. "You were also right about our love being enough. It is. It completes me in ways I never imagined."

He swung her up in his arms. "You keep talking like that and we'll never leave the bedroom today."

They made slow sweet love and Beau stared into her beautiful blue eyes. "Happy?"

"Mmm."

"You're everything that's good in me."

She pushed hair away from his forehead. "No more thoughts about being a bad son?"

"Not a one. I know that events from my childhood

shaped me into the man I am. All I have now are good feelings."

She sighed. "It took us a long time to get it right."

"Yes, and we'll treasure it more because of that."

"Mmm." She glanced toward the ceiling. "We have three bedrooms upstairs and this is a big house. I was thinking that it would be nice for Zoë to have a little brother or sister."

He looked deep into those gorgeous eyes and he didn't see any fear or any pain. All those fears were gone. As he struggled with his emotions, she continued, "My mother said to let you help me heal. My father said not to be afraid to take a risk. They didn't want me to make the same mistakes that they had." She cupped his face. "I can honestly say that I have healed because of you and now I'm not afraid to take that risk."

"I can see that," he whispered, and buried his face in her neck. "The thought of you going through that kind of pain again is…"

She kissed his forehead. "We'll face it together. Isn't that what love is all about?"

"Mmm."

"And I'm not doing this because I need a baby or I feel you deserve one. I'm doing it for Zoë. I don't want her to grow up as an only child."

He raised his head. "You're wonderful." He kissed her long and deep then gazed into her passion filled eyes. "Let's wait until after Christmas and if it's still something we both want, we'll talk again."

She smiled. "I love you, Beau McCain, and I'm never again going to be afraid to say that."

"Cock-a-doodle-do."

At the rooster's crowing, they dissolved into laughter, holding on to each other. They'd come so far and now they would go into the future to a life they both wanted.

* * * * *

My husband could see beauty in a mud puddle. Literally. "Look at that, Louise," he'd say after a heavy spring rain. "Have you ever seen so many amazing colors in mud?"

I'd look and see nothing except brown, but he'd pick up a stick and swirl the mud till the colors of the earth emerged, and all of a sudden I'd see the world through his eyes—extraordinary instead of mundane.

Roy was my mirror to life. Four years ago when he died, it cracked wide open, and I've been living a smashed-up, sleepwalking life ever since.

If he were here on this balmy August night I'd be sailing with him instead of baking cheese straws in preparation for Tuesday-night quilting club with Patsy. I'd be striving for sex appeal in Bermuda shorts and bare-toed sandals instead of opting for comfort in walking shoes and a twill skirt with enough elastic around the waist to make allowances for two helpings of lemon-cream pie.

Not that I mind Patsy. Just the opposite. I love her. She's the only person besides Roy who creates wonder wherever she goes. (She creates mayhem, too, but we won't get into that.) She's my mirror now, as well as my compass.

Of course, I have my daughter, Diana, but I refuse to be the kind of mother who defines herself through her children. Besides, she has her own life now, a husband and a baby on the way.

I slide the last cheese straws into the oven and then go into my office and open e-mail.

From: "Miss Sass" <patsyleslie@hotmail.com>
To: "The Lady" <louisejernigan@yahoo.com>
Sent: Tuesday, August 15, 6:00 PM
Subject: Dangerous Tonight
Hey Lady,
I'm feeling dangerous tonight. Hot to trot, if you know what I mean. Or can you even remember? Look out, bridge club, here I come. I'm liable to end up dancing on the tables instead of bidding three spades. Whose turn is it to drive, anyhow? Mine or thine?
XOXOX
Patsy
P.S. Lord, how did we end up in a club with no men?

This e-mail is typical "Patsy." She's the only person I know who makes me laugh all the time. I guess that's why I e-mail her about ten times a day. She lives right next door, but e-mail satisfies my urge to be instantly and constantly in touch with her without having to interrupt the flow of my life. Sometimes we even save the good stuff for e-mail.

From: "The Lady" <louisejernigan@yahoo.com>
To: "Miss Sass" <patsyleslie@hotmail.com>
Sent: Tuesday, August 15, 6:10 PM
Subject: Re: Dangerous Tonight

So, what else is new, Miss Sass? You're always dangerous. If you had a weapon, you'd be lethal.
Hugs,
Louise
P.S. What's this about men? I thought you said your libido was dead?

I press Send then wait. Her reply is almost instantaneous.

From: "Miss Sass" <patsyleslie@hotmail.com>
To: "The Lady" <louisejernigan@yahoo.com>
Sent: Tuesday, August 15, 6:12 PM
Subject: Re: Dangerous Tonight

Ha! If I had a *brain* I'd be lethal.
And I said my libido was in hibernation, not DEAD! Jeez, Louise!!!!!
P

Patsy loves to have the last word, so I shut off my computer.

* * * * *

*Want to find out what happens to their friendship
when Patsy and Louise both find the perfect man?*

*Don't miss
CONFESSIONS OF A NOT-SO-DEAD LIBIDO
by Peggy Webb,*

*coming to Harlequin NEXT
in November 2006.*

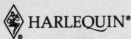

HARLEQUIN®

NeXt™

Entertaining women's fiction for every woman who has wondered "what's next?" in her life.

Receive $1.⁰⁰ off

any Harlequin NEXT™ novel.

Coupon expires March 31, 2007.
Redeemable at participating retail outlets
in the U.S. only. Limit one coupon per customer.

RETAILER: Harlequin Enterprises Ltd. will pay the face value of this coupon plus 8 cents
if submitted by customer for this product only. Any other use constitutes fraud. Coupon
is nonassignable. Void if taxed, prohibited or restricted by law. Void if copied. Consumer
must pay any government taxes. For reimbursement submit coupons and proof of
sales to Harlequin Enterprises Ltd., P.O. Box 880478, El Paso, TX 88588-0478, U.S.A.
Cash value 1/100 cents. Valid in the U.S. only. ® is a trademark owned and used by
the trademark owner and/or its licensee.

5 65373 00076 2   (8100) 0 11266

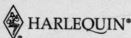

HARLEQUIN®

NeXt™

Entertaining women's fiction for every woman who has wondered "what's next?" in her life.

Receive $1.⁰⁰ off

any Harlequin NEXT™ novel.

Coupon expires March 31, 2007.
Redeemable at participating retail outlets
in Canada only. Limit one coupon per customer.

RETAILER: Harlequin Enterprises Ltd. will pay the face value of this coupon plus
10.25¢ if submitted by customer for this product only. Any other use constitutes
fraud. Coupon is nonassignable. Void if taxed, prohibited or restricted by law.
Consumer must pay any government taxes. Void if copied. Nielson Clearing House
customers submit coupons and proof of sales to: Harlequin Enterprises Ltd., P.O.
Box 3000, Saint John, N.B., E2L 4L3. Non-NCH retailer—for reimbursement submit
coupons and proof of sales directly to: Harlequin Enterprises Ltd., Retail Marketing
Department, 225 Duncan Mill Rd., Don Mills, Ontario, M3B 3K9, Canada. Valid in
Canada only. ® is a trademark of Harlequin Enterprises Ltd. Trademarks marked
with ® are registered in the United States and/or other countries.

52607178

HNCOUPCDN

REQUEST YOUR FREE BOOKS!

2 FREE NOVELS PLUS 2 FREE GIFTS!

HARLEQUIN®

Super Romance®

Exciting, emotional, unexpected!

YES! Please send me 2 FREE Harlequin Superromance® novels and my 2 FREE gifts. After receiving them, if I don't wish to receive any more books, I can return the shipping statement marked "cancel." If I don't cancel, I will receive 6 brand-new novels every month and be billed just $4.69 per book in the U.S., or $5.24 per book in Canada, plus 25¢ shipping and handling per book and applicable taxes, if any*. That's a savings of close to 15% off the cover price! I understand that accepting the 2 free books and gifts places me under no obligation to buy anything. I can always return a shipment and cancel at any time. Even if I never buy another book from Harlequin, the two free books and gifts are mine to keep forever.

135 HDN EEX7 336 HDN EEYK

Name	(PLEASE PRINT)

Address	Apt.

City	State/Prov.	Zip/Postal Code

Signature (if under 18, a parent or guardian must sign)

Mail to Harlequin Reader Service®:

IN U.S.A.	IN CANADA
P.O. Box 1867	P.O. Box 609
Buffalo, NY	Fort Erie, Ontario
14240-1867	L2A 5X3

Not valid to current Harlequin Superromance subscribers.

Want to try two free books from another line?
Call 1-800-873-8635 or visit www.morefreebooks.com.

* Terms and prices subject to change without notice. NY residents add applicable sales tax. Canadian residents will be charged applicable provincial taxes and GST. This offer is limited to one order per household. All orders subject to approval. Credit or debit balances in a customer's account(s) may be offset by any other outstanding balance owed by or to the customer. Please allow 4 to 6 weeks for delivery.

HSR06

nocturne™

HER BLOOD WAS POISON TO HIM…

MICHELE HAUF

FROM THE DARK

Michael is a man with a secret. He's a vampire
struggling to fight the darkness of his nature.
It looks like a losing battle—until he meets
Jane, the only woman who can understand his
conflicted nature. And the only woman who can
destroy him—through love.

On sale November 2006.